Body in the Freezer

Naks-Cos

Copyright © 2017 Naks-Cos

All rights reserved.

ISBN-10: 1542886449
ISBN-13: 978-1542886444

DEDICATION

To the accomplished crime authors of the past who encouraged our minds to roam freely in that world of shadows.

CONTENTS

ACKNOWLEDGMENTS i

CHAPTER ONE 1

CHAPTER TWO 17

CHAPTER THREE 34

CHAPTER FOUR 46

CHAPTER FIVE 59

CHAPTER SIX 72

CHAPTER SEVEN 80

CHAPTER EIGHT 96

CHAPTER NINE 110

CHAPTER TEN 122

CHAPTER ELEVEN 136

CHAPTER TWELVE 158

CHAPTER THIRTEEN 175

CHAPTER FOURTEEN 187

CHAPTER FIFTEEN 197

CHAPTER SIXTEEN 209

CHAPTER SEVENTEEN 221

EPILOGUE 235

ACKNOWLEDGMENTS

To our collective families who gave us time to write this, our first novel!

Naks-Cos

CHAPTER ONE

It was a typical evening in the outskirts of Chennai. And the street was quiet. You might even call it considerate. Not like those busy inner-city streets that are ruled by size and speed. Not a street where crossing it requires an honest prayer to the Almighty, a heart of steel and a fat insurance policy. Not a street where the wheel is mightier than the foot and an accidental death soon gets drowned in the cacophony of horns and beeps and yelling and smog; and in no time, it is back to its usual highway-of-death mode. This was a street where there were only a few cars and bikes moving along at a leisurely speed. They hadn't yet caught up with the lack of courtesy common to the busy inner-city roads and still obeyed the universal rule of a pedestrian having the right of way. Perhaps this was due to the late hour, or perhaps it was due to the low number of vehicles on it, but it was a street where a person could walk across without a worry in the world, except for the ones he started out with. Visnhu stepped on the street with a clear focus – ice-lolly!

Just across the street was a quirky little establishment. This was a popular haunt for young couples wanting to spend time together over a coffee, oblivious to the present and to what the future holds. Their love knew no bounds, but whether they would be bound by the formal tradition of matrimony . . . only future would tell. But the establishment was quite vivacious, full of energy and hope and romance. It stocked snacks and chocolates and flowers and had a coffee machine too. But Visnhu was more interested in the large inviting ice-cream freezer usually stocked with his favorite ice-lolly.

For a guy in his mid-thirties, ice-lolly was his lone guilty pleasure. Visnhu dodged the number of neatly arranged tables and chairs in front of the shop and darted towards the freezer. The shop had a small breakout section, well hidden from the customers sitting at the tables. Only by straining over the counter, could you see a small, but efficiently arranged office. Not cluttered at all; just two large desks, a monitor, a printer, filing cabinets and a few plush chairs.

As was his habit, he first leaned towards the office, expecting to see a mischievous frown from Gopika and at the same time, opened the freezer to pick up his ice-lolly. His face suddenly contorted as he realized that Gopika was absent and his hand picked up a large cold log. A quick look at what he had picked up froze him – a frozen human hand! And in the freezer, a pair of eyes stared back at him lifelessly. He woke up with a shiver.

It was a dark, shabbily kept room that stank of medication. This was his own room in his own house; not the jail cell he had been cooped up for the last seven years. Vishnu blinked and noticed that he was drenched in sweat but thankfully, the nightmare was over. Involuntarily, his hand reached out to the many strips of pills offering chemical courage that he had amassed over time. But even there, his courage failed him. Or maybe it was resolve. Vishnu had realized that mood enhancers and anti-depressants would not keep his nightmares away for long. In the past months, he had waged a battle against his medication dependency and even in this moment of weakness, he did not want to lose the war. Dr Prakash had helped him battle his addictions (no point addressing them as dependencies any more, he thought), but Vishnu's nightmares were beyond Dr Prakash's realm of influence. As a personal favor, out of character for most doctors of the present times, Dr Prakash had suggested that Vishnu take his nightmares to Dr Sujata. Vishnu had his first appointment with her in a couple of hours. He was actually charting out the journey to her office when the thought of getting out on the street led him to the freezer . . . and the frozen hand. He shook away the last remnants stupor and walked towards the wardrobe. Time to have a human interaction.

On the bus, Vishnu found a seat next to a young couple. Not married by the looks of it and having a lovers quarrel. The girl seemed to be bickering about the lingering gaze of her partner, especially focused on other live attractions. And the bickering went on and on and on. Vishnu felt elated. He had found the chink in the guy's seemingly impregnable armor of moral rectitude. Something to discuss with Gopika . . . and suddenly, 'Sir, this is your stop.' The guy seated next to Vishnu indicated that Vishnu had reached his destination. Gopika and the young couple vanished in wisps of smoke . . . figments of his unbalanced mental state. Well, at least he would be meeting Dr Sujata in a few more minutes and she would help him recognize fact from fiction. He desperately hoped so . . .

The address took Vishnu to a sprawling mansion. Old style, with an extensive garden, big French windows, and a great looping driveway. Did not look like a psychiatrist's clinic, but rather than heading back, Vishnu slowly plodded towards the door. A sigh of relief went through his body when he read a clear nameplate just as he was about to reach for the doorbell – Dr Sujata D. P., Ph.D., Professor of Clinical Psychiatry. A soft chime and a few moments later a compact, middle-aged woman opened the door and after asking for his name, ushered Vishnu into a spacious, well-appointed lounge. It was a tastefully decorated room of generous proportions. And the roof-to-wall windows provided plenty of light and an air of openness. A cheerful room. Not something one would expect while envisioning a psychiatrist's clinic. Definitely not in a metropolis where patient care was sold like a tour package.

The shock and confused look on Vishnu's face initiated an immediate query from the lady, but it did not directly address Vishnu's confusion.

'Did you find the place easily?' – Vishnu gave a shy, absent-minded nod.

'Are you thirsty? Would like a glass of water?' – Vishnu nodded again. But there was no movement from the lady. Probably the nod wasn't a clear enough answer. But, Vishnu let it pass. His mind was still reeling from the disparity between reality and expectation.

He wondered if he was speaking to the right person and said, 'I want to speak to Dr Sujata.'

'You are,' said the lady.

'Dr Sujata, the psychiatrist?' asked Vishnu.

'Yep, that's me,' came the reply. Dr Sujata had been observing Vishnu through the slit between the window and the curtains since the time he entered her garden. And it intrigued her. The man was obviously in need of help. But there was something else too. Beneath the shabby, unkempt exterior, a physique that was almost in peak physical condition was immediately evident, just by the way he carried himself. There was a slouch in his posture, but that was not due to a malnutritioned curve in the spine, but rather the burden of a depressed life. Or was it the burden of suppressed guilt, she thought for a moment. And as she had opened the door, she could notice the handsome yet boyish features hidden beneath that scraggly stubble that seemed to sprout in no particular direction. The hair had a tint of grey and so did the beard, but clearly, it was the premature curse of a life being sucked out of this overall strong body, she thought. Was there something to save here, she wondered? Or was it too late? Had hope left this man completely, or had guilt strangled it a long time ago. And just then, she remembered what her colleague Dr Prakash had told her. 'This guy could use your help,' he had said. And Dr Prakash was quite perceptive about these things. He could, just after a few minutes with a patient, tell whether a case could be helped or not. He was also uniquely aware of whether he could help the patient or someone else could. Dr Sujata keenly observed the mannerisms exhibited by this person in front of her. Depressed he may be, unbalanced even, but his posture was steady, unwavering. He seldom made eye-contact, but when he did, it was steady and unabashed. A sign of confidence and innocence; and privileged upbringing, Dr Sujata mused.

Sometimes, there was no other go but to be direct, Vishnu

reasoned. 'This doesn't look like a psychiatrist's clinic and you don't look like a psychiatrist.'

The lady nodded with an understanding smile warming her face. 'What does a psychiatrist's clinic look like? And what does a psychiatrist look like, for that matter?' Unknowingly, Vishnu was now drawn into a conversation. The first one he had in a long, long time. The brain-cells started working and the neurons started to fire. But nothing became clearer.

'I don't know. But this has a homely feel to it. Not like the closeted clinics you get to see in movies,' said Vishnu.

'So, you like movies? What kind? I absolutely love mythological period pieces,' came the reply. And once again, the answer to Vishnu's confusion was as far away as it was when he entered this house! The lines on Vishnu's forehead creased up, but the solitude and the trauma of events past had sapped his confidence. He could not muster up the courage for a sterner query or a harsher voice.

The lady seemingly recognized this and said, 'I have a PhD in Clinical Psychiatry, if that helps. And I don't formally practice psychiatry. I see people via personal reference and chat with them. I find it quite enlightening to meet people face-to-face and have a conversation with them.'

'I suffer from nightmares and Dr Prakash said I should consult you,' Vishnu said this with as much conviction as a lottery buyer has in winning the jackpot.

'Like I said, I just chat with people. And they chat with me. And then, they move on and I don't see them again.' The answer did little to improve Vishnu's confidence. He almost thought of walking out of the house, but the room, the light, the space, the feeling of openness and at the same time, the feeling of coziness and security that it offered were something Vishnu wanted to relish for a few more moments.

'Would you just want to have a chat with me? You have made the inconvenient journey from your house to mine. Seems like a horrible waste to not have a decent conversation.'

Dr Sujata noted the sudden shock on Vishnu's face. She had seen it often, on the faces of people who are jolted back to reality from whatever dream-world they were living in. Dr Prakash had already filled-her in on Vishnu's background and she was interested. How often do you get to talk to a private investigator jailed for murder? Seeing that she was losing him, she queried, 'What happened that night?'

'I DID NOT KILL GOPIKA!'

Vishnu remembered the new smell of their plush office – new paint, new furniture, new computer, air-conditioning on full blast and the smell of freshly blossomed jasmine flowers, a traditional Chennai room-freshener. Gopika looked happy . . . no she looked content, Vishnu corrected himself. She looked content to the point of being smug. They had achieved their dream; well part of it anyway. They had started their own private investigative agency. Now all they needed were cases and they could call themselves private investigators! He remembered vividly how happy they were at that moment – happy that they had their own office and their own visiting cards that said PRIVATE INVESTIGATOR. Vishnu was also pleased that they had a sound fallback position. They had tied up their agency with a Romantic Corner – a shop that stocked snacks and chocolates and flowers and had a coffee machine too. With some chairs and tables spread around, it was going to be popular haunt for young couples who wished to have that quiet moment over a cup of coffee. But Visnhu was more interested in the large storage freezer usually stocked with his favorite ice-lolly. Vishnu was just happy to see Gopika happy, and the fact that he could dive into the ice-lollies any time he wanted (as long as Gopika didn't catch him doing it). Since the time they had known each other, Vishnu had always relied on Gopika for all the decision-making. When it came to decision-making, Vishnu was happy to say, 'She is the Man!' He was a simple soul, he recalled. The love of his life by his side, pursuing the profession he always wanted, a decent income from their joint business venture and an unlimited supply of ice-lollies – to him, that was heaven.

He looked at Dr Sujata wondering what exactly she wanted to hear. Where do I begin, he mused. He seemed lost and was quite thankful when Dr Sujata asked, 'How about we start from when you met Gopika for the first time? Did you guys hit it off immediately? Were you both interested in the private investigator business?'

'Ah, so that is where she wants me to begin,' Vishnu thought. He had skipped a few chapters then. He recalled the day he first laid eyes on Gopika. He could remember that day quite vividly, as if it had happened only yesterday. Little did he realize that it had been more than a decade ago. If only he had known how poignant this chance interaction was going to be. Maybe, he would have never had met Gopika and life would have been so completely different, he rued. They had met by accident, really. Vishnu had just moved to Chennai and he didn't know too much about the big city that was Chennai. He had just secured an admission to a prestigious college in Chennai, or so he had been told. He had made some enquiries and had arranged for a short stay at a guesthouse quite close to the college. It was a low-key, long-term accommodation type establishment. He had some money saved up throughout his schooling and he had paid upfront for a week's lodging. He had hoped to secure something better if possible, within that time. The hostel would be ideal, but he did not want to share a room with someone, and single rooms were premium property at the hostel. He walked up the path he was going to take to the college next morning. He was a careful person, no hiccups at the last minute. He wanted to be there for his appointment with the Principal, on time. He had been born lucky, he thought and then suddenly he remembered his walk along the hoardings right up to the college and a brief look of disbelief, confusion and frustration wafted over his seemingly chiseled features. Had his luck finally run out or had he just denied help from his luck, he thought to himself.

The next day, Vishnu had arrived at the college on time and gone straight up to the Principal's Office. He had an appointment with the Principal to accept the generous scholarship he had been awarded.

Vishnu also asked how the course structure worked. He was basically interested in knowing if he could take courses that interested him rather than follow a set curriculum. As expected, Vishnu found that once the degree was chosen, there was little choice to take courses that were not prescribed or deemed as optional for the degree. Finally, after discussing the rules and regulations in detail, Vishnu found a slight way out. If the timetable didn't clash, there was nothing stopping him from attending any lecture that he wanted to. The only catch was that if that course was not part of his degree, it would not appear on his final transcripts. Vishnu had no issues with that. He was there to learn, not to earn a great degree and hunt for a job. He had already decided what he was going to do in life and he had charted a path that he was going to follow diligently. The meeting was about to conclude when out of the blue, the Principal said something that sweetened his scholarship pot even more.

'As an added incentive, we are also offering a single room at the hostel for anyone who gets this scholarship,' he said. 'We don't want the hassles of room-sharing to hamper the studies and performance of our top students.' Vishnu was overjoyed. Things were actually falling in place for him.

'By the look of it, you wouldn't mind staying at the hostel, I take it?' the Principal enquired with a smile.

'N-no, not at all,' Vishnu stammered with excitement. 'This is wonderful, thank you!'

As he exited the Principal's office, hands held a bunch of papers; registration forms. One for the degree he planned on pursuing, another for the fees being paid by the scholarship; forms for the library and identity card and one more for the hostel room. The food / mess was to be sorted out at the hostel, but even that was paid for by the scholarship, so his savings needn't be touched at this time. He pushed the double flap-doors with his shoulder; his head bent reading through the degree registration form, when he bumped into something soft with a fragrance of jasmine. He was startled and looked up apologizing profusely to whomever he had bumped into and noticed a smartly but conservatively dressed girl frowning at him.

'I am so sorry,' he said again. 'I am just too excited to be here and was reading through all this paperwork. Just wasn't careful enough to look where I was going.'

'Huh,' the girl shrugged and tidied up her hair with a smart flick of her wrist, looked at her watch and just started scurrying away.

'I am Vishnu, by the way. I have just joined this college on a scholarshi. . .,' he said and realized that no one in particular was actually listening. He bent his head again in his papers and headed out to the various administrative offices he had to deal with; asking directions along the way. It took him a good part of the entire morning to get all his paperwork sorted. He was also given a quick tour of the hostel and taken to his room. He was overjoyed to see it. It was a proportionately sized room with sparse furnishings, a table, a chair, a table-lamp, a bed and a cupboard. There were common toilets and shower-rooms down the corridor; something that Vishnu hoped wasn't the case. After years at the boarding school sharing toilets, he was hoping for his own ensuite toilet, but at least had a room for himself. Sharing the toilet wasn't that big a hassle, not yet anyway. As he headed back to the campus he wondered what future aspirations were being held by these young minds mingling around him. Degree selection sorted, scholarship sorted, hostel and mess sorted; Vishnu ran a checklist in his mind. 'Now, need to find the canteen and what goodies they serve?' he thought and was suddenly famished.

Vishnu followed the faded signs that directed him to the canteen. It was a typical college canteen. Young, hungry minds chatting away over hot cups of tea and coffee and plates of omelet, Wada, Idli and sandwiches. Vishnu squeezed through the crowd and made his way to the counter. Even without looking up, the fat, bald guy behind the counter put his palm out. Vishnu ordered a bread omelet and Coke, the guy told him the price, which Vishnu paid and was given tokens for his food. He went to the next counter, handed over the tokens and waited for his order to be ready. The food was ready in no time and soon he was searching for a place to sit and eat. He looked around and found just a lone empty chair. But the chair was facing a girl whose back Vishnu immediately recognized. She was the one he had bumped into just outside the Principal's office. He hesitated for a moment and then made a beeline to the chair. As he stood next to the chair, the girl looked up in what seemed to be irritation. 'Not following you at all, Miss. It is just that all the other chairs are occupied.' The girl craned her neck and checked the veracity of Vishnu's statement and only when she was satisfied that he was speaking the truth did she give a low grunt, 'Huh,' and motioned him to sit. Vishnu sat down and began scarfing down the bread omelet. He looked up to see the girl staring at him, savoring her Wada Sambar. He paused.

'My name is Vishnu,' he said politely. 'I have just been awarded a scholarship by this college to pursue a degree of my choice.'

Vishnu could see the girl's face soften at the mention of a scholarship.

'Hi, I am Gopika and I am here to study Criminal Psychology.' She paused for a while as she had a sip of what looked like absolutely perfect Sambar and asked, 'So what degree did you choose to study for?'

'Incidentally, I was quite interested in Criminal Psychology, but I am more interested in the science of criminality,' Vishnu said. 'So, I am opting for Forensic Science. Mind you, I will be sitting in on courses I find interesting, maybe even a couple of Criminal Psychology courses.'

'Well, here's to new friendships,' he said as he raised his can of Coke in a toast. Gopika giggled and did the same with her cup. And that was their first real conversation.

Dr Sujata looked at Vishnu quite curiously. She made a note to herself – 'Patient has vivid recall of life-events.' She wondered how far she can push him to recall the events leading to that fateful night. As per his case files which she now had full access to, even after so many forceful and almost irrefutable evidences presented during the trial, Vishnu was unable to recall the events that supposedly happened that night. She decided to take a different track, just as a test.

'Do you remember who your first client was?' she asked with utmost curiosity. She could see Vishnu's eyes blank out as he revisited his past and his lips began forming words. Dr Sujata wondered how vivid Vishnu's memory would be this time but analysis would have to wait for later. For now, she listened to every word that came out of Vishnu's mouth with rapt attention.

'Mr. Kapil Shah looked suspiciously towards the Romantic Corner. In a crowd of young people less than half his age, his rotund, pot-bellied dhoti-clad figure stuck out like a sore thumb. It also didn't help that he was there on a slightly delicate family matter.' Vishnu was in full flow, but Dr Sujata's ears pricked. She had just heard something that gave her food for thought, but a pause here would disrupt his flow, she thought to herself.

'Mr. Shah mustered up some courage and walked up to the shop counter and looked at me weird as I was busy doing what I did whenever I had some time to kill.' Vishnu smiled and tried to recall how long it had been since he had indulged in his lone guilty pleasure.

He was about to continue when Dr Sujata couldn't control her curiosity and asked, 'What was that?'

'What was what?' Vishnu asked bewildered.

'What is it that you were doing? The thing that you did whenever you had some time to kill.'

'Oh!' Vishnu's face contorted as he said, 'I was slurping on my favorite ice-lolly.'

'How very child-like!' Dr Sujata thought to herself but also didn't miss Vishnu's uneasiness at the mention of the ice-lolly. But she also remembered that she was face-to-face with a convicted murderer.

'I ushered Mr. Shah into our office and winked knowingly at Gopika who noticed us both walking in.' Vishnu looked up to Dr Sujata and exclaimed with tangible excitement, 'At last! We had our first real client!'

'And then what happened? What was the case? What did Mr. Shah want?' Dr Sujata asked.

'Gopika offered him a seat and asked him if he found the place ok. Mr. Shah cribbed about it being a weird choice for a detective's office,' Vishnu said.

'I apologized and told him that this was the only place we could afford. But Gopika was a bit impatient with all that. She just asked him what he wanted done.' As he said that, Dr Sujata saw Vishnu's face freeze up for just a second. It was such a quick reaction that she blinked and it was gone, his face was back to a blank, lost look. She was curious as to what had triggered that reaction, but then, within the short time she had spent talking with Vishnu, there were quite a few things she was unclear about.

'Mr. Shah looked flustered and didn't quite know where to begin. I had to step in and coax him into telling us what he wanted us to do. I used a tone laced with confidence to put him at ease,' Vishnu said.

'So did he really have a delicate family matter to discuss?' Dr Sujata asked. Her question startled Vishnu and Dr Sujata realized it.

'Well, you said so yourself a while ago, didn't you?' she clarified. 'That Mr. Shah was a bit hesitant.'

'Right. That was just some simple deduction on my part really. We were a new, relatively unknown establishment and Mr. Shah looked quite hesitant to even approach our office. I realized that no one was immediately going to hire us for solving a murder or finding a treasure. Plus, my stint as an apprentice at a Private Eye's office during my college days taught me that the most common investigative jobs were simple background searches, usually related to pre- and post-matrimony. So I guessed that is what Mr. Shah was looking for.'

Dr Sujata pondered on what Vishnu had told her. It did make sense to her, now that he had explained it in detail and asked, 'What happened next?'

'Well, Gopika introduced us and as was standard practice (Vishnu gave a sly smile here. Dr Sujata understood the joke, this being their first client and all), we all signed a binding contract for non-disclosure and client confidentiality. Exactly as I had guessed, Mr. Shah was there to ask for a detailed, but confidential background check for a potential bridegroom for his daughter. He wanted it done very thoroughly and in a manner that would not raise any suspicion from the Rawal family, the marriage alliance.'

'It is quite surprising that for such an important and sensitive matter, Mr. Shah approached you,' Dr Sujata said and realized that her statement could take on a totally different connotation. She immediately explained, 'I mean, you were novices at this. I wonder how or why Mr. Shah even came to you in the first place.'

'You picked up on that huh? We thought that too but Mr. Shah had a very simple explanation. He was an astute businessman and he sensed that we would be eager to do an excellent job, this being our first one and the best publicity in our profession is through word-of-mouth. He also told us that it would be best to have young people do the job as we tended to be more tech-savvy. With the proliferation of social technology – online chat rooms, mobile phones, Orkut and so on, we would be more adept at combing out objectionable material than those old dogs. More importantly, and surprisingly enough, he said all the other private eyes he had approached were a typical male-only operation and he wanted a woman's intuition to guide the search. Gopika and myself as a team fit the bill.' Vishnu's answer was detailed and Dr Sujata admired Mr. Shah's thinking. Who can better judge if a guy was groom-material than a woman? It made perfect sense.

'So, you took the job. And . . .?'

'After agreeing on (what we both thought was a hefty) price, and collecting all the details of the assignment, we bid Mr. Shah farewell. The timeline was seemingly a short one, but as we had no other assignments, we had all the time in the world.' Vishnu paused and looked around a bit hesitantly. As if on cue, Dr Sujata realized what he wanted and stood up.

'Just a minute, I will be back,' she said and hurried away out of the room. Vishnu meant to say something but was left open-mouthed, lips parched. After a full ten minutes, Vishnu was relieved to see Dr Sujata carrying a tray with two empty glasses and a jug with something cool. The condensation was dripping down the sides. She set it down and to Vishnu's relief; it was a jug of ice-cold water. He had hoped for nothing more. 'If you thirst for water, even elixir cannot slake your thirst,' his father used to say. His Dad was a simple man. Vishnu sorrowfully reminisced on why they had drifted apart.

'You were thirsty?' Dr Sujata said and offered Vishnu a frosty glass of cold water. Vishnu took it hastily and gulped down the first mouthful. The cold water hit the spot and relaxed him. He slowly drank the entire glass, every mouthful soothing his throat and relaxing him further. Once done, he asked for more and drank another glass with the same slow soothing rhythm.

'Excuse me,' he said with a bit of shame in his eyes. 'I am not used to talking for so long and was utterly parched.'

Dr Sujata paid no attention to it, possibly because she was very eager to know how their first assignment ended. She just looked at him questioningly as if to say, 'What then? Get a move on!'

Vishnu read the expression perfectly and continued, 'Within an hour (and after another refreshing ice-lolly), we sat around the table to come up with a viable plan of action. Based on the information collected from Mr. Shah and the quick online check Gopika had asked me to get done, we came to know quite a bit about Manoj Rawal. His birthday, friends he usually spent time with, his typical eating and drinking habits (so much for food porn), the sports and celebrities he followed, his political inclinations and so on. Almost everything pointed to Manoj being a young gun from the 21st Century. Average looking, but rich, socially well-adjusted and an up-an-coming businessman.' He stopped and then recalled, 'Gopika said – some girls have all the luck.' He also remembered his retort at the time, 'And some guys do too.' But he didn't say it out loud and Dr Sujata never came to know of it. But she did see that unexplained fleeting expression on Vishnu's face. 'That's twice he has done that,' she noted in her notepad.

'And that's how it all started,' said Vishnu.

'Whose idea was it to have a Romantic Corner along with the private investigator's office?' Dr Sujata asked, deliberately wanting to break Vishnu's chain of thought. Vishnu was slightly startled! He wasn't expecting such a query. He was about to dive into the details of how they had procured the detailed background information for Mr. Shah and how one case led to another and . . . but had completely thrown him off the track. He thought about the question for a while.

'Oh, look at the time! Your story was so interesting; I totally forgot what time it was. Cannot believe we have used up the better part of two hours here!' Dr Sujata said looking at a golden chimes table clock perched elegantly on a handmade teak corner-table. She stood up and Vishnu understood that this was his cue to leave. He stood up as well, and looked at her hesitantly; and then asked, 'Your fees doctor?'

Dr Sujata laughed. 'I did not take your case on for money. I am just doing it as a favor to a friend and mentor; and because I find it quite interesting. Well, see if you can recall what I asked for and we will carry on during our next session,' Dr Sujata said. 'You will visit me again, won't you?' she continued.

Vishnu nodded, 'Yes, I will come in again. Is there an appointment I can book?'

Dr Sujata stretched out to the phone stand, picked up an expensive-looking leather-bound diary and after a brief look-in said, 'How about next Tuesday at 1pm? That is, if you can make it.'

Vishnu nodded . . . 'if you can make it,' she had said!! What else am I doing with my time anyways?

And that was it. Visnhu bid farewell and Dr Sujata carried on with her daily chores. But through the entire day, she felt a sort of uneasiness and couldn't really isolate the cause. And suddenly at 2am she woke up and thought, 'What was the meaning of that fleeting expression on Vishnu's face? And what was it a reaction to? What specific memory had triggered it?'

CHAPTER TWO

The next few days were just a blip in Vishnu's memory. It was the same old dark room, the same voice reminding him of breakfast, lunch and dinner at set times. Nothing had really changed since the day he met Dr Sujata, or so Vishnu thought. But change was afoot. Something deep within him was stirring. For the first time in a number of years, he was actually looking forward to something – meeting Dr Sujata. And then, the day arrived.

Vishnu was back on the bus and looking forward to a few moments in brightness. Dr Sujata's room was comforting if nothing else. And a couple of hours there were quite uplifting and most importantly – free! What was the question Dr Sujata had posed at the end of the chat, he tried to recollect. 'Was it my idea to set up the Romantic Corner along with our investigator's office?'

'I still don't think it is such a good idea,' Gopika had replied, 'I think we should go all in and concentrate on the investigator business. Only if we have nothing to fall back on will we fully focus on making it big as private investigators.'

'We are following our dreams. But, wouldn't it be nice to have a safety net?' Vishnu had countered. He had rarely gone against Gopika's wishes. In fact, he didn't remember an instance where he had actually done anything against her wishes up to that point. But something within him had made him uneasy at the thought of putting all their eggs in one basket.

'I will talk to the agent and get that sorted,' he had told Gopika. Vishnu was never for an argument. But he somehow wanted this to go his way. Anyway, they didn't have enough money to buy the property outright and had to look for a lender. His friend had given him an address. He wondered where this *friend* was now. In fact, he had never seen that friend ever after. That was strange, he thought to himself. But then, stranger things had happened to him since. For reasons known only to them alone, neither Vishnu nor Gopika ever mentioned their parents to each other or to anyone else for that matter. And neither had ever asked the other about it and it had stayed that way. It was one of the factors that had bonded them close together. But the immediate impact of it was that they basically had no guarantor and had to find a lender who did not need one. A few minutes later, Vishnu was at the place where his friend said, some lender would help him out. Vishnu got off the bus and as if in a trance walked up to the gate, then through the garden and buzzed the doorbell.

Dr Sujata opened the door and with a warm smile, welcomed him in. 'What journey were you taking just now?' she asked knowingly.

'I was just going to the lender,' Vishnu replied and seeing that Dr Sujata was just about to pose another question, he added, 'Never mind about that. How are you?'

Dr Sujata was overjoyed at the question and said, 'I am fine, now that you asked me.' She could see that something had changed. Vishnu had actually thought of something normal, consciously. A thought swirled in Dr Sujata's mind but she brushed it aside and noticed Vishnu gazing at her with a curious expression on his face.

'You just showed the first signs of returning back to a civil society,' she said. 'You actually asked me how I have been. Something normal people usually do.'

Normal. Vishnu pondered. How long has he been away from normal? Probably too long, he thought. 'And Dr Sujata thinks I am getting back to normalcy. What about the bus journey I was on just moments ago - - - years ago. Was that normal?' But he kept that question to himself. Dr Sujata was well-prepared this time. She had a frosty jug filled with cold water and two gleaming crystal glasses set on the coffee table. Her notepad and pen ready to jot down poignant facts and . . .

'Hmmm, maybe it is just me but doesn't Dr Sujata look a bit different than the last time?' He made a note to himself.

'Anyways, where were we?' asked Dr Sujata. 'Oh, that's right, you were telling me about how your private investigator business took off.'

'Ah, right. Mr. Narayanan,' Vishnu replied. 'Well, he wanted us to look into Arya's background, the guy his daughter was in love with.'

'Who is Mr. Narayanan? You told me about a Mr. Shah – your first job – where you conducted a background search on a Mr. Rawal,' Dr Sujata interrupted. 'But tell me about Mr. Narayanan if you want,' she continued. Vishnu could sense a slight hesitation in her voice and understood that she didn't want to jump to another case without knowing what happened to the earlier one.

Mr. Shah! What a day that was, Vishnu reminisced. It was after all, their first paid job. And then, he got back to the present and said, 'Oh right! Well, Mr. Shah was our first client. It was all pretty standard. No real skeletons to find. But I guess we did a decent job for very soon, we started receiving similar jobs quite frequently.'

'How frequently?' Dr Sujata asked and Vishnu realized that it wasn't easy to slip something past her.

'Well, all of them really. We kind of specialized exclusively in background searches for potential brides and grooms,' Vishnu said a bit dejectedly. He then looked up to Dr Sujata, met her gaze and softly said, 'So much for being a Private Investigator in India!'

Dr Sujata understood what he meant. All the excitement portrayed in Sherlock Holmes and Hercule Poirot books was just that – bookish. Real life was dull and pedestrian. The hubris of youth had waned away and these two young mystery-junkies had realized that the job of a private eye was no more exciting than that of a typist or a mechanic or an insurance salesman.

'It still is good, steady, honest work,' Dr Sujata offered as solace. 'So, the next case was Mr. Narayanan,' she offered.

Vishnu looked bewildered. 'No! Mr. Narayanan was two years later. We had successfully resolved quite a few cases by the time we met him,' Vishnu said and the expression on Dr Sujata's face was enough to make Vishnu realize his mistake. He was still using flowery language to cover up what they had really been doing for those two years; conducting routine background searches!

He gulped down his pride and just said it the way it was. 'It was another one of those background search jobs.'

'It looks like you guys had by then earned a reputation for these background searches; and a well-deserved one too at that?' Dr Sujata said enthusiastically. 'I am sure it paid well too. Did you still keep the Romantic Corner? Or had your office taken over all of that?'

'Reputation for background search!' Gopika had shouted impatiently. 'There isn't a job titled Background Searcher! Basically, it means we have failed as Private Investigators. Where are the murders? The bank frauds? The jewellery thefts? The unexplained disappearances?' Vishnu remembered that conversation quite clearly. He was ever the optimist. He still believed that at some point in time, they would get some real cases involving fraud, industrial espionage and maybe even murder. But Gopika had always dreamt big. She wanted big cases, big money and big name instantly; and when it hadn't happened even after two years in the business, she was out of patience.

'Agreed it is less exciting, but then it is steady, honest work,' Vishnu had retorted. 'And the money we make isn't too bad either.' But Gopika was having none of it. Such bouts of impatience occurred often with Gopika, but somehow Vishnu was always able to pacify her for the time being.

'Vishnu! Lost in the past again?' Dr Sujata spoke in a very enquiring tone. Vishnu was back to the Now and let go of the Then once more.

'We didn't quite like to think of ourselves as people who could only do background checks. But I guess private investigators lead different lives in books than in reality,' Vishnu said. 'She didn't like the repetitive nature of the job and there was no real excitement, though the money was good.'

'Oh, pity! And Mr. Narayanan had given you a similar assignment, background check. Did that sit well with you?' asked Dr Sujata and followed it with, 'It would start getting monotonous quite quickly, I would have thought.'

'Well, it was a straightforward background check job. By now, we had a method of getting this done and we were so used to it, we could do it almost without thought,' Vishnu said. The results were good enough that they never had to change the method, he thought to himself.

Dr Sujata wanted Vishnu to tell her why he had picked Mr. Narayanan's case in particular for their discussion but thought against directing Vishnu's thought process too much. She just wanted it to play out naturally; wanted to see how Vishnu's mind thought about things; how it analyzed facts and events. So, instead of directly asking 'Why Mr. Narayanan?' she asked 'So how did you go about it? Did you ever uncover any dirt about any of your targets?'

'Not really,' replied Vishnu. 'And that was the main source of frustration for Gopika. She naively thought that we always investigated people of little consequence – you know; average people with no real earth-shattering secrets.'

'Your point being that clients who want people with earth-shattering secrets investigated, pay more money,' Dr Sujata concluded knowingly.

'Well that and also, to find earth-shattering secrets you might have to do exciting things and go to the ends of the world to find them!' Vishnu added.

'A-ha! So you envisioned yourself to be James Bond and Sherlock Holmes rolled into one,' Dr Sujata said in a tone that was just tinged with mockery. And as soon as she said it, she bit her tongue and hoped that Vishnu had not caught it.

'Well, in a sense, she did,' Vishnu said. 'On one hand I was happy that we had a steady business, the Romantic Corner was doing well too and the work we did was not risky; but on the other hand, this wasn't the life we had dreamt of. It definitely wasn't what Gopika had envisioned.'

'So you wished you would get to investigate someone with some skeletons in their closet,' Dr Sujata said in an understanding tone.

'We never tried to conjure up skeletons that weren't there. Never ever! After all, our job was to find hidden secrets, not create them or a mirage thereof.' Vishnu uttered these words with such forceful conviction that it seemed Dr Sujata had accused him of something.

'Of course! Who would do such a thing?' Dr Sujata said. 'So, how did you go about these jobs? Tell me how and what you found about Arya. Any skeletons in his closet?' Dr Sujata was quite keen in getting to know their method. And Vishnu realized that over the years, they had perfected a method that was almost like *A Step by Step Guide to Background Searches for Dummies*!!

'We always started out with a physical identification / confirmation of the subject under investigation. And that would mean I had to go and actually see the person without the person being aware of the surveillance,' Vishnu said. 'I usually followed the subject for some time, either to or from the office or at a restaurant with friends etc. Always keeping my distance. Always without any direct face-to-face contact.'

'So that is what you did in this case too?' Dr Sujata asked, with what Vishnu thought was a tinge of impatience.

'Well, to begin with. Yes!' Vishnu said and continued, 'You know how these software company campuses are set up. Posh buildings, nice walkways, clean open spaces, manicured lawns and gardens and obviously restaurants and coffee places to cater to all those highly-paid software geeks.'

Dr Sujata had seen the phenomena that had defined India's urban rejuvenation of sorts since the Nineties. Many of India's popular retirement cities became global software hubs and entire cities went through a surprising and at times shocking facelift. Chennai, being a metro, did not go through this complete metamorphosis, but there were perceivable changes everywhere. Suddenly, there was this brash, young group of techno-geeks who worked at various multinational software companies and had ample money to splurge on what just a decade ago was deemed a far-fetched luxury. She was impressed to note that Vishnu had in a very limited number of sentences captured the entire geography of what was now popularly known as a *Software Campus*.

'A few lunch-time trips to the company campus told me quite a lot about the food and socialization habits of Arya.' Vishnu was now in full flow. 'I found out where Arya liked to have his lunch and I even found out what he usually favored. But as they say – *Chance favors the prepared mind*. I hit the jackpot just purely by luck.'

'What do you mean, *hit the jackpot?*' Dr Sujata asked in a tone that wasn't quite here or there. At least, that is what Vishnu thought for a fleeting moment.

'I wasn't yet quite sure about how I could get any useful information from Arya's office or colleagues, so I sat down in one of the cafes for a juice. As luck would have it, I saw Arya walk right past me and sit in a remote corner. He had his quick cup of coffee and hurriedly exited the café. Just as he left, he bumped into a couple of co-workers, a guy and a girl. The guy was quite friendly with him but it seemed the girl was slightly perturbed to bump into him. After exchanging a few niceties, the couple sat down at a table right across me and the interesting stuff began.' Vishnu was clearly in the moment and Dr Sujata noticed his glee.

'. . . you that pissed off with Arya? I find him to be a thorough professional,' the guy was saying.

'Huh! Professional, my foot! Ask him to code something in C for a change. Always tooting his JAVA skills!'

'That's ok, Meena. But what is this all about really? Did he pip you for another client-side meeting?'

'I am not that shallow, Puneet! But honestly, how does he manage to go on so many client-site visits. And how come of all places, this client is located in Switzerland! What software company does

Switzerland have? And how come they want him to visit that often?'

'Come on! You know how good he is. And he isn't going to Switzerland next. You are just jealous.'

'Forget me. How about you, Puneet? Did he not put you to shame when you warned him of skipping work?'

'That was just a system error really. I received a notification from our automated attendance system that Arya had been tardy for a while and his log-in and log-out times showed that for a few days, he had worked very irregularly and never for the stipulated eight hours per day. Well, it was Arya who actually found a flaw in the system. Our old system was dumb in that sense. It only logged in the time at swipe-in and swipe-out and considered that there will be no one working for more than twenty-four hours at a stretch. So when Arya logged in at nine in the morning on Tuesday and logged out at ten thirty in the morning on Wednesday, the system only said he worked for one and a half hours, when in reality, he had been working for close to twenty-six hours!'

'Arya said it and you guys believed it. He is the Golden Boy, so everything he says is taken for granted.'

'No, actually the proof was quite strong. Our nightshift watchman Harilal vouched for Arya being present. He had in fact, brought him tea during the night.'

'So, now we believe in what a cheap watchman says. I bet he will say he was visited by Nayantara if I pay him a hundred bucks!'

'Well, now you are just speaking bonkers. On Arya's insistence, I actually tried it and it really did that. The system didn't count up after twenty-four hours.'

'But Arya did go above your head and you were shamed in front of your superior, weren't you?'

'So that is what this is all about, isn't it Meena? Did Arya do that to you some time? And no. It didn't happen quite like that to me. The memo email to Arya was sent by me but the rectification had to happen in front of the HR manager anyways. So, that is what Arya did. He was polite and when we tested the system, he was proved to be correct. In fact, Arya was kind enough to offer correcting the system code all by himself and free of charge too. But it wasn't fair to him to be asked to do more than what was required and we got the maintenance engineer from the system vendor to rectify it. But I am more interested in how he humiliated you?'

'The nerve of this twig! In front of a client, he showed a flaw in my project development outline and the client, pfft, what technical knowledge do they have?! They just gave the project lead duties to Arya!'

'I heard about that incidence, but not quite the way you have put it. I was told it was an open brainstorming session where a group of engineers from our company were hashing out project specifications and requirements with the client. And you all pitched your cases and Arya's case was the one the client finally selected. I must also add that his plan meant that our company maximized billable time to client and still managed to bag the project.'

'Yeah! All because the technical *expert* the client company sent over was a hussy who was more busy ogling and winking at Arya than actually understanding the wool he was trying to pull over her eyes!' After all those years, Vishnu could still vividly recall the expression on Meena's face when she had said that. It was a face full of anger, heavily tinged with envy and a touch of malice. Seldom again had he ever seen such an expression on someone's face, and he had seen plenty. Throughout his trial and incarceration, he had come across revulsion, anger, hatred, disdain, pity; even kindness at times but never that particular mix of emotions that danced on Meena's face at that time.

'So, this Meena was envious of Arya then?' Dr Sujata's question broke Vishnu's chain of thought and brought him out of his dreamworld.

'Huh! Envious would be putting it mildly. She wasn't done yet and ultimately ended up scandalizing Arya.' Vishnu paused and looked down in shame and then slowly said. 'Or so it seemed to me at that time.' He looked up at Dr Sujata and noticed that she had zoned out of their discussion as well and hadn't really heard what Vishnu had said. Vishnu just stared at her with a blank gaze.

'Sorry, what were you saying?' Dr Sujata said all flustered. 'Oh, that's right. Meena. Please continue.'

'I bet Arya is going to spend some quality time with this technical *expert*, going over project specs. Make sure you book a good honeymoon suite for the star, Puneet. He must have a cosy time with the client, if he has to get his point across.' Meena's voice was heavily laden with all sorts of scandalous insinuations. Neither Vishnu, nor Puneet had missed it.

'You are too much, Meena. You will have your fair share of the limelight someday. Don't worry dear, I have all the faith in your abilities.' Puneet pacified Meena but Vishnu, eavesdropping from a distance could sense the lack of sincerity in Puneet's voice. 'Anyways, as is normal with this client, they organize logistics for Arya at their end. If you think a honeymoon suite will help, I can pass on your recommendation through to their HR department!' The mockery was too apparent for even Meena, with all her anger, to miss. Vishnu couldn't stop himself either and gave a low chuckle hoping that he hadn't attracted untoward attention to himself.

'Talk to me when you come back to your senses.' Meena shrieked and hurriedly walked away from the table. Vishnu looked at Puneet and their eyes met for just a fleeting moment. Puneet gave Vishnu a slight shrug and a look that seemed to say, 'Women, right!'

Vishnu quickly looked away from Puneet as if that small visual exchange had just been a figment of someone's imagination, walked up to the counter, paid for his juice and left the café.

'So!' Dr Sujata exclaimed. Vishnu was still lost in thought. He had a tingling feeling that he had just remembered something important and it had just slipped his mind before he could register it.

'So?' Vishnu repeated, not quite understanding what Dr Sujata was asking.

'Seems like there was something spicy going on in Arya's life after all,' Dr Sujata seemed to be a bit excited by the fact that something interesting was coming up.

'And that is what we thought too,' Vishnu said ruefully.

'So you just told that to Mr. Narayanan? And he believed all that?' Dr Sujata asked in a neutral tone. Yet for some reason, Vishnu thought it had a tinge of disgust. Not an overpowering stench but just the faintest of whiff.

'No. Not at all,' Vishnu said indignantly. 'That flimsy evidence would not fly at all. If it did, we could just say we *heard* something and all our cases would be done without ever stepping foot out of the office.' Vishnu couldn't imagine Dr Sujata was naïve enough to think that an overheard conversation with no one to vouch for its veracity would be sufficient.

'So what did you do then? And I am still not clear how this would be termed as direct face-to-face contact,' Dr Sujata queried.

'Well, this wasn't. But then, this gave us enough reason to believe that Arya did indeed have some secrets up his sleeve. I had a long discussion with Gopika on how to proceed further and in the end we decided that I would visit Arya at his office. We were going to do some actual snooping around. I was going to talk to people he interacted with, maybe go through his trash, if possible hack into his email accounts. We were eager to do stuff off the beaten track. We wanted the slightest excuse to get some excitement that was missing from the other previous cases we handled and finally, we thought we had found it,' Vishnu said. Dr Sujata noted that Vishnu's breathing rhythm had quickened.

'I decided that I would visit Arya's office as a *dabbawalla*! It was the least intrusive character we could think of who would raise minimal suspicion. All I was supposed to do was to go in, see Arya in his surroundings, with his co-workers, and in the work environment and then we were going to decide our next move.'

'*If you see anything interesting, do make a note of it. Or take a picture with your cell-phone camera. And don't get caught!* Gopika had warned,' Vishnu said as if in a trance. It was though he could actually hear Gopika say those words to him. But soon, he clawed his way back to reality.

'I just walked up to the entrance gate and started a heart-to-heart conversation with the gatekeeper. I have learned that the strongest bonds humans form after blood-ties are those of commonly shared grief. A cripple relates to another cripple, a jobless person connects with another jobless person and similarly a poor man who works hard to make ends meet, immediately relates with another poor man in the same predicament. It was quite easy for me to get past the gatekeeper, just a poor dabbawalla canvassing IT companies to find employees who would be interested in hot lunches. The gatekeeper was a kind man, but still wanted no trouble and indicated that my entry into the employee work-area would depend on my ability to get past the receptionist.'

Vishnu could actually remember the color of the staircase, the design of the railing and the carpet along the hallway and was quite astonished at the clarity of his recall. For a moment, Vishnu felt like all the haze had lifted and there was a window of clarity.

'Fortune favors the brave – goes the saying, and I was brave. I pushed the door to the reception hall and noticed that the receptionist had just gotten up to go somewhere. She hesitated and asked me to wait for a moment before she returned. I started towards the plush sofa and no sooner had the receptionist closed the door of the lavatory behind her, another door opened and a smartly dressed thirty something walked out. I took the chance and before the door could close behind him, slipped right through to enter what looked like a typical setup for a software company – softly colored walls, bright but not blinding lights, desks with partition barriers, the soft hum of the air-conditioning and an incessant pitter-patter of keyboards. It wasn't a very large area, but it had an air of relaxed roominess.'

'Your observation is quite detailed. I guess it comes with being a detective. You could have been a psychiatrist instead,' interrupted Dr Sujata. Vishnu thought Dr Sujata was either mocking him or was being too kind. But a sort of compulsion to get the story out made Vishnu plod ahead without giving much thought to what Dr Sujata was saying.

'I quickly scanned the work-area and could easily identify Arya. He was standing next to the printer at the far corner of the room. I approached the first desk and asked the lady occupying it if she was interested in a hot lunch delivered to her desk each day in a timely fashion. But even before I could finish my question, I realized the answer would be negative. Thirty-something women with a mangalsutra in their necks and a nicely framed family photo showing a smiling couple with a toddler, seldom have the luxury of ready-made lunches. Most often, they are the dabbawallas for their family! The lady dismissed me with a terse reply and I was about to move to the next desk when I saw Arya intently reading the printout as he was walking back to his desk. He had a sly smile on his face and I would have given anything to know what was on that paper!'

'Presumptuous on your part isn't it?' Dr Sujata enquired. 'You wouldn't know whether the smile was because of what was on that paper.'

'Very true, but for a detective looking for excitement, everything is suspicious,' Vishnu replied. 'I went through two more not-interested and one iffy reply before I stood in front of Arya's desk and asked: Excuse me sir, I was wondering if any of you are interested in a hot home-cooked meal delivered every day for a reasonable price. Arya looked up to me in a daze and in that time, I had read just a couple of words from the paper he had just finished reading while walking back from the printer that was now on his desk – *see you* – **honeymoon**.'

'Wow! Sounds like you got a case with skeletons in the closet after all,' squealed Dr Sujata with all the excitement of a teenager. 'Carry on.'

'I was thinking of how I could take a picture of that paper without anyone noticing it and was thinking of engaging Arya into a conversation about the kind of curries I could offer; when Meena entered the room with a loud huff and dumped herself unceremoniously in a chair about three desks away from where I was. Arya probably noticed Meena entering and looked up to me with puzzled expression. I repeated my question all the while keeping an eye on the paper I found intriguing. My question seemed to have lit a fuse to Meena's anger and she stormed her way towards Arya's desk and started shouting at me.'

'Who let you in?' she asked angrily and in my shock, I dropped my briefcase on Arya's desk.

'I – I – I stammered to come up with an explanation and at the same time got busy in gathering up the contents of my briefcase, that had spilled all over his desk. I was calculating the risk of being caught, but my luck thus far emboldened me and I shoved into my briefcase, that one sheet of paper that had piqued my interest, hoping that no one had noticed my theft. Arya was busy trying to calm Meena down and politely asked me to leave my business-card so that the information could be circulated to all interested employees within the office. I handed Arya a dabbawalla's card I had swiped from a real dabbawalla earlier, just for such an instance and exited the room in a hurry, profusely apologizing to the irate Meena; all the while hoping that my first singular act with a criminal tinge would result in a jackpot!'

'And did it?' Dr Sujata asked. 'Result in a jackpot, I mean.'

'The paper was an email printout from a lady (I recognized by the name used) that said – All arrangements for your visit have been made. As always, the honeymoon suite has been booked and that she was looking forward to seeing him the next day!'

'Well, talk about jackpots; it looks like you hit the motherlode! Meena was correct in her suspicions after all. And Puneet's off-hand comment about booking a honeymoon suite had actually come true,' Dr Sujata said excitedly. 'Did you continue with the investigation and find who this *other* lady was?'

'I took the paper to Gopika who was overjoyed! This is our ticket to more money and some much required R&R at the client's expense she squealed, unable to conceal her excitement. We discussed packing for the travel and the money we would charge Mr. Narayanan for the out-of-city investigation needs. She took a copy of the paper and immediately called Mr. Narayanan to meet up for further instructions. Her conversation was quite short and soon after, told me that she was going to meet Mr. Narayanan. I offered to go with her, but she flatly refused, citing my ineptitude at all matters financial.'

'What happened then? Did you finally get to solve the mystery of the honeymoon suite? Was Arya really cheating?' Dr Sujata asked, almost impatiently.

'I don't know! Later in the evening, Gopika returned in the foulest of moods. I asked her if I was to book tickets and hotel for the travel and she said, the assignment was over!' Vishnu replied. Vishnu remembered vividly, the thoughts he had when Gopika had told him that Mr. Narayanan did not want to continue with the background search any further. Vishnu was in two minds even then. Should he have initiated a chat with Mr. Narayanan or should he have let it go? Was Mr. Narayanan serious about an honest background search or was he simply looking to find an excuse to break Arya and Sita's love-affair? Or did Gopika oversell the facts they had uncovered? He had felt uneasy at the abrupt end of the case then; and that same feeling had returned again when he narrated the story to Dr Sujata.

'Over! But didn't Mr. Narayanan want to conduct a thorough investigation?' Dr Sujata asked.

'It seems that when Gopika relayed what I had overheard Puneet and Meena speak and showed Mr. Narayanan the email I had swiped from Arya's desk, he was furious with Arya and didn't want any more time or money wasted on him by us or Sita. He just asked Gopika to give him a copy of the email, paid the money we were owed and basically told that that was the conclusion of the assignment.'

'Did you or Gopika not go back and convince Mr. Narayanan that more investigation needs to be conducted before any conclusions could be drawn? What happened to Arya and Mr. Narayanan's daughter? Did they get married?' Dr Sujata asked.

'Gopika said there was no use of talking with Mr. Narayanan; that his decision was final. And she didn't want to go back to him with anything. As for what happened to Arya and Sita; who knows. The case was closed. Our job was done. It was not like we were investigating murders or unearthing some sensitive state secrets. It was just a background search for marriage. When the client stopped paying us money and asked us to stop, we stopped. Once we collected our fee, our job was done and we never kept tabs on our clients or targets,' Vishnu said.

'So you don't know what impact your investigations had on your clients' lives; or your targets' for that matter?' Dr Sujata questioned pensively, as if she was talking to no one in particular but herself. 'Well, I thought professional investigators would do that from time to time.'

Vishnu was lost in thought. Gopika never thought of keeping tabs on their past clients. Why would she? Who did that? Not Sherlock Holmes, not Mrs. Jane Marple nor Hercule Poirot! But should they have? And just then, he was interrupted by Dr Sujata again. 'One thing is for sure though,' she said.

Vishnu looked at her puzzled.

'You must be a master in disguise. I mean, for you to be sitting across Puneet and Meena for some time one day and the very next day you came face-to-face with Meena again and she just didn't recognize you. That is a useful skill, especially in your business.' Dr Sujata elaborated and then in the same breath said, 'I am afraid that is all the time I have for today. How about meeting up on Monday? Same time Ok?'

Vishnu nodded unknowingly, bid his good-bye and was back to the bus stop in no time. There was only one thought overwhelming his entire being at this moment, 'What happened to Arya and Sita. And more importantly, what happened to Kamal and Sujay?' But both these thoughts were overridden by another, 'What was it that he had just recognized and then missed registering?'

As he sat in the bus with his head leaning on the window bars, the shrill sounds of traffic faded into a soft background hum and Vishnu recalled the day a young man in a shabbily fitting safari suit clutching a small cheap imitation-leather briefcase in one hand and a mobile phone in the other had sneaked into Arya's office and said, 'Excuse me, I was wondering if any of you are interested in a hot home-cooked meal delivered every . . .'

CHAPTER THREE

Vishnu woke up with a zeal he hadn't shown in quite some time. The trauma of Gopika's gruesome murder, the court proceedings that followed and his subsequent incarceration in a filthy prison for the next seven years had almost sapped him of all the will to live. But somewhere in the deepest pits of his warped mind, he always had this itch of finding what had really happened. If he didn't murder Gopika, then who did! And that had taken him through this long circuitous journey to get back to being a functioning human being first and if possible, a private investigator later. His first stop had been Dr Prakash – the Court-appointed psychiatrist and that had led him to Dr Sujata; who asked weird questions, he thought. Who had proposed the idea of having the Romantic Corner along with their office? Well, it must obviously have been Gopika. She was the one who took all such major decisions. But somehow that wasn't acceptable to some part of Vishnu's psyche. But what did the answer matter. He was no longer a private investigator and there was no more Gopika. There was no more Vishnu either, at least not the carefree, ice-lolly slurping Vishnu of the past, that he vaguely remembered and resembled. But the question Dr Sujata had asked during their recent chat was a worrying one. What happened to the clients and the targets after Gopika and Vishnu had given their investigative findings? That thought had never occurred to him or Gopika in the past. Why would it? Or maybe Gopika thought of it and kept it to herself. He was just not sure about what he knew anymore. But then, who thinks of these things when all was fine and dandy! This was a case of hind-sight 20-20.

But what worries Vishnu slightly was the fact that Kamal and Sujay's case had immediately popped into his mind. He hadn't immediately recalled why earlier, but now he remembered. Sujay's father, their client, seemed to be against the relationship from the onset. He had made his views quite clear to both Gopika and Vishnu. In fact, he was hoping that Gopika and Vishnu would find something in the background search that he could use to annul Sujay and Kamal's matrimony plans. But as far as Vishnu could remember, they were able to find nothing of the sort. It was, once again, the same clean background. No hidden skeletons. But then, why had he remembered that case, he mused. Sujay's father did not look too unhappy when he finally came back to pay up at the office. It felt like Vishnu was missing something, but what – it eluded him. What happened to Sujay and Kamal? Did they still get married against Sujay's father's wishes? Or did they go their separate ways and were leading happy lives? Was there any reason for Sujay or Kamal to hold a grudge against him or Gopika?

Vishnu was, for the first time in almost a decade doing something with purpose. He was going to find out what lives Sujay and Kamal led. In reality, he was trying to find absolution. Absolution from what though? From Gopika's murder? Well, his mind was still not ready to accept blame for that, even after the punishment he bore for the crime. And how was Sujay and Kamal's case related to Gopika's murder, he thought. And why would finding what happened to Sujay and Kamal absolve him of anything? He was surprised that up until the very moment that Dr Sujata posed the question, he had never thought of it. Being a private investigator, he had forgotten a cardinal rule – every action has a reaction – and in many cases, the reaction was more deliberate and striking than the action that initiated it. He shuddered at the thought, but also realized that this was just a strand he was grasping at. Little did he know that this thread would in the end, lead him to understand and unravel the mess that was his life.

Vishnu re-lived the moment Sujay's father had visited their then well-set office. They had done well in past year or so that they had been Private Investigators. They hadn't solved any ground-breaking mysteries but they still managed to have a steady flow of clients. The work was steady although repetitive in nature, but the money was flowing. The Romantic Corner was for all purposes, unnecessary but had now become a part of their establishment and Vishnu couldn't thank his stars less for the storage freezer and his favorite ice-lollies . . . and that thought put a shiver down his spine that chilled him to the bone. Ice-cream freezer – frozen body – Gopika murdered – incarceration – suicide attempts – early release – horror days of darkness – Dr Prakash – Dr Sujata – the well-lit room – Arya and Sita – Sujay and Kamal! And with a jolt, Vishnu was back to the now and in an instant he was lost once again in the past – Sujay's father.

This man was quite grumpy about the whole thing. No sooner had he parked his ample girth in one of the armchairs had he begun grumbling of how inconsiderate the young generation was towards the parents' wishes and the societal norms. He gave them an assignment that had now become a routine for Gopika and Vishnu. A simple background search for a marriage proposal. The father of the would-be groom wanted to know if the would-be bride had any hidden surprises. But his incessant grumbling did not stop. He kept on and on about how he was totally taken by surprise when his gold-plated son Sujay breached the idea of his own marriage, that too with a mere mortal, average girl like Kamal. It seemed that he wanted the background search to uncover something that would deem Kamal unfit to marry Sujay.

The long bus ride came to an end and Vishnu was in a totally foreign environment. Tall buildings, fast cars, honks, huge advertisement banners – this was the same city, but it had left him behind. He remembered what it had been like from a decade earlier, but the city did not. It had chugged along with a rapid pace, always heading for the never-reachable boundary of modernization. Vishnu knew the city when they used audio cassettes and VHS tapes. Now, the city used MP3 players and Blu-ray discs for the same. What did he know about Sujay? Well, not much. He wasn't the subject of investigation, Kamal was. He was in two minds as to whether he should start looking for Sujay or for Kamal. If Kamal and Sujay were married, then they would be living together and most probably would be living with Sujay's parents. Best then to track down Sujay, he reasoned. He then remembered that Sujay's father lived in a bungalow somewhere around this place. Vishnu looked around and thought of inquiring at a grocery store. Not the plush new mini-marts that had sprung up all over the city. This was a typical old-school grocery store. Gunny-bags filled with various grains and pulses, an old grimy counter which had an array of glass containers filled with a multitude of cheap candies and chocolates. A set of cast-iron weighing scales was the center-piece of the counter-top and a shabbily dressed man of uncertain age sat behind the counter seemingly doing nothing of note. This was the shop that used to deliver to your door within a few hours, once the goods-list was given. This was the shop that you paid the bills for the last month, at the beginning of the next. This was the shop where the owner and the pre-twenties shop assistants knew every house in their neighborhood, and more often than not, knew something about the occupants in each house as well.

Vishnu approached the shop and it hit him. He had to buy something and start a conversation with the person sitting behind the counter if he had to get some useful information. That is the way it worked. These shopkeepers were very loyal to their clientele, but once you bought something from them, you became one of their clients and information would flow freely! Vishnu stopped dead in his tracks. He had never really bought anything in a very long time. The last time he had bought something was when he still was a young private eye and Gopika was by his side, he remembered and instantaneously regretted it. Remembering Gopika still had that effect on him. Back to the present, Vishnu reminded himself. I have to buy something that would start a conversation without raising any unwanted eyebrows. And such a simple decision took some time.

Vishnu laughed at himself.

'Some detective you are,' he said to himself disdainfully. He had a sly smile and went up to the counter and said, 'A loaf of bread and a bottle of jam.' The shopkeeper got up at his own pace and started putting the two things in a plastic carry bag.

Vishnu was about to start his line of questioning but before he could begin the shopkeeper asked, 'Have you moved into the lodge across the street recently? I haven't seen you before.'

Vishnu couldn't believe his luck. 'Yes, just moved in. Trying to find my bearings, but cannot do that on an empty stomach,' he said.

The shopkeeper laughed and nodded knowingly. 'There is the Ganesha Hotel a couple blocks away, if you are keen. Good food at a fair price,' he told Vishnu.

Vishnu had noticed that stall as he had walked over. It was a typical joint frequented by the lower middle-class. Not something young software professionals or any well-to-do guy would drop by. Suddenly, he realized something. 'You don't look like a well-to-do guy.' The line of questioning had to change.

'Do you know where Mr. Kamat stays?' he asked and was surprised that after so many years, he could instantly remember the name of Sujay's father. It gave him a sense of achievement and filled him with temporary pride.

'Mr. Kamat? You mean the one who owns a printing press in Saidapet? Why? Do you know him?' came the barrage of questions from across the counter.

'No, not really. But I was told he is looking for a driver,' said Vishnu.

'Oh yeah! Well, you see the lane next to the new high-rise across the street. Just take that lane and follow it to the end. Then turn right and it is the third bungalow on the left. You can't miss it. It has a beautiful wrought iron gate.'

Vishnu picked up the bread and jam, thanked the shopkeeper for the directions and started towards Mr. Kamat's house, all the while thinking of how he would find what happened to Sujay and Kamal.

He reached the house, marveled at the generous proportions of the bungalow and the intricate wrought iron gates and was about to open them when a thought struck him and he retreated back the way he had come.

He will have to talk to Sujay directly, he reasoned. But definitely not in the current form. Vishnu headed back to the dark corner of his home. But he had to change back to his suave self if he had to interact with the real world. He had to get back to reality, make himself presentable to decent society. A shave and a haircut and a grooming session, a few appointments with the tailor or a fashion boutique should sort it out, he mused. And thus started his transformation, from a psychologically troubled murder convict to a functioning human being. It wasn't an easy transition and what Vishnu thought to be just a matter of moments turned out to be a matter of days. Just the physical appearance wasn't enough he realized. He had to become comfortable in his new skin. Get used to the clothing and the expensive shoes. To the etiquettes and mannerisms of a well-groomed gentleman; and above all, to the clean-shaven handsome face that stared back at him when he looked in a mirror. That meant he had to reschedule his appointment with Dr Sujata. He did not want to face her without an answer to the question she had posed. 'So you don't know what impact your investigations had on your clients' or targets' lives?' she had asked.

Vishnu's transformation was going to be put to the test today. He had walked up to Mr. Kamat's lane and as if on cue, he saw Mr. Kamat leaving in a car. He saw a security guard close the gates behind the car and hurried up to the gates. 'Is Mr. Kamat home?' Vishnu asked.

'Which one sir? Senior or Junior?' his question was answered by another question.

'Junior? You mean Sujay? Vishnu asked skeptically, hoping that he had come to the right Mr. Kamat.

'Yes sir. He is home. Who shall I say is asking?' the guard confirmed and queried further.

Vishnu was both relieved and excited all at once. Excited that he had found his quarry and relieved that Sujay was living with his father. But that could still not be the whole story. Was he doing well? Was he a family man? Questions such as these started boring holes into his relieved mind and he started formulating a way of getting them answered. But to keep the conversation rolling, he said, 'No, I was here for Mr. Kamat Senior. He looks after the printing press isn't it?'

'Oh, well. You just missed him. That was him in the car. But if you want to talk business, you can talk to Sujay sir as well. Let me get him for you.' The guard insisted.

So Sujay was actively involved in the business. That was a good sign, Vishnu thought and continued, 'No need. I will talk to Mr. Kamat at his office then. It would be nice if I could talk to them both together though.'

'You can do that after ten o'clock. Sujay sir will drop the kids to school and head for office after that,' the guard filled in.

Vishnu felt a new sense of calm wash over him. Sujay was actively involved in business, happily married to Kamal and they had school-going kids. And that is it he thought. All is well. Suddenly, a cute kid in a chequered school uniform came running out of the door and straight towards the guard. And right behind him, a lady in a wrinkled just-out-of-bed gown called out, 'Arya . . . get back in here this instance and pack your lunchbox!' The little boy stopped in his tracks and turned back and said, 'Coming Ma.'

'Sujay sir's kid is very naughty,' the guard muttered and for the lady's benefit said out loudly 'You can meet Sujay sir at the printing press directly,' as he hurried back to retrieve the kid to his mother.

Vishnu was stunned! Mrs. Sujay was definitely not Kamal! He quickly gained control of his faculties and decided to head straight to the printing press. He wanted to find the right vantage point so that he could see Sujay get out of his car and walk towards the press – the perfect time to bump into him and start a conversation. But first he had to find the exact location of the press. He had a head start there.

He knew the area where it was supposed to be located and he also knew that Mr. Kamat owned it. In the old corners of the city such as Saidapet where the press was located, history had a high value. Vishnu was sure that Mr. Kamat's press, which was quite an old establishment, would be quite easy to find. He started thinking about the way the conversation was going to unfold. And something else had made him uneasy too. Something he had heard when he was talking to the guard at Mr. Kamat's bungalow. But he couldn't pinpoint as to what it was. Something the guard had said? Something he had seen – other than the fact that Sujay's wife was not Kamal. 'Well, it will come to me,' Vishnu thought.

And that was almost an hour ago. In the meantime, Vishnu had located the entrance to the press and at this very instance was seeing Sujay park his car and walk towards the direction of the press. Vishnu thanked his stars for the city traffic. Parking was choc-a-bloc and Sujay found a place relatively away from the press entrance. Vishnu quickened his pace seemingly looking to the opposite side of the road and bumped into Sujay, letting his briefcase fall noisily to the dust covered footpath. 'Watch where you are going,' Sujay admonished and was about to get past him when Vishnu picked up the briefcase and said, 'Apologies sir, I am trying to find my way to . . . hang on, you are Sujay aren't you?!'

Sujay was taken aback and looked at Vishnu with a big question-mark on his face. 'Sorry, do I know you?' he asked sheepishly.

'You are Sujay aren't you? Sujay Kamat?' asked Vishnu.

'Y-Yes. Sorry, and you are . . .,' Sujay queried.

'No wonder you have forgotten me. It's been ten years almost. I am Prabhakar, classmates with Kamal. How is she, by the way?' and just as he finished, Vishnu realized that Sujay's face had gone distant and bitter.

'I don't know. You say you were her classmate, so shouldn't you know how she is doing?' Sujay replied in a clearly annoyed tone.

'I am sorry; I was away for most of the time. You know, the H1-B – Green Card route. Wasn't able to visit my homeland for a decade and now that I am here, the memories come flooding back,' Vishnu said with a nostalgic look on his face. 'I remember you and Kamal were going to be married then. What happened?'

'Well, I don't want to talk about that gold-digger. Good riddance. I have moved on and am happily married to someone who loves me, not my money,' Sujay said.

'Oh! Kamal, a gold-digger? I would have never guessed it. Anyways, best of luck to you.' Vishnu said and walked away.

It was a very brisk walk. Kamal was a gold-digger, huh! That thought did not sit right with Vishnu. He had actually conducted a thorough surveillance and even recorded some of Kamal's conversations with her Dad and nothing to indicate Kamal being money-hungry was evident. On the contrary, Kamal was very much in love with Sujay for the right reasons. Something must have changed. Or maybe Kamal was a much superior actor than what he had given her credit for, Vishnu thought. Anyways, now his work had increased. To answer Dr Sujata's question, he will have to see how Kamal was doing.

That was the easy part. Vishnu knew exactly where Kamal lived, at least before he was sent to jail. He made a beeline to Kamal's house and played the same trick. He posed as a long-lost classmate of Kamal's and luckily, her father was extremely forthcoming with information. 'Kamal is happily married and settled in Cape Town. Her husband is a spice trader. She visits every year with her daughters,' he said and went on and on. He told Vishnu how she was very much involved in the family business and how she balanced her business engagements with her family commitments. He also let in very proudly how she had started a small scholarship scheme for needy kids in the schools around their locality and was also planning to extend some substantial financial scholarships for higher education. This did not sound like a gold-digger, but that didn't matter as much. All was well with both Sujay and Kamal. Sujay was well and happily married and Kamal was doing great too. It was weird that Kamal and Sujay were not married to each other. And it was weirder that Sujay thought Kamal was a gold-digger though all evidence pointed to the contrary. As far as he could tell, the background search he and Gopika had conducted had not destroyed either Sujay or Kamal's life.

There was something that was still haunting him, something he had heard during the course of this investigation. But what? It was so near and yet so far away. Anyway, the one bright spot was that he had an answer to Dr Sujata's question. With a slightly lighter heart, Vishnu came back to his room and found it dark. As was his habit, he once again began his sojourn into his past. College days! Good times all around. He had already decided to be a Private Eye and had also chosen courses he thought were going to be invaluable in his career. To gain valuable hands-on experience, Vishnu had taken on an apprentice's post at a reputed detective agency in Chennai. It was only when Vishnu offered his services for no salary did the owner of the detective agency agree to allow him to work there. He recalled that most of the time he spent was boring and all he did was read reports of past or continuing cases and a bit of filing. He soon realized that most investigative work in India revolved around pre- and post-marital background searches. There was a spattering of other work such as corporate espionage, kidnapping, theft etc., but that wasn't enough to pay the bills. People would avail the services of a private eye for such crimes simply to avoid the complication of involving the police and the law. He was reading through a post-marital investigation report. The case was on-going and every other day, a detective from the agency would add to the report. It was a simple case of the husband suspecting his wife of adultery and wanting proof of it. Read in bits, everything seemed to indicate to the same conclusion. But Vishnu had all the time in the world. When he read the entire report, a different scenario emerged. It was the wife who had hired the private eye to create the illusion that her husband was unjustly suspicious of her and his suspicious nature and jealousy was bordering on harassment – clear grounds for divorce and a hefty alimony cheque.

Vishnu was so pumped up with this finding that he did two things the very next morning. First, he called the lady in question and asked her politely but in no uncertain terms to stop her treachery. Secondly, he bragged about his incisive observation skills to Gopika during their lunch hour.

'Are you sure about this?' Gopika questioned. 'It surely sounds quite diabolical.'

'Well, I just told the lady what is what. If I see that the contract has been terminated, I know I was right. If my boss fires me, I might be wrong. But looks like I am right,' Vishnu said just as a middle-aged lady, clearly oozing of wealth, greed and boredom came and stopped next to their table.

'You are Vishnu, correct?' she said as she pulled up a chair and sat down haughtily.

'I am sorry, you are . . .,' but Vishnu couldn't finish his sentence.

'Look, I don't have time for two-bit guys like you,' she said as she shoved her hand into a bejeweled purse she had with her. In an instant, it came back out clutching a thick wad of currency notes. 'Here is ten thousand rupees for your silence.' She noticed Vishnu's hesitation and added, 'There is another ten thousand in it for you once I get my divorce.'

Vishnu was left aghast. 'Keep your money, cancel the contract and find a truer way of getting divorced. Just say you are bored of the relationship!'

'Idiot! You have done well in uncovering my deceit. That doddering old fool you call boss was too blinded by the money and the routine of a job to see through my ruse. Don't spoil it for me and bite the hand that is giving you a gold biscuit to chew on!' she was now shrieking, all the time totally oblivious to the fact that Gopika was sitting just on the other side and within earshot.

'So, you want to get rid of your husband and still want to keep his money!' Vishnu said utterly nauseated at the uninhibited greed this seemingly cultured lady was showing.

'Who doesn't want money?' she said looking at him with

contempt and said, 'Except few idealistic brats like you!'

'Leave now,' Vishnu said and stood up and gestured to Gopika, 'Let us go. It is Criminal Justice 101 in five minutes.'

As they left, Gopika had turned back to look at the lady. Vishnu did the same and saw the lady glaring at him, seething in anger.

'That was a lot of money she was offering for you to do nothing,' Gopika said.

'Yeah! Funny, isn't it?' Vishnu said. 'Obviously, she thinks shutting my mouth with twenty thousand will earn her crores in alimony. You should see her husband. Boy is he loaded!'

'Well, you could ask for more then,' Gopika said paused and then went on, 'Or why not go directly to the source. I am sure if her hubby finds out his wife's treachery, he will reward you more handsomely!'

Vishnu looked at Gopika to see if she was serious, but she was looking nowhere in general and so Vishnu just laughed out loud and said, 'You are really funny!'. And off they went to the lecture hall. On reminiscing on it for a bit longer Vishnu realized, it was from that time onwards when Gopika and Vishnu had actively started discussing setting up a Private Investigation Agency together.

CHAPTER FOUR

Vishnu rang the buzzer as always, expecting Dr Sujata to open the door and let him in. The door opened and Dr Sujata stood there with a quizzical expression. She was taken aback and that amused Vishnu a little. 'I am Vishnu. May I come in?' he asked politely.

'Oh Vishnu! Yes, yes, please come in. I was just surprised by this new look,' she said. 'You have cleaned up quite nicely.' And though surprise was clearly evident in her tone, something else was hidden in there, but Vishnu, in all his excitement, failed to recognize that.

'Our background searches had no adverse effect on the lives of people. I just checked and both Sujay and Kamal are doing great!' Vishnu blurted out.

'Who are Sujay and Kamal? We didn't talk about them before, did we? Last time, we spoke about Arya and Sita. Are they all related?' Dr Sujata asked.

'Are they related?' thought Vishnu to himself. 'They somehow seem to be,' he thought but somehow, he was unable to grasp the thread that connected them. It was something he had heard. 'No, they are not related. But this is the case where Sujay's father indicated that it would be better if the marriage could be broken. We had said that we will not fabricate false evidence to that effect and we didn't. In fact, the background search showed no reason for Sujay and Kamal not to get married. But . . .,' he trailed off.

'But . . .?' Dr Sujata prompted.

'But it is strange that they are not married to each other,' Vishnu said pensively. 'Doesn't really matter! They are married to different people and are leading happy lives individually. So all is well.'

'Do you know why they are not married to each other?' asked Dr Sujata. 'What about the rest of your clients and their targets? What about Arya and Sita?'

'I don't know,' admitted Vishnu.

He thought that in cases where there was no problematic evidence uncovered, neither Gopika nor Vishnu could be held accountable for the aftermath. He explained this to Dr Sujata and added further, 'Mr. Kamat, Sujay's father, wasn't in favor of their relationship to begin with. Maybe he was able to convince his son out of it. Just to be sure, I need to look at what happened with John and Sanjana. That was a stinker!'

Dr Sujata realized that though Vishnu's external appearance looked neat and tidy, his mind was still very much cluttered and his focus wavered all over the place. Rather than direct him back to Arya and Sita, she decided that Vishnu's subconscious would be the best guide for their conversation. She did wonder why Vishnu was running away from Arya and Sita and was also intrigued by why John and Sanjana's case had initiated such strong emotions in Vishnu. 'Stinker!' he has said. Something was definitely off. But Dr Sujata wanted Vishnu to open up completely and prodded, 'Is this the last case before Gopika's mur. . . death?' She had stopped herself from using the word *murder*, but hadn't done so quite soon enough. Hurt and pain was clearly visible in Vishnu's eyes.

'N-Not the last one.' He hesitated for a second and said, 'Maybe you can consider this as the last one with two sub-cases. Anyways, it did involve the same client – Mrs. Devi.'

Dr Sujata was intrigued. 'John and Sanjana it is,' she said. 'Tell me everything about their case. Are they related to this Mrs. Devi you just mentioned?'

'Mrs. Devi was Sanjana's mother. She came to us with a very weird request. She was a single parent, a widow by the looks of it and rich too as we found out later. Anyways, she was very much against their marriage and so she wanted us to just break the romantic relationship between John and her daughter, Sanjana. Find or fabricate evidence, she said. As expected, she did not want anything to be tied back to her,' Vishnu elaborated.

'So did you find any evidence?' Dr Sujata asked 'Or did you fabricate it?'

'We did a bit of both,' Vishnu replied sheepishly.

'What? . . . How?' Dr Sujata seemed confused.

Maybe, she had taken Vishnu to be a person of unwavering morals, but suddenly Vishnu's apparent admission of forging evidence had shaken her up. People surprise you all the time. As the well-known adage in inter-personal relationships goes - *Never assume you know the psychology of a person under all situations. Assumption is the mother of all fuck-ups.*

With some uneasiness, Dr Sujata looked at Vishnu, but he had already started his monologue.

' . . . usual background check first and then see what we need to do, Gopika had reasoned. I was totally against any forgery and so I was hoping that some evidence that would make Sanjana break-up with John would be unearthed.' Vishnu clammed up after that, seemingly lost in thought. Did we do something wrong? Why did it not feel like it at that time? The evidence was quite strong enough and all they had done was given it a bit more substance. And this train of thought was abruptly halted by Dr Sujata's query, 'Well, did you? Find some evidence I mean.'

'In a sense,' Vishnu hesitated. 'A quick search into John's recent activities aroused a strong suspicion that he was involved in at least a one-night stand with Shalini. Might have been something more substantial too, but we were also given a timeline by Mrs. Devi. She wanted all this wrapped up within twelve days – a deadline Sanjana had given her. John was moving cities due to a change in employment and Sanjana was adamant on accompanying him as his wife. She had told her mother, Mrs. Devi; that either she could organize their wedding or John and Sanjana were getting married by registration. The pitfall of being a rich adoring mother to a pampered daughter, Mrs. Devi had claimed ruefully.'

'Just a suspicion? So what did you forge?' asked Dr Sujata.

'We didn't have to really,' Vishnu quivered. 'We were fully convinced that John and Shalini were having an affair and in due course, we could have found the necessary evidence. Mrs. Devi was visibly and understandably agitated. She wanted nothing to do with John for her poor gullible baby daughter. And who could fault her. She was a loving mother who did not want a cheat to marry her only daughter,' Vishnu elaborated.

'During one of my stakeouts, I found John and Shalini seemingly holding hands just for a brief moment, and as soon as they thought someone was watching them, they let go of each other. There was also an instance where John had a hand on Shalini's back as he coaxed her into a taxi. On another occasion, I photographed them together on a park bench,' he said. 'All were quite harmless. You know, the cheesy movie kinds.'

'Seems like John and Shalini were really painting the city red!' Dr Sujata said indignantly. 'I would call that an affair, no problem.'

'Well, it might have been that. Or they might just have been good friends or a visiting cousin or . . .,' Vishnu was out of breath. 'In any case, all those photos were taken on the same day!'

'So what?' Dr Sujata asked. 'He was two-timing Shalini for sure.'

'Maybe he was, but we will never know that now,' Vishnu said. 'I gave the pictures to Gopika and was off for the day. I was planning to pick up the scent the very next day and confirm our suspicions, but Gopika had already jumped the gun. She had contacted Mrs. Devi in my absence and it seems Mrs. Devi was convinced. She paid for our services, took the photographs and that was all we ever heard about John and Shalini and Sanjana.'

'Well, that is no forgery at all,' Dr Sujata looked at Vishnu quizzically. 'You took pictures that were real and just gave it to your client – this Mrs. Devi.'

'As private investigators, we must be thorough and we must have evidence for everything we put in front of the client,' Vishnu said sincerely. 'It seemed to me like all we had, was a conjecture with no concrete proof. Gopika should not have been that hasty. One more day would not have made a major difference.'

'So, Sanjana believed them? So much for true love.' The sarcasm was apparent in Dr Sujata's voice.

'I know, right. That is what I reasoned as well. If their love was strong, Sanjana could always deny the evidence or question it at least. But by the looks of it, she didn't and Mrs. Devi was back in our office with another job – our final one.' Vishnu shuddered at the thought.

'So you don't know for sure what Sanjana or for that matter, John's reaction to those photographs was?' Dr Sujata asked.

'Why is this lady always asking for what happened after?' Vishnu thought to himself. Nothing happened to Sujay and Kamal and by the looks of it, nothing happened to Sanjana either, for Mrs. Devi was back for the next job soon enough. John was a two-timing bastard anyways and he would have carried on with Shalini and might have found someone else to two-time. What is Dr Sujata's obsession with the aftermath? Vishnu was just on the verge of being annoyed when Dr Sujata, almost reading Vishnu's mind said, 'But more importantly, you said Mrs. Devi came back to you?'

Vishnu recalled the day he saw Mrs. Devi heading back to the Romantic Corner. She saw Vishnu leaning on a wall slurping down an ice-lolly, seemingly lost in thought. But as soon as Mrs. Devi started up the couple of steps that would lead her to the counter, Vishnu recognized her and a quick frown appeared and almost immediately disappeared and Vishnu had said, 'Mrs. Devi? You are here again so soon. Is everything alright?'

Mrs. Devi looked a bit hesitant. They had managed to deliver on her previous request; but what she had in mind now was much bigger and riskier and more serious. And obviously, she hadn't seemed sure whether these low-level private investigators who only did background searches for marriage proposals could manage what she was going to ask of them. But, she was going to ask them anyway.

'Well Vishnu, I have a problem,' she had said mysteriously.

Vishnu's interest was piqued, but he was also quick to realize that subtle connotation. Mrs. Devi had said she had a problem; but she had not said she thought they could solve it for her. It had made Vishnu feel a bit uneasy, especially when the last job they did for Mrs. Devi involved a few intimate pictures of John and Shalini. He had wondered how it had all gone, but thought against asking about it directly to Mrs. Devi. Instead, he had invited her in and said, 'Please come in to the office Mrs. Devi. We can discuss your problem there with some confidentiality.'

Gopika's eyes first squinted suspiciously and then enlarged with excitement. She probably recalled that Mrs. Devi had been very generous in their remuneration, the last time she had availed their services. 'How nice to meet you so soon, Mrs. Devi,' she had said with a warm smile and looked quizzically at Vishnu who was just having the last licks at his ice-lolly. She looked at him in frustration and Vishnu understood it all too well. 'These ice-lollies will be the death of me,' she used to say when Vishnu's obsession with these cheap ice-lollies would occasionally become a nuisance. 'Mrs. Devi has a problem,' Vishnu had told Gopika, who seemed to be relieved by that.

'Please have a seat Mrs. Devi and tell me more about your problem?' she had said.

'You know I am a single mom. Well, I also run a successful business and I have run it quite well thus far,' Mrs. Devi explained. Both Gopika and Vishnu nodded – Gopika with the eagerness to hear more about what Mrs. Devi wanted and Vishnu with a feeling of unease that he couldn't pinpoint to at the time.

'Well, like most businessmen, I would like to be more well-to-do than I currently am, if you get my drift,' Mrs. Devi had continued with a sly smile and saw that both Gopika and Vishnu knew exactly what she meant.

'And to be more well-to-do, I need to win large contracts which are awarded at the end of a competitive tendering process,' she had elaborated. 'And in my area, I have two main competitors that I need to beat.' She paused, mainly to catch her breath. Her sallow complexion and wavering posture did not give the appearance of the strong-willed steel-nerved businesswoman she clearly was, Vishnu had thought at the time. A couple of hits at the inhaler and Mrs. Devi continued, 'Sometimes, I succeed and at other times I don't. But a good businessman succeeds all the time and so I thought it would be great if you could dig up some dirt on each of them that I could use to my advantage.' Mrs. Devi looked first at Gopika and then at Vishnu. Both of them were musing Mrs. Devi's pitch very seriously. But just as Gopika shifted in her chair to say something, Mrs. Devi had interjected, 'It is serious industrial espionage I am looking for, not a run-of-the-mill background search.' She had used her most condescending tone to full effect and the reaction was immediate.

'We don't just perform run-of-the-mill background searches, Mrs. Devi,' Gopika had blurted seemingly agitated. 'We are fully capable of carrying out any kind of investigation as required by the client,' she had said indignantly.

'No offence intended, dear,' Mrs. Devi had said, 'From one businesswoman to another, I am fully aware of the struggles you would have faced to set up and run this establishment. But you are not aware of the dangers involved in industrial espionage.' Her tone was grave and her face was extremely serious. 'People kill for such sensitive information and they are ready to kill to ensure that such information does not fall into the hands of their competitors.'

'All you want is for the two competitors to be out of the race, isn't it?' Vishnu had asked, slightly bemused. 'Let us just use the age-old movie trick. Murder one and set it up such that the other takes the fall for it.'

Gopika had seemed very annoyed at Vishnu's frivolity. She seemed afraid to lose Mrs. Devi as a client, had she taken it as an affront that Vishnu was so flippant about the whole thing. She had half expected Mrs. Devi to just get up and leave and had begun damage-control, 'I am sure Mrs. Devi doesn't mean anything that drastic. Apologies Mrs. Devi, my partner here has just had a rush of sugar from his ice-lolly going to his brain. He doesn't mean it. Please continue.'

To Gopika's surprise, Mrs. Devi wasn't perturbed at all and continued, 'Well, that would be the best solution Vishnu, if it could be done. I can negotiate a buy-out of both their companies from their families and I will be the sole player in the game.' Vishnu was left aghast, and so was Gopika, it seemed. 'If someone could come to me and say that was possible, I would make him a millionaire right there and then. It isn't unheard of in the business, happens at times. But the catch is to pull it off without raising any suspicion. And I don't think you guys could do that. Against that kind of opposition, you need a lot of brains and money. I could provide the money, but even then, you guys stand no chance.' Mrs. Devi had seemed very excited and at the same time was agitated that these measly private investigators could even joke about something this audacious.

'It behooves one to even joke about within limits, Vishnu. Gopika, your partner seems to think too highly of your collective intelligence. You need to rein-in his unfound enthusiasm,' the mocking tone Mrs. Devi used had cut through Gopika like a dagger made of ice. Cold and stinging. And Gopika wasn't going to take this abuse lying down. 'We could do it Mrs. Devi. If the price was right, we could get away with murder easy!'

There was a stunned silence! Vishnu couldn't believe where his thoughtless, outlandish joke of a suggestion had suddenly morphed into an idea that was under serious consideration. It was revolting to the core for him. Casually thinking of murdering a person and framing it on someone else. 'We are detectives, not killers for hire and this is real life, not reel life,' Vishnu said agitatedly. 'We will do what we have always done – a thorough background search. And these business-types always have some skeletons lying around in their closet. All we need to do is find them and use them as leverage.' Vishnu hoped that this *legal* option would be agreeable and will be sufficient to get both the women off their murder route.

'If someone comes at you with a knife, would you defend yourself or not?' Mrs. Devi prodded.

'Defend, of course! But not kill,' Vishnu retorted adamantly.

'And what if someone killed Gopika? Would you kill that person then?' Mrs. Devi had touched a raw nerve and she knew it.

'W-Well, first I will need to know why the person has killed Gopika. I mean that is a very extreme step . . .,' he was about to stammer out his plan of action when Gopika glared at Vishnu and asked incredulously, 'You have a step-by-step plan of action? Really?! Even when someone murders me!!'

Mrs. Devi had a sly smile on her face. She had touched the right nerve! In a very calm voice, she said, 'It is all very hypothetical, no worries. Don't take it personally. I will find some other solution, now that you have given me things to ponder,' she said mysteriously, stood up and slowly started walking out of the office.

'Wait, Mrs. Devi. We could pull it off, you know. As I said, for the right price.' Gopika had stood up and hurriedly followed Mrs. Devi to the door. Vishnu was too stunned and appalled to have a reaction and just sat in his chair.

'No dear. You could, but not with him,' and Mrs. Devi's voice had lowered to almost a whisper as she said those last words and continued, 'My father always used to say – there are some things a man can do and then there are some things a man can't do, know them both. How right he was! Well, now you know.' The sting in Mrs. Devi's last sentence was too naked to be hidden. And with that, she was out of their sight, but unfortunately, not out of their minds.

'I just couldn't believe that Gopika would have such a cavalier attitude about murder,' Vishnu said. He was clearly shocked even now.

'But was Gopika really serious about it? Or was it just a big misunderstanding?' Dr Sujata asked. Her tone almost verged on it being a rhetoric question.

But Vishnu was too engrossed in his own thoughts to recognize the intonation. His mind floated back to those turbulent times and he could feel the bile rise up to the back of his throat. He somehow managed to push the acrid liquid back down and said, 'She was!' He didn't continue. He couldn't continue was more true. His mind was numb.

'So did you go back to Mrs. Devi?' Dr Sujata asked.

'What?' Vishnu asked half in trance, 'No,' he replied just coming out of it. 'I thought she loved me and we were partners at work and partners for life.'

'So you convinced her out of it? But then, why was this your last case? Did you guys stop being private investigators?' Dr Sujata had a series of questions.

'We spent a few days, or was it weeks, not talking to each other. We could hardly face each other. I tried to convince her that murder, whether or not we could pull it off without being suspects, was still amoral. And Gopika said, this is the business we are in.'

Vishnu recalled, 'What morality are you talking about? We have a trained army. And the training is facilitated by our own elected government and paid for by us, tax payers. And the training is mostly about how best to kill humans. All the armies of all the countries do the same,' Gopika advocated. 'Why is it easy to hang a person for one murder but not easy to hang Pol Pot for the Cambodian Genocide? Morality is relative and the age-old adage holds – *You are a criminal only if you are caught committing a crime.*' He had no real argument against it.

'We are in the business of solving mysteries, finding things . . .,' Vishnu had pleaded. 'We are not killers for hire. We are simple people with good hearts. We don't kill people. We don't even talk about killing people. How can you easily agree with Mrs. Devi's proposal?'

Dr Sujata seemed to clearly fathom the sorrow Vishnu was experiencing. In a matter of a single conversation, his entire world was upturned. Gopika, who Vishnu thought to be his soulmate, had shown that her moral make-up was in no way in-sync with his. But, Dr Sujata wanted to know more and asked, 'So what did she say?'

Vishnu was back in Dr Sujata's room, mind and body and continued narrating his woeful tale. He recalled what Gopika had said. 'It is a gauntlet thrown down by that doddering old hag, Mrs. Devi, and I intended to pick it up. I can fully plan and execute any task I put my mind to.'

'What confidence!' Dr Sujata mused loudly. 'I would have loved to meet Gopika. That is a unique personality.'

'We never met Mrs. Devi again, but I and Gopika just started drifting apart from that day onwards. We were never the same again,' Vishnu said in a sad tone.

'So . . .' Dr Sujata trailed off, hoping that Vishnu would pick up the thread. But when that seemed not happening any time soon, she posed her complete query. 'So you guys parted ways? Shut down the office?'

'Nope. Though I wish it could have gone that way. One day Gopika just talked to me about Vignesh,' Vishnu blurted.

'Vignesh?' Dr Sujata asked visibly surprised. Dr Sujata had read the case files in detail. When Vishnu was accused of Gopika's murder, he had claimed there was another person in the office with him. The person was allegedly a new partner Gopika had proposed for their agency and his name was Vignesh. Vishnu had urged the police to find Vignesh and they never did. No one ever saw anyone else except Vishnu. Dr Sujata had seen such cases quite often. People suffering from trauma had often invented events and people to fit a story their mind was ready to accept. And Vishnu had never been ready to accept that he had murdered Gopika. Vishnu's delusions had come back. Vignesh had returned. The psychological analysis at the time had concluded that Vignesh was just Vishnu's alter-ego, the other side of the coin, the other personality residing in the same body.

'According to Gopika, just the two of us were probably too limited in our coverage of cases and some new blood was needed to infuse vitality and zeal back into the agency.' Vishnu shuddered at his own casual mention of blood. 'Gopika said Vignesh was a candidate she was grooming to be a partner at the agency. She was looking for a new partner in *our* agency.' The stress on the word *our* and the wince Vishnu had when he said that wasn't lost to Dr Sujata. She was good at reading such seemingly imperceptible body language.

'I think we can afford another person at the agency.' Gopika had exclaimed suddenly without paying any heed to the stunned look on Vishnu's face.

'I have scoped out a promising candidate. I think we can be excellent partners. As you are also a part of this agency, I think you too must meet him and see that you are comfortable working with us.'

That sentence broke Vishnu's heart. Suddenly he was *you* and not one of the *us*. He knew then that they had drifted apart, but he was still a romantic, a decent guy. And he was still in love with Gopika. And love, as they say, is an addiction. And addicts seldom realize that their addiction is the cause of most of their problems. Most often, addicts think of the addiction as the refuge they seek from all their problems.

Vishnu had decided not to make a big deal about the whole *new recruit* thing. He thought playing it out calmly would be the best. 'Do we really need a new person? And can we afford to pay him?' Vishnu asked.

'Of course! We can,' Gopika chirped in. 'And I clearly see you are fatigued doing all the field-work by yourself. Some help would reduce your burden.'

Vishnu was seething inside. Not at Gopika. Well, she was a darling young girl oblivious to the devious ways of the world. He was mad at Mrs. Devi for putting ideas in his beloved Gopika's mind. All Gopika ever wanted was excitement and Mrs. Devi had cherry-topped excitement on a plate full of danger cake. And he also blamed himself; for he had planted the seed that grew into this poisonous tree. But for now, play it cool, he said to himself.

'Anything you say dear. Just get him on board. If you think he is a good fit, he sure will be.' Vishnu said with the same sheepish look that he used to have when he agreed with anything Gopika asked of him. But he had to expend a lot of self-restraint to refrain from smashing the glass-top table he used to work at.

'No. You are an equal partner in the agency. I think you meet him first before we decide on anything.' Gopika still maintained the silky tone. 'I am sure you will find no issues with him though,' she added.

'Sir, this is the last stop!' someone had nudged Vishnu and he was back in the bus. Vishnu looked up to the conductor startled. He was just talking to Gopika, no wait, wasn't he in Dr Sujata's living room talking about Vignesh?

'Sir, you must get out here. This bus will not make any more trips today. It is going in for maintenance.' The conductor half looked like he was preparing himself to wrestle Vishnu out of the bus.

'S-sorry, I must have dozed off.' Vishnu said standing up and started walking down the aisle of seats towards the exit when he suddenly turned and asked, 'Where is this?'

The conductor gave Vishnu details regarding his current location and also gave him directions to catch another bus that would lead him to his destination. Vishnu thanked him and in no time was on another bus when his mind floated away.

'So who do you want to look into? John and Sanjana? Or Vignesh?' Dr Sujata had asked.

Who indeed? he thought.

CHAPTER FIVE

The improvement in appearance was almost immediately apparent, except for Vishnu. From being a sickly, unkempt, shabbily dressed person, dour and devoid of any zeal for life, Vishnu now seemed to be an average Joe. Nothing too spectacular in itself, but the transformation from a walking corpse to an average Joe was nothing short of a miracle! Vishnu's room looked much neater than before. And the face that stared back at him when he shaved in front of the mirror was a healthier one. The eyes had slowly started showing a slight glint of excitement, maybe even joy. Vishnu was subconsciously settling into a routine. He had his breakfast and was thinking of what he could recall about John and Sanjana. He remembered Mrs. Devi mentioning something about her business and that John was planning on moving cities for a job. He half hoped that finding what happened to either of them would be as easy as finding about Sujay and Kamal.

In the storeroom, he found the old case files, just where he was told they would be. It took him some time in digging out the one he was interested in. From there, he extracted the details of the company John was working for as well as the name of the company Mrs. Devi owned. Finding John would be quite difficult, he thought, especially if John had moved cities. But finding Mrs. Devi and thus, getting to Sanjana looked more straightforward. After all, how difficult could it be to track down a rich businesswoman, he mused.

Vishnu alighted from the bus and was in for a shock. Instead of finding the sprawling industrial complex he had envisioned, he was faced by a posh high-rise complex. Luxury sky-scrapers, expensive boutiques, high-end cars and manicured lawns and gardens were all around him. Whatever had happened to Mrs. Devi's industry, he thought. It wasn't the wrong address for he had checked it twice before leaving home and so, he enquired at one of the boutiques that seemed to be selling nothing in particular. The lady behind the counter affirmed that Vishnu was in the right neighborhood. But he felt as if the entire neighborhood had just packed up and left!

He must have been thinking out loud for a more wizened man approached him from behind the counter and said, 'You are absolutely correct, sir. Had you been here just seven years ago, this was just a big industrial wasteland.'

'Do you remember who this land belonged to?' Vishnu asked hesitantly, almost knowing the answer even before he asked.

'Some poor industrialist I think, who was run out of business by the Chinese. This Made-in-China boom made paupers of a great many rich bastards, sir.' The man across the counter gave Vishnu the popular lesson in the history of world economics.

'Do you know the name of the person though? A Mrs. Devi perhaps?' Vishnu made another try.

'Who knows sir! These out-of-business industries change so many hands, it is hard to know who owned it. In any case, we moved in three years ago. I ran a catering business in the city for years, but the posh high-rises is where the business is these days. Birthday parties, colony get-togethers, family functions, baby showers, marriages, engagements, you name it. Are you looking for caterers, sir? Leena, give our rate-card for sir to look at.'

And before Vishnu could say another word, a fat velvet-bound booklet was thrust into his hands.

'Very reasonable, sir. And we cater for westers tastes as well. Modern people such as yourself like pizzas and burgers and sandwiches rather than Pongal-Wada. Have a look, sir.'

'No, no – that's all right. I just came here to meet someone. Don't need any catering services, sorry.' Vishnu was quite apologetic.

'Have a look anyways, sir. We take orders anywhere in the city. Maybe you want to have your kid's birthday party.'

'Not in the near future. Not married yet,' Vishnu said.

'Then your engagement party, sir,' came the immediate reply. The old-guard might have moved from the old part of the city to these plush premises, but the old-school clingy salesmanship had not been given an upgrade yet, Vishnu thought amusedly and made a beeline to the door. And as soon as he had done so, he realized the fix he was in. Mrs. Devi would be difficult to track down and that was supposedly the easy part. A wild thought entered Vishnu's mind. He wondered if Mrs. Devi's competitors had turned the tables on her and run her out of business! Had the hunter become the hunted after all? And then his excitement vanished. The hunter *had* become the hunted, he thought to himself. Only, he was thinking of the wrong hunter! *He* had gone from dreaming of solving crimes to being a convicted criminal! Once that thought was pushed out of the mind, Vishnu realized a more pressing truth – John would be impossible to track if he had moved cities! But maybe not, he thought. The company John worked for at the time was a well-known multinational. Vishnu thought he ought to give it a try.

At the company's entrance was a sprawling open-space with sofas and potted plants littered seemingly randomly, but tastefully. A small semi-circular counter was manned by a comely twenty-something girl who gave the air of being more important than she really was. She was looking intently at her computer screen and talking into her wireless mouthpiece as Vishnu approached her. He was thinking if he had the right approach. Should he have waited outside and accosted a random employee, he thought? May be the receptionist would just call the security and lead him out, he feared. But what happened was a complete surprise.

'Yes sir, what can I do for you?' the receptionist asked with a flirtatious smile.

'I am not sure if you could help me out. I am looking for a friend of mine whom I haven't been in touch with for almost a decade.'

And Vishnu half expected the girl calling up security. Instead, the receptionist said, 'Oh that is so nice of you to try and reconnect with your friend. I can definitely try searching the employee list if you can give me the name.' The flirtatious smile was back in full force.

'The name is John.' Vishnu said and wondered what had brought about the eagerness and the flirting in the receptionist's behavior. Maybe that was the remit of the job, he thought. Or maybe she was just being helpful and he mistook her helpfulness as flirting. He had been away from human interaction for a long time anyways.

'Just John?' the receptionist asked. 'Could I get the last name as well please?' It was a question Vishnu was dreading. Somehow, he had missed John's last name, but before he could think out loud, the sweet voice said, 'There are three Johns on our payroll currently. Oh, by the way, do you know your friend still works for us?'

'He used to work here about a decade ago and then was supposed to move to another city and that's when I lost touch with him,' Vishnu said. 'I was wondering if you could tell me what his current status is, or maybe give me a forwarding address if you have one on record.'

'No need for that, I know exactly the person you are after!' the receptionist exclaimed. 'It has to be Mr. John D'Souza. He is the Vice President for Operations. He did a stint at our Bangalore outpost for three years during the time-frame you talk about and came back a star. Let me patch him through.'

'No no. Don't do that. I want it to be a surprise. Could you give me his home address at all? It will be great to see John and his family after all these years.' Vishnu couldn't believe his luck. To find John in the same company after so many years was not something he had expected. And it was funny how he immediately remembered John's last name as soon as the pretty young thing had uttered it. He was preoccupied with his thoughts and as a result, he missed out on a few words the pretty young thing had spoken.

'. . . Shalini madam too. She works here as well, as the Head of Logistics. Hi-fliers both of them. A true power couple.' The receptionist was an open bank vault! If only everyone was this open about information, Vishnu thought . . . we would have to change our locks and passwords every day, came a cynical response from his detective brain!

'Hmmm. Their address is not on file. Must be something to do with the HR system upgrade we went through a few weeks ago. Not all personnel records have been migrated to the new one yet.' The statement lacked conviction and Vishnu half-thought that the receptionist was simply stalling. But before he could think of a response, the receptionist said, 'If you give me your contact number, I could find the address for you and give it to you over coffee.'

'Well, this is definitely flirting,' Vishnu thought. But just then, something she had said just exploded in his brain and he stammered, 'I . . . that's all right. I will come back later.' And he was about to turn around and walk out when the sweet voice asked, 'How about tomorrow, at five in the evening? That's when I get off work.'

'Ok,' he said absentmindedly and walked out quite briskly. He paid no attention to the longing stare that followed him out of the reception area. The stare had followed a smartly dressed man in Bally shoes, a Patek Phillipe Complication casually adorning his wrist and the Montblanc fountain pen that he had unclipped from his breast pocket to jot down John's address in his Moleskin diary.

The receptionist had said Shalini! Clearly! Shalini! Vishnu thought. John had married Shalini and they both worked for the same company. So, John cut his losses and married Shalini. Good, Vishnu thought. The photos they had provided to Mrs. Devi had surely worked. Mrs. Devi would have been happy, Sanjana didn't elope with John and he married Shalini. That was a good outcome, he thought as he headed home.

Dusk fell softly on Vishnu's abode and the soothing rays of moonlight led him into his turbulent past, even without his knowledge.

'Why do you not approve of us taking on the job Mrs. Devi offered?' Irritation was clearly audible in Gopika's voice. She was that sort of a person. Simple joys would ring out like melodious bells in her voice, Vishnu reminisced. That is what had attracted him to her in the first instance. 'I won! I won fifty rupees,' she had shouted, the first time Vishnu had noticed that – Gopika had won a raffle ticket in the College Gathering. But that same jingle-bell voice could turn frosty and gravelly at the slightest of discomfort or annoyance.

'We solve crimes, Darling! We don't want to start committing crimes,' Vishnu said patiently. 'Let us stick to what we do best. We have enough work and enough money to keep us well-fed.'

'I cannot understand where you got your pathetic working-class morals and ideals.' Disgust was clear in her eyes when she said this. 'Keep us well-fed! Is that all you ever want? What a loser way of life! Can you not have any bigger ambitions? Can you not dream of something better than just being well-fed?'

His almost blue-blood birth had insulated Vishnu from the tribulations of poverty. But on a whim, he had spent three days and three nights without food, just to experience real hunger. He had not been able to control his hunger on the fourth day and had scarfed down a King's lunch and dinner in one go. But that experience had taught him something he never forgot. He knew that as long as he does not sleep hungry, he was doing well. And it also enlightened him about how privileged he had been. Something a lot of us never really appreciate. If you can afford three square-meals a day and have a roof to sleep under, you belong to the top one percent of the world's population. And he thought the love of his life would at least acknowledge it.

'I yearn for more exciting cases. I even dream we will at some point be consulting the police on some crime investigation. But I always think of us as crime investigators. Not criminals.' Vishnu was surprised that he had the nerve to put up an argument against Gopika. But this was something he felt strongly about; probably more strongly than anything else. 'We are good people with morals,' he continued. 'We should not be stooping to the level of committing murder. I am appalled to even think of it!' His voice had grown louder, but he was oblivious to it.

'I don't see what's wrong in it?' Gopika continued with her argument. 'I know I am good at it and with your help I could have easily done it. And what morals are you talking about? All we do is pry into other people's private affairs. If only I could get my Vishnu back.'

'I am your Vishnu, Darling,' Vishnu said patiently, 'But I do not approve of murder.'

'My Vishnu never disapproved of anything I said!' Gopika shot back. 'I think I need to find *my* Vishnu again,' and she stormed out of the office too.

My Vishnu, he thought. Surely, his ears were not playing tricks. He had clearly heard the slight but noticeable slant Gopika had put on the word, *My*. I am Vishnu, he mused. Who is this *My* Vishnu? He thought as he absentmindedly opened up the storage freezer and started slurping on his favorite ice-lolly, pensively.

And that was seemingly the last conversation he had with Gopika as his partner. For soon, she was going to introduce him to *My* Vishnu – only his name was Vignesh! And it all started when she said, 'I think we can afford another person at the agency.'

'Dinner is ready, Thambi. Would you want it to be served here or would you be coming down to the dining table?' Vishnu stirred and came out of recalling his past. And he first thanked his luck. He didn't have to sleep without food tonight!

The dinner was done and he went to the balcony. The cacophony of calls coming from all sorts of nocturnal critters, from all directions was loud but at the same time soothing. It made the night seem more vibrant and lively. He spent some time collecting his thoughts and also realized this was the first instance in a long while that he had come to the balcony for leisure. After a while, he ducked back to the storeroom, where all the case-files they had worked on were stored. He then began the very slow but meticulous process of filing them in chronological order. The floor was littered with dust covered boxes and papers and half-open folders, but between the cracks of this mosaic, sections of a luxurious hand-woven Persian carpet were peeping through. He sat in the chair and stared at the littered floor. 'Rewind! Rewind!' he said to himself. The events in his recurring nightmares were clearly etched in his mind. His arrest for Gopika's murder, his futile attempts to direct the authorities to find Vignesh – the real culprit, his long incarceration, the multiple suicide attempts, suicide watch and solitary confinement, release . . . the whole lot. What he wanted to recall were the events between his fight with Gopika and his arrest for murdering her. Where did Vignesh come from? And where did he disappear? Why couldn't anyone find any evidence of his existence? Was he just a figment of his own imagination, just like the court-appointed psychiatrist had repeatedly asserted. When did he first hear the name? Did he really meet him? He had to find answers to these questions if he wanted to redeem himself of all blame . . . if he wanted to get a semblance of his old life back!

That day had started out ominously. He came into the office to find no sign of Gopika, which was odd. On the rare occasions that he had to run some early morning errands, Gopika would always beat him to the office. But today, even after a very late start to the day, Gopika was not at her usual seat. He tried calling her cell-phone a number of times and found no answer. He went to the storage freezer, stuck his hand in and picked up his favorite ice-lolly. And started thinking what he could do to pacify Gopika. He loved her and he thought she loved him too. But suddenly Gopika had changed. Or had she? Was this the *real* Gopika as opposed to *my* Gopika? The thought made him smile. It was a sad smile though. The irony of it, he thought. That she was looking for *my* Vishnu and now he was looking for *my* Gopika! But this time, he wasn't going to back down. His love had blinded him but he began realizing deep down in his subconscious that he was going to lose her at some point. Somehow, he never had the guts to confront the reality, but the time had now come. And the pain of finality was almost unbearable. He had made up his mind – to give it one last chance.

It was quite late in the day, almost evening, that Gopika showed up and was quite surprised to see Vishnu. 'You still at the office!' she stumbled across the door and went to her chair without any more small talk. As was her habit, she poured herself a glass of water from the jar that sat at the corner of her table. It was identical to the one Vishnu had on his. And seeing Gopika drink made him thirsty too. Involuntarily, he followed Gopika's lead, poured himself a glass of water, sipped a little and realized that he wasn't thirsty after all.

'I have been waiting for you the entire day. I think we went off the track yesterday and I was wondering if we could talk it out,' Vishnu said in a very tired voice. It amused Vishnu to realize that all he had done throughout the day was ponder; and just that had tired him out!

'I had some time to organize my thoughts too,' Gopika said and it gave Vishnu a sense of hope. But the next sentence shattered it. 'I realized that the way we work, the way we approach things and what we want in life are quite different,' she said.

'So overnight, you think we have nothing in common! After all these years of being together?' Vishnu was incredulous. He had never thought of Gopika to be that unreasonable. Yes, she was a tad overbearing and he pampered her by agreeing to her every whim, but to be adamant about murder! The thought revolted him.

'Well, not really. We worked well so far,' she said, 'And we will in the future too. But obviously, there are some things one can do and there are some things one can't do. You say that yourself.'

Vishnu nodded. It was something his father used to say and damn, it was the same thing Mrs. Devi had said as well. He lived by it and over the years, Vishnu had realized that it was an irrefutable truth.

'I think we should just find someone who can do things you cannot do,' Gopika said.

Vishnu was stung by this statement. And he angrily said, 'And what about things you cannot do?'

'Well, that is why I have you,' she said. 'I can do the thinking but I cannot do the fieldwork as well as you can,' she added. 'Don't you see? It is a compliment! But surely, I cannot expect you to be able to do everything.'

'You mean I cannot commit murder! And you want to find someone who can!' Vishnu's shock knew no bounds and his voice reflected that. How can this woman whom I have loved for so long, talk about killing someone she doesn't even know in such a matter-of-fact manner, he thought.

'Well, I have already found him. I was going to ask him to come over tomorrow to meet you, but now that you are here, I will just call him over for now,' she said. And before Vishnu could register a complaint, she dialed a number on her mobile and spoke a couple of sentences in quick clipped tones and hung up. 'He will be here at half past eight tonight. I have given him our office number so he will call up if something changes. Take down his mobile number if you want to call him up if you change your mind about meeting him.'

'Well, if you have decided you are going ahead with this, why do you need my approval at all?' Vishnu argued as he jotted down the number Gopika gave him, his rage clearly boiling over. 'Just take him on and be done with it. I will not associate myself with murderers, so I think it is time for us to part ways.' And as he finished the sentence, he felt drained of all energy.

'Darling!' Gopika said in her cloyingly sweet voice. 'I am not talking about murder. That job is no longer ours. I am just talking about sharing the case load. And maybe increasing our capabilities of doing certain things you might not find comfortable doing. He is just like you. You will see. You will hit it off famously with him. And you will get to spend more time with me at the office.'

'So why do we need a new guy anyways? And who is this guy? What is his experience?' Vishnu was confused.

He couldn't make out what Gopika was playing at. But all those thoughts were drowned by the carrot Gopika had so wisely dangled.

' . . . you will get to spend more time with me at the office,' she had said. And that had enticed Vishnu into thinking irrationally. He was back to being in love with Gopika and he was once again sure that she was in love with him. And before he could ask Gopika what the guy's name was, she had slipped out of the office. Something she had to take care of, she said – women problems.

'I will be back later though. And we can have a very late dinner together,' she said without even looking back.

'Dinner . . . as if!' Vishnu said, probably in too loud a voice, for the person, Ganesh, they had employed to run the Romantic Corner gave him a quizzical stare before he ducked into the shop freezer to get scoops of some yellow-colored ice-cream. Butterscotch, Vishnu thought and ducked into the spare storage freezer to get his favorite ice-lolly. 'As long as I am waiting, let me at least have an ice-lolly,' he said to himself.

Vishnu waited . . . and waited . . . and waited some more. At the stroke of 8:00pm, Ganesh ducked in to Vishnu's office to let him know that he was heading home. It meant Vishnu had to lock up shop; a common occurrence as detective work would continue late in the night as well. It is funny how every minute feels longer if you are waiting for someone past the set time. He looked at his watch for the tenth time. It was just 8:40pm. The guy was ten minutes late and counting. What kind of a guy is late to meet his prospective boss for the first time? But then Vishnu was usually late for all his University Exams. And Chennai traffic at this time was atrocious too. And who is to say how the new recruit was going to get here. If he was using public transport, ten minutes delay was nothing. But he had a cellphone. He could have called up easy. And just as he was thinking, the shrill ring of the office phone on his desk jarred him and he answered – almost too quickly, he thought. He should have waited for a couple more rings, just so he didn't sound too eager or desperate. But it was already done.

'Hi, is this Vishnu? Hello, I am stuck in a traffic jam due to an accident about fifty meters from where I am and haven't moved an inch for the past forty minutes. My battery is dying and I might not be able to call back. But I will meet you tonight for sure. Please wait for . . .,' and the line went dead. Vishnu didn't even have time to acknowledge his presence and yet, he didn't know the guy's name.

And already there was a hurdle in Vishnu meeting this fellow. And to pass time, Vishnu started thinking about hurdles. He was an avid hurdler during his college days, one of the top three hurdlers in the state. 'In Sanskrit, a hurdle to complete a job is known as a *Vighna* and Lord Ganesha is also known as *Vignesh* the remover of all hurdles,' Vishnu thought to himself. And suddenly wondered why that thought had ever popped into his mind. He had never studied Sanskrit formally. 'Did people still do that?' he wondered. 'Why would they study Sanskrit at all? And what do they work as?' And so his thoughts wandered. But his mind did flash a word from time to time, faintly, in the background, almost imperceptible but there – *Vignesh*!

'Hi, I am Vignesh,' someone was saying and he acknowledged.

'Excuse me! Hi, I am Vignesh,' this time it was a bit louder. And that annoyed Vishnu. He had just acknowledged the greeting. But then he felt someone shaking him and he woke up with a start.

'Sorry I was late. I am Vignesh.' The man in front of him was a lean, well-kempt and taller than average. About six feet, Vishnu thought. Just slightly shorter than himself, Vishnu computed and was full of needless glee.

'Sorry to keep you waiting. I was quite badly stuck in traffic. It was horrible. And the rain messed things up even more. I had to just park my bike and catch a bus and then buy an umbrella to get here from the bus stop without being soaked.' This guy doesn't stop talking to take a breath, Vishnu thought to himself and was about to open his mouth to say something when the guy in front of him had started off again.

'Sorry. You must have dozed off. Tiring day? Madam had told me that you were quite busy but I couldn't help it. My phone is dead. I am hoping it isn't soaked, just battery gone.'

'Wh—Whaa...,' Vishnu's voice was coarse. The awkward sleeping position had made his mouth dry and he involuntarily pushed his hand forward to the jar of water on his table. There was a fantastic water cooler in a corner of the room, but both Vishnu and Gopika usually drank from the jar in a tumbler made from real glass. The plastic cups the cooler dispensed water in somehow didn't hold favor with either of them.

'Oh! Sorry Mr. Vishnu. Here, have some water,' the guy in front of him offered a glass of water from Vishnu's jar.

Vishnu took the glass and drank almost its entire contents before ducking out and said, 'Thanks! What did you say your name was?' and as he said it, his mind came back with the echo, *Vignesh*!

'I always find drinking water after I wake up from my sleep to be really refreshing. Cold water wakes you up wide awake. Of course, if you drink it at the wrong time, your sleep gets delayed too, or so I have heard. Anyways, I hope you are ok to chat with me about the job. Actually tomorrow, I am up for another interview. Need a job. This is my first choice though. I have always dreamt of being a detective. Do you guys get a . . .'

There was only so much chatter Vishnu could take. He impatiently raised a hand and signaled the other man to stop.

'Please, hold on! I have just woken up and my brain cannot process all those words at that speed yet. You need to slow down a bit. One sentence at a time till I am fully awake, and first things first. I didn't catch your name yet,' Vishnu said.

'Oh, sorry again. I must not be apologizing all the time. Sorry. Well there, I did it again. Oh yes, my name is V-i-g-n-e-s-h . . .'

Vishnu was woken up by Ganesh. Vishnu blinked and realized that he was slumped over on his desk and his cheek was wet with the dribble that had oozed out overnight. He saw Ganesh standing across his table with a quizzical look on his face. 'What sir? No dinner with madam in the night?' he asked. And that was when the real nightmare had begun.

That was the last thing he was thinking of before Vishnu dozed off into a land of no dreams, deep sleep where there is just tranquility and peace.

CHAPTER SIX

Vishnu was a bit uneasy during this visit to Dr Sujata. It wasn't anything about himself though. But it made him uneasy. It was something that he couldn't quite put a finger on. And he looked around quizzically to the now well-known environment he was in. The same room, the same couch, the same openness and Dr Sujata sitting in her favorite chair. But it wasn't openness he felt, more like emptiness. And the light somehow seemed to dull the imagery rather than bring it to focus. And Dr Sujata thus looked paler than she usually did. Maybe a stray cloud had cast its shadow he thought, but the Sun shone brightly and he could see the wet lawn gleaming outside. What is it then? Vishnu thought to himself and his mind started to form an image and just then . . .

'So, did you find out anything about John or Sanjana or Vignesh?' Dr Sujata asked.

And the image that had started to form in his mind vanished in a wisp of smoke. He was so close to finding why he had been uneasy and suddenly, that chain of thought was broken. And new links were forming. John and Sanj. . . Shalini, he thought to himself.

'I didn't think it would be that easy, and I wasn't expecting what I actually found!' Vishnu said, back in the groove. 'John and Shalini are married to each other. Quite happily by the looks of it. What's more, they work for the same company John worked all those years ago!'

'Wow!' Even Dr Sujata hadn't expected the stroke of luck that had come Vishnu's way. 'So John married Shalini after all. No more two-timing for John then. That's excellent – I mean for you. One more case followed-up. No issues there.' And she looked at Vishnu's almost crestfallen posture. 'I mean, there would still be other cases to follow-up, I am sure. Don't give up now. Did you find anything about this Vignesh?'

Vishnu thought he noticed a hint of doubt in Dr Sujata's tone. It seemed like she too didn't believe Vignesh existed. Vishnu couldn't blame her. During the initial investigation before his incarceration, he was unable to convince anyone of Vignesh's existence anyways. Vishnu looked at Dr Sujata and the clever psychiatrist she was, she immediately understood what that look meant.

'Don't be confused by my intonation, Vishnu,' she said soothingly. 'At this point, I only have your case file to go on. I haven't yet heard *your* side of what happened.'

Once again, the slight slant on *your* was not lost on Vishnu. Anger welled up within him. Not aimed at Dr Sujata's disbelief in his version of the events, but at himself and his inability to convince even one other soul about Vignesh's existence. But that thought had taken quite some time and Dr Sujata offered, 'Tell me what happened on the day after you met Vignesh.'

The nightmare, Vishnu thought. He had lived it every single day ever since. It had basically turned the past seven odd years into one big nightmare. He was so used to being in the nightmare that he had forgotten how to really live and function like a normal human being. Dr Sujata had shown him a way, he thought. But she was also pushing him back into the nightmare. And he was scared of it. For these repeated journeys into those fateful days had given him no clues to Gopika's murder. No answers to any of the questions. No new hints regarding who killed Gopika. And the more empty journeys he went on, the stronger he believed in the ghastly. That he had, in fact, murdered Gopika! And that made him throw up almost instantaneously. He hurried towards the toilet and spent a good five minutes in cleaning and composing himself. He came back and saw Dr Sujata looking at him in a way he had never seen before. Was it malice? Or glee? Or pity? Vishnu thought. Or was it concern?

Apology?

Dr Sujata looked down for a second and looked back up and Vishnu thought – apology. 'I am sorry if it hurts to reminisce on those days, Vishnu,' Dr Sujata said. 'We could do it some other time if you are not up to it today.'

'But we have to do it?! Isn't that what you mean?' Vishnu asked irately.

'Well, if you are interested in finding answers, yes,' Dr Sujata said. 'It is a crucial part of your story. And revisiting might trigger something that could lead to the murderer.'

Vishnu recognized the absence of two words in Dr Sujata's statement – *us* and *real*. 'Could lead *us* to the *real* murderer.' That is what he was hoping to hear. But clearly, he had to convince Dr Sujata that he was innocent. He desperately needed someone to believe in him.

'Well then, here we go, deep into the rabbit hole,' Vishnu said and had an ironic smile on his face. 'Alice in Wonderland reference at this somber moment!' he thought to himself.

'I was woken up by Ganesh, our hired help who looked after the Romantic Corner,' Vishnu started. 'But I don't remember if Ganesh asked me anything specific about anything. I must have just asked him to buzz off or something, I don't really remember. But . . .'

'It says here that you said, *What dinner? I never had any dinner with Gopika*. And just as he was leaving the room to attend to a customer, he heard you say, *Looks like I will never have dinner with her anymore*,' Dr Sujata interjected.

'I don't remember saying that,' Vishnu said quite irritably. 'I do remember calling Gopika frenetically the entire day. And I might have left some clearly angry messages on her voicemail.'

'Yes. The police did find a number of extremely angry messages on Gopika's cell-phone. And their flavor wasn't in your favor,' Dr Sujata added. 'And surprisingly, not once did you mention Vignesh in those messages!'

That had been a point of contention during the court proceedings,

Vishnu recalled. And it was probably a long and strong nail in the coffin that buried his innocence. 'Why would you call Gopika twenty three times on that day, threaten to never see her again and never ever mention Vignesh in any of those messages? Especially, when you claim that you met him just the night before,' the Prosecutor had argued.

And Vishnu recalled now, what he had realized then. He was so mad at Gopika that he spoke of Vignesh in terms of *Your* Vishnu. She had been tardy for two days in a row. And she had hinted at the fact that Vishnu had lost his usefulness to her and that she had already found a replacement. Furthermore, the fact that she had shamelessly sugar-coated the insult of casting Vishnu aside by using the promise of more time together in the office and the make-up dinner and never followed it through, had irked Vishnu. Add to that, the confused state he was in that morning where he was unable to separate fact from fiction. Had he met Vignesh? Or was it all just a dream? How much of it was a dream? Had Gopika ever mentioned Vignesh by name?

And so, Vishnu narrated the events of the previous evening. He told Dr Sujata about Gopika's late arrival, her comment about *My* Vishnu, her mention of Vignesh, setting up of the meeting and her enticing dinner invite. He skipped the events of that fateful night, for fateful they may be, they were still hazy. And Dr Sujata heard it all with rapt attention. It all made sense to Dr Sujata. It also wasn't anything new that she had heard. The case files had mentioned as much. The description of events during the days before and after the murder were all confirmed by the intensive police investigation. The events of that fateful night, however, were in dispute. She was, for now, satisfied with his retelling of the events that led to the discovery of Gopika's body.

Vishnu, on the other hand, was dreading the part that was about to come – Gopika's body in the storage freezer that stocked his favorite ice-lollies, all evidence pointing towards him being a spurned yet psychopathic lover, his swift but conclusive conviction and incarceration.

'I called at Gopika's hostel and enquired, but they had not seen her since the previous night,' Vishnu continued.

'But the watchman confessed that Gopika had sneaked in for a change as she had a dinner date with you later that night,' added Dr Sujata. 'In fact, she told the watchman that she was starting a new life. At least that is what the watchman remembered in his sworn testimony,' she continued.

'Yes, he did, didn't he,' Vishnu said drily. 'And of all the days and all the twenty odd women who stayed in the hostel, he remembered what one woman was going to do that particular night!'

Vishnu looked at Dr Sujata and she looked at him for a moment before she quickly lowered her gaze and said, 'Weird; but weirder things have happened. Anyways, I am a bit thirsty and am going to get some water. Would you want some?'

And that is when it hit him. The emptiness was not in the room, nor was the fadedness or the gloom, it was in Dr Sujata's eyes! 'Did she think he was guilty and therefore a lost cause?' Vishnu thought. 'Was he really the murderer? Had he just invented a story to bury his own guilt?' he questioned himself as he had done on numerous occasions. People were known to do that. But then he realized, that was not it. The gloom in Dr Sujata's eyes seemed to come from within. It looked like she wasn't gloomy about the case. It was as if gloom had just engulfed her entire persona, but the reason eluded him for now.

'So, Gopika definitely planned on meeting you that night for dinner,' Dr Sujata said coming back to the room. She took her time to rearrange the cushions before taking her usual seat.

'Or at least that is what it looks like,' Vishnu said and as soon as he had said this, his brow furrowed. When he said it out loud, it made clear sense, but he had never thought along those lines in these past years. 'It *looked like* Gopika had planned on meeting me for dinner that night,' he said to himself.

'But she also didn't want to be present when you were going to meet Vignesh,' Dr Sujata said. It was a statement rather than a mere observation. Wow! Another simple statement that he had never clearly appreciated. Dr Sujata definitely has the knack of getting new information out when it seems there isn't any more to get, he thought. And suddenly, he was elated. A glimmer of hope crossed his mind. Maybe Dr Sujata was the push needed to absolve him of the crime he was accused of. Maybe, with Dr Sujata's guidance, he will be able to unearth some facts that will clear-up the mystery about who murdered Gopika. Well, a mystery in his own mind, he recalled disheartened. For the world, Gopika was murdered by Vishnu!

'What else do you remember from that night?' Dr Sujata asked. 'Anything particular that you might have missed out during your trial? Something you thought of during your incarceration or afterwards?'

'No,' Vishnu said with a sad finality. 'I have recalled the events of that night and day a thousand times since and I don't remember anything I haven't said before. I think Vignesh must have drugged me and murdered Gopika.'

'But there is no proof of that. And why has no one found any trace of Vignesh ever since?' Dr Sujata's question was a poison-tipped arrow that had hit the bull's eye. This was the very same question the Prosecutor had demanded an answer for. The same question his conscience had kept on asking ever since. The same question that was as yet unanswered.

'I mean, isn't it weird that Vignesh appeared out of the blue when you had a spat with Gopika and disappeared immediately after she was murdered?' Dr Sujata asked.

Vishnu had a *You too, Brutus* look on his face. Dr Sujata was hinting at the same diagnosis that the court psychiatrist had proposed. That Vignesh was just an alter-ego Vishnu had created in the presence of hatred towards Gopika. Once Gopika was gone, the trigger was gone and Vignesh had vanished. The room started to suffocate him. The light started to burn him and his throat was parched. But then, he realized something that he hadn't realized as clearly ever before.

'All I need to do is find Vignesh,' he said.

'WHAT!' Dr Sujata exclaimed and then quickly composed herself and said, 'Oh, right. Once you find him, you will have all your answers.'

Vishnu took leave from Dr Sujata and headed home. That last reaction from Dr Sujata had confused him. It seemed as if she was incredulous at Vishnu's conclusion; finding Vignesh after all these years. But she had somehow composed herself and indicated that Vignesh had all the answers. That was not quite it though. Something in her tone or mannerism was just beyond Vishnu's grasp and he couldn't really identify it. Nevertheless, he had made up his mind. He would not stop until he had convincingly found who Gopika's murderer was. What else did he have to pass his time anyways, he mused. He had all the money and all the time needed for a lifetime. And for once, he also had a goal.

He took a fresh folder from his study and loaded it with the high-quality marble paper he was so fond of writing on and headed to the storeroom. Here, he started reconstructing the events of that fateful night and day. He also had a copy of his case files to fill in all the available or rather court-accepted evidence. It went something like this –

Gopika came almost in the evening (Ganesh testified to that effect) – Gopika discussed setting up a meeting between me and Vignesh (court acknowledges no evidence in this regard) – Gopika called Vignesh from our office, in my presence to confirm a 8:30pm appointment (no evidence of such a call exists in Gopika's call logs) – I waited for Vignesh who didn't show up for a long time, then gave me a call to say he was delayed due to traffic (no accident reported and the phone call came from a cell-phone that was triangulated to be within the signal radius of the Romantic Corner, seemingly indicating that I had called myself! Furthermore, there was a time difference of two hours between the call and my actual claim of meeting Vignesh. So what was Vignesh doing for two hours?) – Gopika had given me the number claiming it to be Vignesh's (Police investigation showed the SIM was registered in my name and bought using my own identity papers! The phone was later found with Gopika's frozen body) – Vignesh called me using the same SIM to tell me that he was going to be late for our meeting that night – No direct link connecting to Vignesh ever found – Next day I called Gopika a number of times (23 as per the court-accepted cell-phone records) and left angry voicemails and never mentioned Vignesh by name – Court-appointed psychiatrist proposed a split-personality diagnosis and put me in for incarceration with rigorous psychiatrist care. No psychotic episode ever since and so I had to endure the full jail term – Psych evaluation concluded that as the trigger (Gopika leaving me due to my ineptitude) had been removed, the split persona never recurred. The Prosecutor argued that there was no way of knowing if it was a true case of split-personality or if I was putting on a fantastic act.

Vishnu read and re-read his notes meticulously. He was trying to find one gap, one opening, one loose knot that would unravel the mystery. Vignesh seemed to have planned it all. He had murdered Gopika. But why?! It had all started with a plan I had proposed to solve Mrs. Devi's problem, as a joke. Mrs. Devi liked it and shockingly Gopika had agreed to implement it. Though Gopika was all for doing it that way, Vishnu had hated the plan. He hated the fact that Gopika even considered it, hated Gopika for pursuing it and hated himself for not being able to see Gopika for what she was – an immoral and cold-hearted human being. How had he not seen that? Or maybe he had, but couldn't really accept that his only love in life – Gopika – was so unworthy of his love. He definitely didn't accept that. But someone else had seen through Gopika's silky sweet exterior. Vignesh had!

CHAPTER SEVEN

Vishnu felt the rush of excitement that he had not felt in a long time. He was actually doing something fruitful regarding his guilt. He was going to find out one way or the other, the person responsible for murdering Gopika and destroying his life. And the clues were hidden in the notes he had just drawn up. So he re-read the notes again. This time squinting at each and every letter of each and every word. And again, there was just one point where he stopped. It was the same hurdle that he couldn't get over. It was the same irrefutable fact that had condemned him during his trial, all those years ago. The SIM that was used by Vignesh to call him that night was bought under Vishnu's name using Vishnu's own identity. It was something that he had argued around. He didn't remember buying the SIM or the phone and his fingerprints were not on it either. The Prosecutor had turned this argument around to prove that this was a meticulously planned murder and Vishnu was not suffering from any personality disorder. Cause if he had, he would not have had the presence of mind to ensure that *Vignesh's* cell-phone was devoid of any fingerprint evidence. His defense lawyer had further argued that if that was the case, how Vishnu could have been so stupid to buy the SIM under his own name. But the Prosecutor had also twisted this and claimed this was just a part of Vishnu's split-personality act put up to confuse the Court. Though the evidence against Vishnu was strong, it could be construed as purely circumstantial. Vishnu's defense lawyer had done a decent job of portraying Vishnu as an innocent victim of the evidence stacked against him. He had sowed the seed of doubt but hadn't quite been able to convince the Court of Vishnu's complete innocence. It was under these circumstances and the lack of an eye-witness to the actual murder that Vishnu had avoided the death penalty. He was, however, convicted of manslaughter. Furthermore, due to the manslaughter charge, the rule of reduced punishment for time well-served also applied and his fourteen-year incarceration was reduced to seven.

He decided that the cell-phone and the SIM were the only openings he had so far. He had to find how a cell-phone and a SIM bought using his identity had fallen in the hands of Vignesh. And so he listed all the possibilities:

1.   Vignesh stole my identity documents and bought the SIM.
2.   Vignesh forged my identity documents and bought the SIM.
3.   Gopika had decided to hire Vignesh and had bought the SIM and phone for him. That was quite odd, but then most bills for their office were set up in his name. That was because he owned the entire premises – their office as well as the Romantic Corner. Maybe Gopika had overreached her powers and bought the SIM and phone for the use of the new partner – Vignesh.

There was a fourth possibility, but Vishnu shuddered to even let that thought peep into his mind just yet. According to the Court of Law, that wasn't a possibility – it had been the generally accepted truth. Vishnu was Vignesh! Vishnu just focused on the three possibilities he had jotted down and said to himself, 'If I add to this, the fact that Gopika was murdered and Vignesh has never been found there can be only one conclusion – Vignesh murdered Gopika and I was blamed for it!' But then his shoulders slumped over. 'That isn't anything new,' he thought. He had survived the past years solely on that belief. And now, he was going to find Vignesh and hand him over to the law for proportionate punishment and absolve himself of the heinous crime he was accused, found guilty of and punished for.

It was late in the night and he had all the energy in the world to spend on his case. He decided to tackle the third possibility first. If Gopika had bought this SIM for Vignesh under Vishnu's name, she might have put a note in their employee records. And if she had bought this for Vignesh, she should have already decided on hiring him. Which meant she should have detailed notes about Vignesh's personal details in the Employee Folder. He wondered. As far as he knew, that folder only had the details of himself and Gopika, for they were the only employees of their agency ever. But with the clearer mind-set enabled by Dr Sujata, Vishnu thought this was something worth checking. Had he mentioned this during the trial? He wondered. Maybe he had or maybe he hadn't.

He found his old computer from all the boxes strewn around and to his surprise, it started with an immediate click! This clunky old desktop was like an old hammer – it just worked. After a few minutes of warming up and going through the login screen, it took a few more minutes for the system to be fully operational – that was Windows back then. On the screen was an icon labelled *Employee* that was sitting right below an icon labelled *Trash Can* and Vishnu's heart fluttered for a second as he double-clicked the *Employee* icon. But then, just as he had foreseen, there were just two files in the folder: one named Gopika and the other one named Vishnu. 'Couldn't have been that easy anyways,' Vishnu said out loud, but there was no one else to listen to his frustration. He leaned back in the chair and started going through the events once again. And he realized something quite liberating. He no longer dreaded the nightmare that was his past life. He was in fact looking forward to dissect his nightmare piece by piece until it unraveled its mystery. A sincere thought of gratitude towards Dr Sujata crossed his mind and then he was back in his nightmare. Gopika had come in late – they had an argument – Gopika talked about a prospective new partner – talked to him over the phone – gave Vishnu a phone number and Vishnu had jotted it down - - - BANG! It hit him like a cannon ball. Gopika had never mentioned Vignesh by name!

It had taken him all these years to come to this realization. Gopika had never mentioned Vignesh by name! He repeated this sentence over and over again before his brain could fully assimilate the implications of this finding. That could really mean one of three things:

1. Vignesh was not his real name.
2. The Vignesh that he met might not have been the person Gopika wanted Vishnu to meet.
3. Vignesh really was a figment of his imagination – his other persona!

The third possibility really chilled him to the bone. It seemed like every time he unearthed a new nuance of the mystery, the possibility that he really was Vignesh who had killed Gopika would raise its ugly head like the nine-headed Hydra. And every time he cut one head off, three others grew in its place. The deeper he dove into the labyrinth of his own nightmare, the more realistic the possibility of himself being Gopika's murderer began to sound.

But he had decided not to lose hope until absolutely all avenues had been exhausted. And he thought back. One fact remained unchanged even after all the reruns of his nightmare – Gopika had given him a number for the prospective new partner he was supposed to meet that night. And he had written it down in his diary. And he had that number in front of him, in the diary that he had written it in, in his own handwriting. How could he forget? It was the last thing he had ever written in that diary. A stray thought slid into his mind and soon became an idea. The idea was put into action and before he knew it, he had clicked the search icon for the entire C drive of the computer and typed the number Gopika had given him. He pressed enter and the waiting began. His thoughts had wandered all over the place. Mr. Kamat and Arya and John, then to the jail and his solitary confinement, Dr Prakash and finally Dr Sujata and the slight uneasiness he felt when he met her today. The slight gloom on her face, the almost imperceptible change in her body language, it made him uneasy that he couldn't put a finger on what had changed. The search result didn't give him anything. He wasn't expecting too much from it, but then every shred of new information would prove helpful, he thought. They were private investigators, but they hadn't yet mastered a good book-keeping system and a lot of stuff was either written down or just filed away in their collective memories. He had to look at the case files. And the thought sent a shiver down his spine as always. He had to dig up the past.

The storeroom where he kept all his past was as always, dimly lit. Somehow, he wanted to keep his past out of focus. But Vishnu had realized that if he wanted any internal peace, he would have to look at each and every event in his past life very carefully, under the harsh glare of critical thought. And the first thing he did, was turn on the brighter florescent light bulb. The boxes strewn all over the floor were pieces of the puzzle he had to solve. And then there were letters and papers and files and receipts and all kinds of office stationery and furniture cluttered all over. Yet, he had spent the past few days in dating and labelling the boxes, at least the most relevant ones, to indicate their contents. He picked up a box labelled *Letters* and searched for a place to put it down. He could see that the *Letters* box he was holding had a pile of letters from all over the place, but the top envelope was an unopened one with the name of some woman he had never heard of. By the looks of it, the envelope contained a greeting card. But he paid no attention to it and kept looking around for a place to put down his burden. He finally found one, right on the armchair. He high-stepped a couple piles of paper and a stack of boxes to reach the chair and placed the box down. As he turned back and the lettering on a file caught his eye. *Report of the Post-mortem Examination*, it read quite clearly and it stunned Vishnu. He picked it up unknowingly and began to read.

He couldn't believe he was reading a coroner's medical examination report about Gopika! He remembered listening to all the gory details of the report's findings in court. He could still feel his ears ringing with the arguments and the counter-arguments he and his lawyers had made against the case presented by the Prosecutor. But this was the first time he had actually held a copy of the report in his hands. It was quite prudent of his defense attorney to store all the evidence and proceedings of his trial diligently. It was a big piece of the puzzle and would be most helpful in charting a way ahead. His father had always wanted to appeal the judgement and was happy to escalate it right up to the apex court of the land, but Vishnu was in no mental state to undergo the same torture of questioning again and again. The fact that Gopika was killed and disposed of in such a fashion had sapped his life. Moreover, that he was found to be the murderer had broken him and left him a husk of his formal self. He had ceased to be human from then on and had tried many times to end his suffering once and for all, and failed. But now that he had a clear goal, to get to the bottom of this mystery of who murdered Gopika and why did it look like he had done it; he had gotten back to a semblance of someone living. Still a husk, but that husk was soon filling up with something nourishing. He peered into the report.

Some relative gory images with hand-drawn markers were also stapled in. All the findings were listed in a sterile, dispassionate medical language. But to Vishnu, this wasn't alien. He had studied human anatomy and physiology as part of his Forensic Science degree. The report listed the skull fracture and the massive blood loss as the cause of death. The identifiable marks on the body and the effects of the body being frozen solid and then defrosted were also mentioned. Freezing and unfreezing had ruptured many of the internal cell walls and membranes. It was also mentioned that the freezing had begun before rigor-mortis had set in. And on certain parts of the body, there were freezer burns where the body had come directly in contact with the cold metal of the storage freezer. There was also *the* puncture wound right on the vein on her left forearm. Vishnu's mind floated back to the courtroom where he was standing in the witness box and the Prosecutor was asking him some seemingly innocent queries.

'Mr. Vishnu, do you know if Gopika ever donated blood?' the Prosecutor has asked and the seemingly out of context query had thrown him off.

'Donate blood? You mean like the Red Cross – Blood Bank kind of thing?' It was more of a rhetorical question really. What else he could mean, Vishnu thought. 'No, never! Gopika had a strong aversion to needles.'

'So can you explain why she has a wound that resembles a needle prick on her left forearm?' the Prosecutor continued.

'No, I can't,' Vishnu said, but then suddenly remembered something and said, 'No wait! She said she was going out to sort out some woman issues. I didn't pay much heed then, but maybe she had some blood test done or some inoculation administered.'

'Or maybe this Mr. Vignesh sedated her?' the Prosecutor continued.

That threw him off! He had never thought of that. 'Yes, maybe he did.'

'So he sedated you by making you drink cold water and then when Gopika came along later in the night, he sedated her by injecting an untraceable chemical into Gopika's circulatory system, then crushed her skull in, spattered her blood all over the floor, then cleaned all the blood and put her dead body in the ice-cream parlor's storage freezer and then disappeared.' The Prosecutor had succinctly summarized the entire series of events and Vishnu realized how ridiculous it all sounded, but the Prosecutor wasn't done yet. 'The police department made enquiries regarding Gopika's whereabouts since after she left her office.' And he summarized the findings. He told the Court how Gopika had returned to her hostel to pack a few things. She had paid off her dues and on the way out had thanked the watchman and handed him a generous tip. When he had enquired why she was going out that late, she had said that she was heading out for dinner with Vishnu and then gleefully exclaimed, 'I am starting a new phase in my life!' The watchman had heard these words often from girls who were moving out of the hostel to get married and had assumed as much. He knew that Gopika and Vishnu were in a relationship for quite some time and thought Gopika was going the same way; marriage and settle down with her boyfriend. And that is when it dawned on Vishnu. This was all going against him.

'So you and Gopika were going to move in together?' the

Prosecutor asked.

'What? No! I would have wanted to, but she wasn't ready yet,' Vishnu said dejectedly.

And then the seed of doubt was sown. 'The Prosecution proposes that you had promised to move in with Gopika. That you were going to use that pretext to get Gopika drop her guard just enough for you to kill her. That you were then going to dispose the body in a secluded spot and no one would be the wiser. After all, without a body, it is next to impossible to prove a crime and you very well knew that no one was coming looking for Gopika; not even her parents!' That statement had not only sown the seed of doubt, but also sealed Vishnu's fate. The argument was a convincing one and had no flaw in itself.

'Why would Vishnu want to get rid of Gopika?' Vishnu's defense lawyer had queried. 'And if he did, why kill her? Why not just break it off?' he had argued further.

But the Prosecutor had the answer for this that would paint a darker picture than Vishnu or any of his defense team had hoped for. 'Such is the state of things,' the Prosecutor argued. 'For a rich guy like Vishnu, Gopika was just a use and throw away item. And rather than deal with the emotional wreckage and clinginess of these innocent girls, just disposing them off was a more preferable option for these inhumane characters.' It was a damning argument. And one which was further fortified by the countless number of similarly themed movies and TV serials.

But Vishnu in his desperation questioned the Prosecutor's logic instead. 'And what untraceable sedative did I inject into Gopika? And why did I still stash her in our own Romantic Corner's storage freezer?'

'Clever, Mr. Vishnu. It is a film-goer's pipe dream to find an untraceable sedative. You initially thought of killing Ms. Gopika by injecting a big enough air-bubble into her circulatory system. But when Ms. Gopika realized what you were doing; she resisted and there was a struggle. You pushed her and she hit her head on the table corner. The wound bled profusely, but more importantly was serious enough to be lethal. You then planned to clean up the bloody mess and transport the body to be disposed of but it was too late and you realized that there was sufficient activity on the street, paperboys, milkmen, auto-rickshaws, tea-stalls, that you couldn't transport the body without being seen. So you hid it in your storage freezer to be disposed the following night and then went through the elaborate charade of searching for her the rest of the day. It was just happenstance that Ganesh, your shopkeeper, wasn't comfortable with Ms. Gopika's disappearance, especially when he had heard you quarrelling the day before. He had also heard Ms. Gopika tell you about returning for a dinner together that very night. But, the very next morning when he asked you about how your dinner with Gopika was, you brushed him off saying you didn't have dinner with her that night. Ganesh has also testified that you were angry and muttered that you will never have dinner with Gopika again. It was just by chance that Ganesh had stumbled on Gopika's corpse. He had opened the storage freezer to replenish some ice-cream flavors in the store freezer when he had received the shock of his life! Gopika's frozen corpse staring blankly at him; her frozen hand extending upwards towards him, as if asking for help. Had Ganesh not called the police, you would have disposed of Ms. Gopika's body and she would just be one more number in the statistics of missing people.' The Prosecutor's explanation was convincing and the theory was bulletproof. Vishnu had dug his own grave.

No motive could be proven for Vignesh to kill Gopika. In fact there was no proof that Vignesh ever existed. All the evidence was circumstantial but strong and the Prosecutor was an extremely wily character. He didn't seem to be aggressive at all. He never adopted the interrogative or accusatory tone. He skillfully elicited all the responses from Vishnu and then weaved a convincing story of Vishnu's deceit and rage and guilt that had led to Gopika's death at Vishnu's hand. The Court had returned a judgement of manslaughter and Vishnu was saved from the death penalty. In the end, Vishnu was sentenced to fourteen years of rigorous imprisonment. Due to his deteriorating mental health, his multiple suicide attempts and for his time served without incidence, this actual incarceration lasted seven years. Then came Dr Prakash who directed him to Dr Sujata and that had led him to where he was standing today, Gopika's post-mortem report in his hand.

As he put down the post-mortem report, his brain was back on track and he started looking for a case file. Any case file, just to get his mind off the post-mortem report he had just read. He started opening up the boxes strewn close to his feet and he saw the name on a file – NarayananAS. Arya! He remembered. It was perhaps the only case he hadn't revisited since he had started his therapy sessions with Dr Sujata. It was a straightforward case at the outset but then something had happened. And something about the abrupt way in which the investigation was terminated made Vishnu uncomfortable.

He focused on Arya's case file, not because he was looking for something specific, but because he just wanted to not remember Gopika and her gruesome death. Vishnu had always found it weird that Gopika, who was such a techno-geek was adamant on keeping regular hard-copy paper folders for all the cases they took on. It stemmed from her habit of writing a regular diary, he recalled. At the time when digital diaries were all the rage, he had even gifted her one on her birthday, only to note five months later that she had still not even powered it on! Personal diary has to be hand-written, she had told him. 'Writing a diary is more than the thoughts and the scribbles and the doodles and the emoticons,' she had explained. For her, it was also a record of how her hand-writing changed with her moods. He knew that the computer case files were quite sparse, for he used to populate those and he wasn't that great at book-keeping anyway. But the paper-folders were always very meticulously maintained – receipts, photographs, film rolls and later SD cards, phone logs; basically everything that was relevant to that particular case. And as he began reading the folder he realized that Gopika also had her own hand-written comments to go along. *Need to get to Arya's*

Office - Vishnu to look into it, she had written on one page. *Need to push Vishnu to get evidence,* she had put down on another. *Meena!? Could be useful?* was on another one. As he flicked through the pages and receipts that were neatly filed and dated, he came to the printout of the email he had so cleverly lifted from Arya's office. He went down the memory lane and his chest swelled up reminiscing on his ingenuity of how he had sneaked into Arya's office and under everyone's very noses, had been able to procure this seemingly scandalous document. **What a catch! More money?** said a sticky note written in red ink in what Vishnu recognized immediately as Gopika's writing. And yet, it was almost scratched out by a frustrated, angry pencil with the words, *No go! Need to rethink approach for next time,* written in an equally neat methodical hand.

Vishnu remembered that event vaguely. He had given the email's printout to Gopika that day and she was elated. She was going to speak to Mr. Narayanan and see if he would be happy to fund a field-trip for both Gopika and Vishnu to gather more evidence. But in the evening, she had a gloomy look on her face and had tersely informed Vishnu that Mr. Narayanan had decided not to pursue this any further and had terminated their services. For a moment, Vishnu had noticed the disappointment in Gopika's eyes. She had been dreaming of a sponsored fact-finding mission for so long. And that very dream had vanished into thin air in an instance. Vishnu had thought of just sponsoring a short outing for the two of them on his own and getting Gopika back to her cheerful self, but had thought against it. Their fledgling business wasn't yet set enough to bear the financial burden of a romantic outing and Vishnu didn't want to go back to his ancestral money-pot to cover the expenses. *If only I had told Gopika about my family's background and the immense wealth I was the sole inheritor of,* he mused. *Maybe things would have been different. We could have been a wealthy, married couple, maybe a couple of kids, farm-houses and holiday homes wherever Gopika fancied, cars,* foreign visits, whatever she had ever wanted, he thought. And suddenly, a thought that had been scratching the insides of his mind for all these years began its irritating scratching once more, 'Did Gopika ever truly want me? Or did she just see me as a means to an end?' Nonsense! He thought to himself. He loved Gopika. 'But did she really love you?' came back the scratching query. And he didn't have a clear answer.

But he had realized something new. Only now, he had completely forgotten what he had realized! He bent down to put the file in the box when his eyes glossed over the file below – Mr. Kamat. He picked it up intriguingly. Sujay had angrily claimed that Kamal was a gold-digger, after him for his money. But Vishnu's recording of her conversation with her father was quite the contrary. As a private investigator, Vishnu prided himself in being able to read the person quite correctly and he had always thought Kamal was sincere and truly in love with Sujay. He thumbed through the pages to see if there were any pearls of wisdom Gopika had put down and he wasn't disappointed. The usual comments about directing Vishnu to do some things, getting some more information from Mr. Kamat were apparent. But one comment caught Vishnu's eye. *What does Mr. Kamat want? Verify if there are financial implications to a positive or negative result.* Gopika had written. And that didn't sit well with Vishnu. The task was to conduct a thorough and honest background search. Why would there be any financial implications at all, he wondered. And what positive or negative result was Gopika referring to? His pace quickened and he started turning over the pages of the folder at a more frenetic pace, quickly scanning over every page to read if any such comments featured. And then in a transparent plastic sleeve, he found the audio cassette he had recorded Kamal's conversation with her father. That conversation had made Vishnu believe beyond any doubt that Kamal was truly in love with Sujay and not his money. 'Just as I thought,' Vishnu said to himself, 'Kamal was not a gold-digger.' Behind the cassette but in the sleeve was a small piece of paper. *Kamal's conversation* it said and just below it was Gopika's comment, *Can be used either ways.*

Vishnu was extremely uncomfortable reading that comment. What ways was it going to be used, he thought to himself. But he had started painting a scenario already. He hoped it was not true, but the recent meeting with Sujay made it hard to ignore. He turned over another page which was just a copy of a food-bill he had filed in during one of his outings regarding the case and was astonished to see another plastic sleeve with yet another audio cassette. He did not recognize it, nor did he remember ever seeing it or Gopika mentioning it. Why was there another cassette at all, he wondered. Did Gopika make a copy of the cassette to give to Mr. Kamat? And if she did, why hadn't she given it to him? Why was it still in the folder? Just when all these questions began crowding up Vishnu's brain, he saw another small piece of paper that was in the sleeve. It said, *Paydirt!* Vishnu was utterly confused. Mr. Kamat had not seemed too happy about Kamal and Sujay's relationship and he just wanted Kamal's background search to result in some objectionable facts that he could use to leverage his precious son out of the relationship. As far as Vishnu recalled, his recording of Kamal's conversation with her father or any other aspect of her background turned up no issues that could be used by Sujay's Dad to object to their relationship. And yet, Sujay seemed somehow convinced that Kamal was a gold-digger and he had not married Kamal after all. Vishnu had been surprised to learn that Sujay's thought of Kamal as a gold-digger, but the word *Paydirt* followed by the exclamation mark that he saw of the cassette made him a bit more uneasy. Something definitely did not fit right. 'I have to listen to this tape first to make any sense of this,' Vishnu thought out loud and quickly scanned the room for the tape-recorder.

He remembered his trusted old Panasonic RX5030 Boombox that he had used during his college and later his private detective days. It was one of those old technological dinosaurs that just never broke down. He had played tapes after tapes incessantly on his Boombox all through his college years. And from time-to-time he had used the same Boombox to listen to various clandestine recordings he made during his years as a private investigator. He scanned the room and saw a small glint of metallic grey at the very far corner, recognizing it immediately as his trusted Boombox. He hurriedly picked it up and almost immediately was restless with frustration. He didn't see the power cord attached to the Boombox. Now, he had to search for batteries he thought and instantly, he remembered. Like most people of the day, the battery compartment was the place where the power cable was neatly coiled and stored for safe transport. He opened the battery compartment and was both relieved and amazed to see the power cable as expected. Old habits die hard, he mused. He plugged in the power cord, loaded the cassette and was about to press the play button when he remembered the periodic ritual these tape-recorders needed for the supposedly *crystal clear stereophonic sound*, they needed their heads to be cleaned! Kids of this age would not even know what that means, he thought amusedly. In the era of Blu-Ray disks and MP3-players, the tape-recorder was as old as the Pyramids! But, he continued with the process. He opened the cassette compartment and with a small piece of paper that he wetted with his spit, wiped out the rectangular metal head that would ride the magnetic tape and read the recorded sound. The paper came back with a small black smudge. Good call, he thought to himself. He closed the compartment and hit play. At first, there was nothing except background noise and the sound of the spool-wheels whirring slowly in the Boombox and then the recording started playing back. Vishnu listened to it intently as he immediately recognized the soft, twangy voice as that of Kamal's. It wasn't a particularly long recording, just about four minutes give or take. But when it finished, he looked aghast and his jaw dropped. He couldn't believe what he was hearing. Utterly bewildered, he rewound the tape and played it back. Then again. And again. What he heard nauseated him to the core. He could clearly recognize that this was a doctored version of the original recording he had obtained of a conversation between

Kamal and her father. In the original recording, it was clear that Kamal was in love with Sujay and had no regard for Sujay's wealth. But this doctored version projected an exact opposite image. It seemed that Kamal was a scheming gold-digger who, with her conniving father had planned all along to entice a rich guy like Sujay to get married and partake in all his wealth. In this doctored version, it sounded like Kamal had succeeded in doing just that and was gloating about her hold over Sujay. 'And for some reason, Gopika had deliberately hidden this from me,' Vishnu thought. And this was ***Paydirt***!

With a visibly disturbed mind-set, Vishnu started rearranging the boxes the way they were and picked up the box which had the unopened envelope. He focused on it and was surprised that it was addressed to Gopika. It peaked his interest and he opened it carefully. He was surprised to see that it was a Thank You card profusely thanking Gopika for saving someone's life! His eyes widened and his mind was no longer fuzzy, he was now fully focused on this new surprise that had fallen into his hands. He inspected the envelope the card came in. It had a return address and a name Kasturi, clearly written at the back. On the front, it was addressed to Gopika at their office address. A couple of postal stamps were barely visible under the dark smudged post mark. The date intrigued him, for it was a few days after his initial arrest all those years ago. He was mildly taken aback at finding unopened mail addressed to Gopika after all this time. He re-read the message written on the card. Apparently, Gopika had donated blood to this woman who had undergone a labor-related surgery and had saved the life of the woman and her child. Something did not sit right with Vishnu. In almost five odd years that he had known Gopika, he had never once seen or heard Gopika donate blood. In fact, the one time that he had tried to recruit her for a blood donation campaign, she had backed out claiming that she was scared of needles. On the one hand, he had just found out that Gopika had looked at all their cases as money bags and nothing more. In fact, with total disregard for truth or the impact her forgery would have, it looked like she had doctored a recording of a relevant conversation and presented it to the client. This had somehow resulted in *Paydirt*. And here in his hand was a card sincerely thanking the same Gopika for saving two lives by a timely donation of blood. Vishnu lay down on his bed and closed his eyes. Tomorrow, he would have a lot to talk with Dr Sujata.

CHAPTER EIGHT

Dr Sujata's sessions had definitely paid off. Vishnu was on the quick path to recovery; though he hadn't quite realized it himself. He was soon getting back to a respectable routine. After his customary morning exercise and ablutions he sat down for breakfast, and saw the spread in front of him. Boiled eggs, buttered toast, the aroma of freshly brewed coffee, Appam and fresh creamy coconut milk – the breakfast of royalty, he thought. The fine bone china cutlery and the authentic silverware complementing the hand-brocaded tablecloth and his trusty manservant waiting for the signal to start serving. The piping hot coffee came first. Good, old-fashioned pure South Indian Filter Coffee – ambrosia to a coffee lover like Vishnu. He remembered how he used to absolutely love his coffee; just like his father. He was picky about his coffee grounds and how it was made and the right proportion of decoction and milk, just like his father was too. But for reasons known to Vishnu alone, he had shunned away from coffee for quite some time. Then, came the phase of ice-lollies, he reminded himself and shuddered. He was about to crawl back into the deep, dark wormhole that his life had been through for the past decade but then, the waft of strong, freshly brewed coffee took him all the way back to his childhood.

Vishnu reminisced on his childhood. It sounded cliché but he really was born with a golden spoon in his mouth. His ancestors were a rich and powerful line of landowners, Zamindars as they were known back then. Unlike most Zamindars of the time though, Vishnu's forefathers were well-liked by their workers and they were quite intelligent when it came to matters of money. Just when the newly independent India decided on implementing land reforms to redistribute the lands more fairly, his grandfather executed a master stroke. He put in place a plan to "exchange / transfer" a substantial chunk of his arable land in the countryside with, at the time valueless, dry, arid rocky wasteland at the outskirts of several towns and cities namely Madras, Madurai, Pondicherry, Coimbatore, Salem and Vellore. And over a period of decades, the landscape changed. His grandfather taught his son, Vishnu's father, everything he knew about wealth management and wealth generation. Vishnu's father was a quick study and had his own ingenious mind. He realized the perils of being a well-known rich guy in a developing India and aimed at becoming the wealthiest person in the state that no one knew about. And that is when a stroke of luck came about his way.

During the time of British India, surnames were a dead giveaway of a man's caste. And an independent India soon realized that caste was one of the great dividers of men, of communities. And the wise leaders of the state of Tamilnadu engineered a collective social mindset where the society slowly did away altogether with the surnames. No more caste identification based on surnames. And that played nicely into Vishnu's father's plans to become anonymous. All these years, the large real estate portfolio that his ancestors had amassed was under the umbrella of the ancestral surname, a surname that he was inadvertently forced to distance himself from. And thus began an era of selling prime pieces of real estate for a silent partner's share in a range of businesses. Vishnu's father's idea about being the silent partner was a very unique one though. In most businesses he had a stake in, all his partners were silent about his involvement and all his partners were deemed silent by his final word, relayed to his partners through his trusted lieutenants. By the time Madras officially became Chennai on the 17th July 1996, Vishnu's father had almost achieved his goal. When he had waltzed into the gates of a posh new township at the outskirts of Chennai, just before its official inauguration at the hands of a Kollywood on-screen power couple, he was stopped by the security guard who demanded an invitation letter for that posh event. When Vishnu's father produced it from his well-worn leather attaché and presented it to the guard, the guard had checked the list of attendees and ticked off a name without giving much thought to it. And as he saw the traditionally dressed and seemingly out-of-place man walk up to the ceremony hall, he wondered why on Earth had this peasant-looking fellow been invited to this star-studded event. Little did he know that this peasant had pocketed more than seventy percent of all the profit that was generated from the sale of each apartment, bungalow and shop within that township. And Vishnu had seen all of this with his very own eyes; for he was the young boy holding the peasant's hand, walking all excited, looking behind to see the look of repulsion and confusion on the security guard's face. He had asked his Dad why he never showed any outward affluence. For all onlookers, Vishnu's Dad was still a peasant, albeit a relatively affluent one, who had somehow managed to hold on to a substantial piece of fertile agricultural land at his native place. He still lived in the same, large, old but well-maintained ancestral home. The only difference was that the farming had changed from bullocks to tractors and the market had moved from the village to the city. To facilitate the sale of the farm produce, upkeep of machinery and such, several people from the city would visit the Zamindar's home from time to time. And the Zamindar had a beaten-up Ambassador car that would ferry him to and from the city when needed. His Dad had said, 'Many in this world are rich Vishnu, but few have power. Fewer still command respect and a select few command awe. When you grow up a bit, you will realize that not being known as a wealthy person when you really are one of the wealthiest around is a kind of power many seek but few achieve. I was lucky to achieve it and one day, you will inherit it. Your charm might get you many friends my dear boy, but your seemingly middle-class status will test how good of a friend, they really are. Once you have tested their mettle and loyalty, you will have the power to make them kings. Never do that, for there can be only one king. Make them your trusted lieutenants and they will forever be indebted to you. That is real power my boy.'

And that was the last heart-to-heart conversation Vishnu ever had with his Dad. They returned home to a pall of sorrow. Vishnu's mother had suffered a sudden heart-attack and was unconscious. By the time Vishnu's father could arrange for an ambulance to move her to the hospital in the next town, it was too late. The massive attack had basically killed off most of her heart muscle and her heart had just given up. Vishnu was devastated, as was his father. Though he was fully engrossed in his business affairs, he had loved his wife very dearly. And the only way he knew of overcoming his grief was to be more engrossed in his work. The finality of his mother's death affected both Vishnu and his father equally deeply, but they both interpreted and reacted differently. His Dad reckoned that if he too met the sudden death his wife had, Vishnu would be left all alone in the world, a thought he dreaded. To that effect, Vishnu's Dad started putting all his efforts into establishing a safe future for Vishnu. And that meant not just a ton of money, but a ton of money along with constant sustained source of a ton of money and loyal, knowledgeable people who would manage it all. To organize such a vast empire required all of his time; time that he should ideally have spent with his only son who had been traumatized by the sudden loss of his mother. With a heavy heart, he decided that Vishnu would go to boarding school. It would be just for a few years till he could establish the empire he wanted Vishnu to inherit, he envisioned. He could clearly see the seething hatred for his plan in Vishnu's eyes. 'But he is just a boy, what does he know?' he thought to himself and soldiered on. Little did he realize that his seemingly high-handed approach of sending Vishnu away would end up creating a festering wound in Vishnu's psyche and ultimately morph into an unbridgeable chasm between them. Money with all its enticing power is just never enough, and the never-ending quest for Vishnu's safe future continued. All the while, Vishnu became more and more distant and soon started resenting his family's wealth.

There were a few hushed conversations regarding Vishnu's father tying the marital knot once again. But these conversations were summarily squashed by him clearly and with the conviction that everyone else soon realized, could not be budged. 'I can barely take care of Vishnu now and you want me to take care of an additional woman!' he had argued. Or at least that is what Vishnu seemed to have heard. In a few days, his father had decided that Vishnu was to get educated in the best boarding school the country had to offer, far away at the foothills of the Himalayas. Vishnu resented every bit of all that had happened. He resented that despite all the wealth, his mother could not be saved. He resented that his father thought it was a burden taking care of his only child and he resented that his father had decided to send him to a place thousands of miles away, without ever discussing it with him. It was a resentment that had shaped his future. It made him more self-reliant than the rich, pampered brats he schooled with, but it also distanced him from the only person who truly cared for him; his father. It was a fact he realized much later in life when he saw that his father was ready to move Heaven and Earth to get him acquitted of Gopika's murder. He saw the pain in his father's eyes when all else had failed and he was sentenced to serve a life sentence. But he also realized that his father was the only person in the entire world who believed in his narrative; in his innocence.

It was during his boarding school days that every schoolboy's favorite pass-time first became Vishnu's escape and then became Vishnu's goal – detective novels. Hardy Boys, Nancy Drew, The Three Investigators, Miss Mary Jane Marple, Sherlock Holmes, Hercule Poirot and Mme Precious Ramotswe took him on a journey of adventure, mystery, crime and sleuthing where he forgot all his pain of loss and abandonment. Many pre-teens and teenagers go through this phase and then outgrow it. But with Vishnu, it was a bit different. He hadn't stumbled upon the exploits of these legendary detectives as a pass-time. He had used these exploits as a refuge from his sorrow. Also he had at times overheard his Dad use words like *investigate, background history, validity check, verify details, professional investigator* and *private eye*; which kind of suggested that these things did happen in everyday life. And that led to a thought being planted deep within him. He wanted to be a part of this world of shadows; to be able to peel away the layers of deceit and uncover the truth. And he thought he could do better than these sleuthing legends. So just like many other schoolboys, he started writing his own detective stories; and had penned down a few pages worth of what he thought was a mindboggling mystery when a thought hit him. 'How am I better than these guys?' he mused. Over the years, he had matured enough to now realize that Sherlock Holmes was just a figment of Sir Walter Scott's imagination as was Miss Jane Marple Agatha Christie's. 'What these authors couldn't *do*, they *wrote*,' he said to himself. But he was better than them. He decided that he was going to *do* stuff, not just *write* about it. That is when he made a decision; he chose a path his life would tread. He was going to be a Private Investigator! Validation of whether he had it in him to be one came some time later.

Sherlock Holmes studied forensic science quite ardently. In fact, he was the first person who made it a science; and it helped him make these seemingly amazing deductions which for him were just *Elementary*! Vishnu decided to follow the great sleuth's footsteps and soon realized he was in luck. The World and Science in general had moved on since the Victorian Era that Mr. Holmes lived in and formal degrees in forensic science were readily offered at reputable institutions of the 21st Century. Vishnu decided to study forensic science and when he had let his Dad know of his preference in a terse one-liner, his Dad seemed to have paid no cognizance. Vishnu's Dad had amassed such wealth and established such a resilient empire, that it didn't really matter what education Vishnu pursued. At the time, Vishnu was surprised at his lucky breaks for he had readily been accepted to the top forensic science program in Chennai and was even offered a scholarship. It was only now that he wondered whether that was all his father's doing. It was during his college days that he had met Gopika who was pursuing a degree in criminal psychology. Their interests complimented each other and they had hit it off.

'Did you forget anything Thambi?' Vishnu was shaken by the question and blinked out of his trance to see his trusty old manservant by his side. He was probably the only one who called Vishnu by that honorific in the house. 'No, nothing Aiyya,' Vishnu replied using the title he had used since childhood, for Aiyya had been with the family since before Vishnu was born. After the death of Vishnu's Dad, Aiyya had loyally overseen the family's businesses in the absence of its rightful heir. 'I didn't forget anything. I just remembered a lot though,' he said as he started descending the large marble steps to get to the driveway and in moments, he was out of his house and into his car. A mansion really, right in the middle of a huge plot of land. The fact that such a large piece of land could be owned and used just to build a single dwelling so close to the crowded metropolis that was Chennai vouched for Vishnu's wealth; something he had no regard for. Wealth changes people. Sometimes, it entices people so that they value wealth above everything else. And sometimes, it makes them value everything else. It had the latter effect on Vishnu. He had shunned his family's wealth for quite a long time, and that is how he had become a private investigator. 'And that is how you got into this mess,' he reminded himself.

He sat in his car and his driver knew exactly where to go. Vishnu had used his services to get to Dr Sujata's house the last time around and had asked to be dropped a few blocks from her home, right at the bus stop. It was the same bus stop he had got down the first time he had visited her. Vishnu was casually, but expensively dressed as usual. Only high-quality linen is what he wore most of the time, for it was lightweight and breathable. He wondered why such a perfect fabric had not caught on in the hot humid regions of South India. He rang the doorbell and as if on cue, Dr Sujata opened the door and let him in. For a moment, both Vishnu and Dr Sujata paused and absorbed the changes that manifested in each other's appearance. Dr Sujata saw a more confident, healthier looking Vishnu. Her eyes gleamed and just for that brief moment, her face gave away something she didn't want to – or at least that is what Vishnu thought puzzled. He couldn't really put a name to the emotion that he had just seen on Dr Sujata's face. He tried but failed. No word he thought of could accurately capture what he felt he had seen her face go through. And Vishnu was taken aback by that; and by the fact that Dr Sujata was looking a bit paler than the last time he had seen her. Or was it just that his own improving mood and his overall well-being was deeming Dr Sujata's well-being to be inferior to his own? He couldn't tell, and that moment was gone.

'Hello Dr Sujata? How have you been?' Vishnu greeted.

'I am doing well, Thank you. By the looks of it, you seem to have gotten over the gloom quite well. Do you have any new clues to follow?' Dr Sujata went directly to the point.

Vishnu found that a bit odd. Usually, Dr Sujata would allow Vishnu to dictate the flow of conversation and only occasionally steer the topic if it started meandering. But today, she was a bit more direct and her attitude almost bordered on impatience; as if she was in a hurry to get it over with. He wondered if her look of tiredness was real and if that had anything to do with her directness.

'I have found a few things in the past few days and I was about to pursue one today, had we not agreed to meet up,' Vishnu said; but the slight quiver in his voice was not lost on Dr Sujata.

'You have found a few things? But you are not sure what to do with them?' Dr Sujata coaxed.

Vishnu was relieved. The lady is still as sharp as ever, he thought to himself. Maybe her frailness and her directness were just tricks played by his own mind. 'Yes. I have uncovered three things, all equally puzzling,' he said. The tone of his voice wavered a bit but it wasn't clear if it was due to indecision or excitement.

'So, you found anything about Vignesh? Or is it something else?' she asked seeming quite eager but at the same time, she seemed to be on edge. Again, tricks of your mind, Vishnu calmed himself.

'I found out that Gopika had a habit of jotting down some comments in the case files. They make for an interesting read. Well, they make for a shocking read really,' he said.

'Shocking? How?' she enquired.

'Well, she has made comments on the case files and they reek of greed. It seems like all she was looking for was a big payday, with no concern about what was ethically correct, about what the truth was, about anything really,' Vishnu said in a somber tone. His gaze was watery and fixed at nothing. He was clearly in pain, but there was a tinge of hate lining his voice, something that had never happened when he talked about Gopika, she thought.

'And what is the next thing you found?' she queried.

'The next thing just proves that I did not know Gopika very well. I came across an audio recording we had used during one of the cases; Mr. Kamat's if you recall. Well, this one was clearly doctored to show that Kamal was a gold-digger when in reality the original recording proved beyond doubt that she wasn't one.' Vishnu's heart sank as he said those words. It was when he said those words out loud that their impact was felt. Gopika was a heartless abomination of a human and money was all she cared for.

'And you are sure Gopika doctored it? And benefited from it?' Dr Sujata asked. Her eyes showed a flash of anger but no real surprise. It seemed that she had already come to realize the truth.

'Y-yes!' Vishnu stammered. 'No one else could have done it. And Gopika had written **Paydirt** on the cassette. It seems like she used a doctored tape to get more money from Mr. Kamat!'

'You both did!' Dr Sujata interrupted, 'Get more money, I mean. Though why you needed all that money is beyond me. You come from a decently rich family, isn't it?'

'I was never in it for the money and I never really cared about money,' Vishnu said. 'I was in it for the investigation and the thrill of it all and that is all I did. I wanted to be a private investigator since schooldays. Gopika took care of all the accounts and I don't even know how much money we made in our businesses.'

'Such cavalier attitude towards money, and the trust clients put in you,' Dr Sujata said and Vishnu couldn't make out whether it was pity or hate or just abhorrence. 'Of course, you come from a well-off family and money might not have meant that much to you. But for Gopika, it was a completely different story by the looks of it. After all, you know how that story goes right?'

Vishnu remembered the time when Gopika's parents' testimonial was admitted in the Court. According to it, Gopika had always been a hot-headed child prone to extreme adamant behavior. One fine day, just after her schooldays she had a major argument with her parents regarding how they wanted her life to shape up. Coming from a traditional middle-class family, her parents had wished for a simple graduation and then an arranged marriage with a suitable groom celebrated by a grand function, kids and the rest of it for Gopika. And Gopika was totally against that. She wanted to meet people, earn money and go places. When neither side seemed to retreat, Gopika had just demanded her share of the inheritance from her family so that she could move out of the house and start life on her own. When her father vehemently rejected any such arrangement, Gopika had stolen the family jewels and whatever cash she could lay her hands on and promptly left town. She had brazenly left a note to that effect too. Her Dad had been furious and wanted to report to the police, but it was Gopika's mother and close well-wishers who had advised against it. Gopika only had one sibling, an elder sister who wasn't yet married. Reporting to the police would have tarnished their family name and finding a suitable groom for their elder daughter would have been almost impossible. Collectively, they took the decision to erase Gopika from their life and live as if it was a single child household. It had worked well. In fact, when approached by the police during the investigation and trial phase, Gopika's parents had strenuously requested that their statement be considered by the Court in absentia and that they remain anonymous. They did not want anything related to Gopika ever to come back to them. For them, Gopika had died a long time before she was murdered.

'Yes,' Vishnu said sheepishly. 'I had no idea about that till it was raked up during the trial. We never discussed our past or our parents.

That was one of the pillars our relationship was built on.'

'That might be, but you can clearly see the motivation, can't you?' Dr Sujata asked. 'With all her familial support structure gone, she was just trying to secure her own future. And money is how you do it. Nothing wrong with that,' Dr Sujata stated matter-of-factly.

'No, nothing wrong at all – as long as you do it ethically,' Vishnu said with some emphasis. 'But it looks like Gopika was going to use confidential information from people's lives and tweak it around if needs be to get more money out of clients.'

'Like I said, you will not understand it. You have been well-off all your life,' Dr Sujata said calmly.

Well-off! Vishnu thought to himself. Did Dr Sujata know how rich he really was? Well-off wasn't even close to his family riches. Maybe I should have just let Gopika know of it too, and she would be alive and we would not be where we are now. Or maybe we would never have come together. Or maybe Gopika would still be the greedy bitch she was turning out to be and he would have hated her for it; maybe even killed her out of hate. And he would be in the same situation as he was in now. Only, he would have known he was the murderer! What a sobering thought indeed.

'Hello! Cat got your tongue?' Dr Sujata brought him back to their conversation. 'So what are you going to do next?' she asked. She was intrigued as to what else Vishnu had managed to dig up. But first, she still wanted to know whether Vishnu had made up his mind about Gopika and said, 'You said Gopika tampered with evidence connected to Mr. Kamat's case. It could be a one off.'

'I wish!' Vishnu's reply ended with the sigh of a broken man. But almost immediately, she could see the anger seething in his eyes as his breath quickened and he continued, 'It isn't just that one case. I thumbed through Mr. Narayanan's case file too. That's Arya and Sita's case,' he added quickly noticing a look of confusion on Dr Sujata's face. 'The way I interpret Gopika's notes in that one, it seemed like she wanted more money out of it but couldn't, because Mr. Narayanan terminated our services.'

'Well, you did the background search on Arya and gave the results to Mr. Narayanan. Why would he still retain your services in the first place?' Dr Sujata asked.

'We hadn't completed the background search yet, at least not according to me. I just found an email indicating that Arya might be having an affair. But we wanted to confirm it first. I gave the email to Gopika who presented it to Mr. Narayanan to ask if he was ok with us investigating more, which would incur additional costs,' Vishnu said, and Dr Sujata looked at Vishnu but what she was really looking at was Vishnu's naivety.

'But Mr. Narayanan just asked you to stop the investigation and you never went back to the case for a follow-up,' Dr Sujata insisted. It was more of a statement than a question. She had heard this all before and it seemed like she didn't have too much patience for the same stuff. What is new she wondered.

'Well, yes. Until now!' Vishnu said.

Something like a bolt of lightning seemed to surge through Dr Sujata as she immediately bent forward intent on listening to the new piece of information Vishnu was about to disclose.

'Nothing too exciting really. Gopika had scribbled in something to suggest that she might have used a different approach to get more money out of Mr. Narayanan,' Vishnu said these words with bitterness. Dr Sujata was surprised by the tone in Vishnu's voice.

'It is a business after all. Your goal is to make money, isn't it?' Dr Sujata said.

'But not at the expense of our duty. Not at the expense of morality or the truth!' Vishnu said with gusto.

'Anyway, why does it matter now? I am wondering where this is going really. Is this the third thing you wanted to tell me?' Dr Sujata asked.

Vishnu quickly ran through how he had accidently found the unopened Thank You card which had been sent by a lady named Kasturi, thanking Gopika regarding a life-saving blood-donation she had performed. Dr Sujata listened to the story keenly and was processing the facts to get to a useable result when Vishnu began speaking again about the whole affair.

'Gopika was never one for donating blood and I also found that there was a small needle prick found on Gopika's dead body,' Vishnu explained.

'It looks like she had a change of heart and donated blood; the card and the prick prove that she did. So what?' Dr Sujata looked confused with this seemingly irrelevant line of discussion.

'It just doesn't feel like the same person,' Vishnu said. 'The same Gopika who was after money to the extent that she could tamper with evidence, fiddle with people's lives really, was also donating blood to save life when she was so against it in the first place.'

'People do weird things for weirder reasons. They are not predictable machines. It is the chaos that makes people and our lives in general interesting,' Dr Sujata said. 'Maybe Gopika was really the person deserving your love and her greed for money wasn't as deep-rooted as you think it was?'

Vishnu's face was that of a tortured soul. 'I so want to believe it, but what about the tampered audio recording and all those notes she scribbled in the case files? I could not believe that Gopika would stoop to such low morals just for money. Cheating clients!' Those last words escaped Vishnu's lips with a gasp.

'Was she only cheating clients?' Dr Sujata asked and Vishnu gave her a quizzical look.

'I don't understand,' Vishnu said honestly. 'Who else was she cheating?'

'Don't you remember what she did when her demand for her part of the inheritance upfront was denied by her parents? She just stole whatever she could from them. That was just before you met her in college, I think,' Dr Sujata offered. 'It seems like her greed for money was slowly but surely building up. I mean, she had come to a point where she had fabricated false evidence to make a few extra bucks. And you said she looked at all the accounts related to your business.' Dr Sujata paused for effect, and effect she had.

The expressions on Vishnu's face transitioned from confusion to understanding to something that looked like rage and then immediately to one of pitiful hate, abhorrence some would call it.

'Anyway, Gopika doesn't seem like a person who would donate blood . . . if there wasn't anything in it for her.' And with that, Dr Sujata ended her analysis of Gopika's character.

Vishnu's heart cracked. It was like the final nail in the coffin. After all those years of love, trust and partnership with the only lady in his life, it had all come down to this. He no longer trusted anything he knew about Gopika. In fact, the only thing he fully believed in now was that he never really knew Gopika at all. He bid farewell to Dr Sujata after arranging for a follow-up meeting and walked out towards his car with a heavy heart. He was going to have to investigate Gopika.

CHAPTER NINE

Vishnu got out of his car. As had been his habit, he asked his driver to drop him a couple of blocks away from the address he was interested in. It was a typical middle-income apartment complex. Not dilapidated, but not spic and span either. Three floors of middle-class families. Six apartments, two each on a floor. Windows shut, air-conditioners humming full throttle. Typical summer. He climbed up a flight of stairs and knocked on the door. A woman in her mid-thirties answered the door, opening the door just enough for Vishnu to see a very small part of the living room. Vishnu saw the immediately wary look on the woman's face, but as soon as she saw this well-groomed and well-dressed individual, her look softened. Vishnu didn't waste any time.

'I am sorry to bother you madam, but do you recognize this Thank You card?' he said and handed over to the woman at the door. The door opened even further and now Vishnu could see a well-worn sofa and the corner of a coffee table peeking behind the woman's substantial girth. The woman took the Thank You card in her hand and almost immediately her demeanor changed.

'Of course, I remember!' she exclaimed. 'How can I not?! This lady was a God-sent angel who saved my life twice over!'

Vishnu looked at the woman quizzically and the woman seemed to have understood the cause of confusion. 'I mean she saved my life and that of my kid.'

'So you met her? Talked to her?' asked Vishnu.

'No. I was under anesthesia in the ICU. My Mom spoke with Ms.

Gopika. She told me about her.' The lady suddenly clammed up and looked at Vishnu. 'Why are you asking, sir? Do you know her?'

'I did,' Vishnu said somberly. 'She died almost the same time this card was sent to her. I only just found it in her things, unopened. After reading through, I felt the urge to come talk to the sender. I am sorry if it is a bother.'

'What! Oh My God! Died how? Such is luck. These angels come to Earth just to do such wonderful deeds and then, they are called back to heaven. What can I say? I am so sorry for your loss. Please come in, have a glass of juice.' The lady opened the door to usher him in. 'You should talk to my Mom. She is the one who met Ms. Gopika. Will be very sad to hear about her untimely death.'

Vishnu was about to take a step into the house when he stopped going further. 'Can I talk to your mother then?' he enquired. 'It will give me some peace of mind to hear about Gopika.'

'Well, my Mom doesn't live with us,' she said, 'but do come in and have a glass of juice. I will get you her number and address in the meantime,' she insisted.

'I wouldn't want to impose,' Vishnu said politely. 'If you just get me your Mom's address, I will be on my way,' he said. 'I have some errands to run in the afternoon and if your Mom lives in the city, I can get done talking to her before I do anything else.' Vishnu's eagerness was clearly audible in his voice and the lady nodded in understanding.

'Just a minute,' she said and ducked into another room, leaving Vishnu standing at the apartment's door, wide ajar. Vishnu only had to wait for a couple of minutes when the lady came back with a hastily torn piece of paper with something scribbled on it. 'This is the name, address and telephone number for my mother. Visit her whenever you want to. She seldom goes out of her home. I have put down her telephone number too, but the line is dead, so she will not receive anything if you call.'

Vishnu thanked the lady and set out to his next destination – the address he was given. He wondered what he was going to achieve pursuing this line of enquiry, but something in his mind told him this was the right way to go about it. For a brief moment, he was not bogged down by the cloud of doubt about Vignesh or Gopika or his split-personality or anything else. All he wanted to know was how Gopika was roped into donating blood. The thought that Gopika committed a selfless act was like a soothing salve to the wounds Vishnu's psyche had borne when he read through her notes on their case files and listened to the doctored audio recording in Mr. Kamat's case.

Vishnu's driver knew the city like the back of his hand and had no trouble in getting to the address given. As always, he stopped a block away from the place and directed Vishnu to the house. They were in the very old part of the city. Open gutters and old single-storey homes lined the street for most parts. Some of the homes had been replaced by a few multi-storey apartment complexes and office blocks. But all this was old-school. It still had retained the old-city feel. Two wheelers parked haphazardly, an overflowing rubbish bin right next to a distribution transformer – just a typical old part of an Indian city. Vishnu knocked on the solid wooden door a few times before any movement was evident on the other side. A lady probably in her mid-sixties opened the door and looked at Vishnu quizzically. And just before Vishnu could open his mouth to get the first few syllables out, the lady cut him short, 'No one home. Come back some other time.'

Vishnu stood there bemused. He had just elicited the most typical response to anyone unknown knocking on the door. Vishnu immediately said, 'I just spoke to your daughter Kasturi. I am not selling anything.'

The mention of her daughter's name made the lady stop and take notice. But it was clear that she was still quite wary of the stranger. Obviously, identity theft and confidence tricksters were getting common by the day and just knowing someone you were related to wasn't enough to open any doors. Vishnu quickly gave more information, 'I am here to talk to you about the blood transfusion your daughter had during labor. It so happens that my friend, Gopika, was the donor,' and he took out a photo of Gopika from his wallet. The introduction and the photo seemed to soften the lady's stance but still there was a bit of wavering. Vishnu finally took out the Thank You card and handed it to the lady along with the piece of paper on which her daughter had scribbled her name, address and phone number.

'Actually, Gopika died around the same time this card was posted and I was away for all these years. Only now, I took charge of her belongings and I found this Thank You card. I just thought it will be good to know more about Gopika and her final days.' Inadvertently, a tear dropped down his cheek and that was the door opener!

The woman looked at the sincerity in Vishnu's eyes and asked him to come in. Vishnu had to bend down to enter and at the same time had to high-step over the threshold to avoid being struck in the shin by the raised door-frame. When he entered, he noticed that it was a room almost exactly as he had imagined. The two small windows on either side of the door were the only source of natural light which was dimmed out by the faded and thin curtains made up of some cheap synthetic saree. The room was relatively spare in furniture and what was there was almost as old as the lady if not more. The saving grace was what seemed like a very well-maintained Murphy radio, the net antenna and everything. Vishnu remembered that a similar piece was also his father's treasured possession where he would often listen to Radio Ceylon. 'Have some water, Thambi,' the woman offered. Vishnu drank a bit, but the lukewarm water in a funny smelling stainless steel tumbler wasn't too inviting and he politely set it down.

'So tell me what happened. Ms. Gopika is dead?! I simply cannot believe it. She was so young! And a really nice girl.' The old woman seemed visibly moved, but Vishnu could see that there was something more.

'Yes, she was. She died in a terrible accident,' Vishnu said and that lump in the throat that comes up when people lie was a large one. 'I really don't want to remember it again, it was too traumatic. Instead, I would love to know how you met her,' he redirected the conversation.

'She was a God-sent for me and my daughter. And we only met her by accident. My daughter had suffered a catastrophic bleed during her emergency C-section and was requiring a lot of blood. And as they couldn't fix the source of the bleed, all the blood they pumped into her was just gushing out. A stage came when the hospital ran out of the right type of blood and it seemed as if there was no way to save my daughter.' The quiver in the woman's voice was quite evident. It was as if she was experiencing the horror all over. Vishnu felt for the woman, what she must have been through.

'I thought Gopika had never donated blood in her life, something about her being scared of needles or something else,' Vishnu probed.

'Yes, I remember she said that to the nurse. And so, she wanted the nurse to describe to her in detail each and every step of the process; how and where to insert the needle, where to tie the tourniquet if needed, how to pump the fists to aid blood flow and when to stop. Weird,' said the woman.

'Why weird?' asked Vishnu.

'Sorry, I should not have said weird with Ms. Gopika being dead and everything. But she didn't seem interested in how the blood is stored or typed or whether it is being used immediately or any such thing. I was there with her, thanking her profusely for her kindness; but she seemed to be paying no heed to it whatsoever. All she was interested was how to get the blood out, how much maximum can be drawn in one go, how will she know she had drawn out too much and what is the minimum recovery period. I also offered her some money for the blood donation, but she didn't seem very interested. I asked for an address from the hospital's register to send out our thanks.' The old woman was exhausted with that long monologue and stopped to have a drink of water. It was the time Vishnu needed to process all that he had gleaned so far. Gopika wanted to know how the blood is drawn. And suddenly a thought occurred to him and he asked, 'So, Gopika wasn't called to the hospital on that day to give blood?'

'No. They were getting blood from anyone with a matching blood group and she happened to be there and kind enough to be willing to donate. It may be fate, but hers was the last bottle of blood required. The doctors said it was nothing short of a miracle. But once Ms. Gopika's blood was pumped in, the bleeding subsided and stopped soon after.' The woman's response didn't clarify the query Vishnu had in mind.

He remembered that Gopika had ducked out on that evening citing woman's issues; and his mind immediately strayed on needle prick mentioned in the post-mortem report. He had always thought that the hospital trip and the needle prick were connected and that it was something Gopika had planned for. After hearing the story from the mother, he realized that the needle prick could have been due to this spur-of-the-moment blood donation that Gopika was roped into. He just wanted to make sure of this, as this would punch a hole in the case the Prosecutor had built against him by convincing the Court that this needle prick was due to Vishnu injecting Gopika with an air-bubble. 'Do you remember the date of this event, Amma?' he asked.

'Of course! How can I forget the day my only grandson was born and my daughter cheated death,' and she gave the exact day, date and time that it all happened and that is when Vishnu realized why something within him made him pursue this. He had uncovered something new after all! Gopika had donated blood, contrary to his knowledge about her aversion to needles. And from the description of the wound in her post-mortem report, it could be from another blood-donation that she went through on the day she died, rather than it being the entry-point of an injection that was allegedly administered by him; or it could be the untraceable sedative administered by Vignesh. It didn't get him any clarity but it did tell him one thing. Gopika had secrets that he didn't know of. What other secrets Gopika had kept from him, he wondered and the thought made him uneasy. He had to get back to the storeroom in his mansion that stored his past. Maybe something in those storage boxes would lead him to unravelling the mystery that surrounded the existence of Vignesh, he thought. He bid his farewell and walked back hurriedly to his car. His obedient driver had been waiting patiently for Vishnu to return and deftly navigated the Chennai traffic to get him home.

Vishnu had a quick chat with Aiyya and after making arrangements for a quick dinner to be sent up to the room, ducked into the storeroom where everything from his past was stored. This was the first time he had a nice, long look at all the boxes and realized the amount of life they documented. 'So many cases,' Vishnu thought to himself and then suddenly stopped at the sight of a box labelled *Ice-cream Parlor*. He was intrigued. That was definitely no case file and he just couldn't guess what that box would have contained. He hurried up to the box, and as always, had to step over a few other boxes to get to the one he wanted. He opened it half expecting to see unused ice-cream cones and spoons and plastic cups, but instead what he found was a neat stacks of what he immediately realized to be receipt books. 'Accounts!' Vishnu said out loud, 'Obviously!' Every business needs to have a record of its finances. That was a fundamental requirement of any business, he said to himself. And he remembered Gopika gratefully for taking care of all the financial paperwork, leaving him to do the interesting sleuthing – the work he really cared about. But now, he wasn't so certain. After his recent discovery of Gopika's ever increasing greed and Dr Sujata's not so subtle hint that Gopika might also have cheated Vishnu, he shuddered in anticipation of what he would find.

'There should be a set of accounts for the investigative agency too,' he thought and remembered how he had invested all the money in the establishment. Gopika basically came with nothing, and yet, she ran the business like she owned it. A hint of bitterness had seeped into his thoughts as he looked into the accounts. He had always been least bothered about the financial side of the business, he recalled. But the current revelations about Gopika keeping secrets from him had suddenly made him look carefully at everything she had ever done, and book-keeping was one of them. Gopika had always treated finance to be a realm ruled solely by her and though it hadn't bothered Vishnu at that time, now he was apprehensive. Within a few minutes, he could put his hands on a set of passbooks. It took him a further few minutes to get a hang of reading the entries in the passbooks. They were simple affairs with basically four columns, Money In, Money Out, Current Balance and Date. Vishnu looked at the figures in the first passbook and started recollecting some of the expenses. The monthly payment for his apartment as well as Gopika's hostel were immediately recognizable, so was the salary paid to Ganesh, the helper manning the ice-cream parlor. Both Gopika and Vishnu had fixed equal salaries for themselves and that deduction was also something Vishnu recognized. He was amused to recall that the salary he typically paid his driver nowadays, was close to twice what they made in those days. And then there were some expenses that would have been bills for utilities such as loan payments, electricity, telephone and internet.

Nothing untoward for the first few pages of the passbook, but then he found a fixed amount being withdrawn every month like clockwork. He scanned the rest of the passbooks hurriedly and he looked up stunned. The withdrawals had continued steadily for the entire period that their enterprise was in operation. It was a substantial amount! Gopika was basically fleecing Vishnu all that time. She was stealing money that belonged to both of them. 'Why does that surprise you?' he thought to himself. He recalled all that he had uncovered about Gopika recently and it all added up to one thing – Gold-digger! He wondered what he would have done if he had found out the treachery back then. Would I have had the guts to confront Gopika? And if I did, surely she would have had a seemingly convincing explanation, maybe a nest egg for those difficult times, maybe a retirement plan or some such floozy thing. And such was Gopika's influence on Vishnu, that back then he would have accepted any explanation without question. Would you do it today? He asked himself. He wondered what his reaction to the treachery might be if he had known about Gopika then what he knew of her now.

With a heavy and agitated heart, he went to bed, with a half-empty stomach. Vishnu was so sick to find out that the woman he loved and trusted had basically exploited him as a source of income and nothing more that the dinner Aiyya had sent up to the room was just not appetizing anymore. He thought of why Gopika would have needed the money. 'Would it have been a secret savings account?' he thought to himself. Or was it that she had another secret in her life, something that was worth blackmailing for, he thought. But if she was being blackmailed, why would she be killed? As the passbooks showed, the withdrawals had continued regularly to the very end, so why kill the duck that laid the golden egg? He quickly dismissed the thought of blackmail, but he couldn't come up with an explanation that satisfied his tumultuous mind. Luckily for him, sleep overpowered his senses and he went into a deep, soothing calm. When he woke up, he could still feel the bitterness in his heart, but the heaviness had abated. He woke up with more energy than he thought he would have and he had a clear agenda for the day – Arya!

He remembered very clearly where Arya had worked and bolstered by the way he had found out about John and Shalini, Vishnu thought that starting at Arya's place of employment was a good bet. He quickly realized that his suave persona and the air of dignified wealth was a fabulous door-opener. He could just walk up to the reception, leave the twenty-something receptionist in awe of his handsomeness, sign his name and enter, asking for the manager. He had tried to get information about Arya from the receptionist, just as he had done in John and Sanjana's case, but the receptionist was new at her job and didn't know quite how to work the system. She was however, helpful in allowing Vishnu to enter the main work area and meet with the HR manager. As with all managers, the HR manager also had an air of being busy about her and asked her secretary to help Vishnu with his query. Vishnu was led to a cramped desk just outside the HR manager's cabin where a young man in his late twenties stood up to acknowledge his boss's request. Vishnu smiled at the role reversal. He had half imagined the HR manager to be a man in his middle age and the secretary to be a young lass. Vishnu put forth the query regarding Arya. The small talk he had in the meantime let Vishnu know that the HR secretary had joined the company about three years ago and so he just had to look for past records in the stores downstairs. He ordered a coffee for Vishnu and asked him to wait for him as he left to go to the storeroom. Vishnu sipped his coffee and stood up to have a look at the layout of the work-space. It was quite a bit different than the one he remembered from all those years ago when he had swiped the printed email from Arya's desk. And he couldn't quite place where Arya's desk would have been either. His mind wafted back to Gopika and the withdrawals and the doctored tape and Dr Sujata, when suddenly he was shaken by, 'Found it sir! Sad really.'

The HR secretary was panting and sweating, but his voice had cracked not due to exhaustion, Vishnu recognized. It was excitement mixed with something else. 'Mr. Arya is no more, sir,' he said in a somber tone.

It took a minute for Vishnu to realize what had been disclosed, but he still wanted to be sure and asked, 'No more working in this company? Has he given any forwarding address?'

'Sorry sir. No more as in dead. He died in a road accident it seems. There is a forwarding address though, if you want it. Here, let me write it down for you. Actually it is so sad . . .,' the secretary continued with words of condolence, but Vishnu couldn't hear anything further.

Vishnu was stunned and his mind wafted away from what was being said. During his investigations, he had found Arya to be quite a happy-go-lucky type of person. Death in a road accident seemed totally unfair for a guy with all that promise. But then life is seldom fair, Vishnu recalled. His own life was the apt example of that adage.

'Does it say when he met with the accident?' Vishnu asked.

'Yes sir. It sure does. He was still an employee of this company then and so the company footed all the medical bills. By the looks of it, he was a highly valued employee. He was taken to the best hospital in the city, but his stay was quite short. The company had kept detailed medical reports of him,' he said and saw the confused look on Vishnu's face. 'They did that probably for the insurance claims, nothing surprising.'

'Can I have a copy of the medical records?' Vishnu asked and by the look on the secretary's face realized that he had overstepped his hospitality.

'Er-r, I will have to ask my boss, sir. These are official company documents and I cannot freely give it to people without proper authorization. I hope you understand. Just a minute and I will clear it with madam.' And the secretary started to get up from his seat.

Vishnu put a reassuring hand on the secretary's shoulder and said, 'It doesn't have to go any higher really. I am not investigating anything and this will not create any trouble for anyone. Arya was a dear friend whom I lost touch with due to my travels, and this will just give a bit of closure for me. I am sure Geetha will be ok with it. Of course, if you need to get approval from her, please go ahead.'

Vishnu immediately realized that his gamble of calling the HR manager by her first name, which showed that he knew her quite well, had paid off. He hadn't met the HR manager ever in his life before today, but had only picked up her name from the nameplate on her desk.

The guy hesitated and then said, 'I will make a quick copy. It is just a few pages really. Looks like there wasn't much they could do.'

Vishnu collected the medical records, thanked the secretary and ducked into the HR manager's cabin to thank her and put in a good word for the secretary and walked out of the building. Arya had died in a road accident. He wondered how Sita was coping with that or whether she had totally gotten over it all and was living a happy life. Whatever be the case, he would have to be careful not to approach her directly and reopen Arya's memories. He looked at his watch and realized it was almost time for his session with Dr Sujata. He was not really happy, but he was in high spirits. The past few days had been quite productive and he had quite a bit of stuff to talk about with Dr Sujata.

CHAPTER TEN

He got into his car and his driver knew what to do without Vishnu needing to tell him. Vishnu spent the time of the journey in carefully skimming through the copy of Arya's medical records that he had just acquired. Skillfully, his driver navigated the streets of Chennai and stopped where he always did, a couple of blocks away from Dr Sujata's house. Vishnu walked in through the gate and was surprised to see Dr Sujata outside in the garden. Perhaps it was the blazing Sun or the high humidity or his own tiredness, but he thought Dr Sujata was looking sick. It was a surprising thought, he realized. He hadn't thought she was tired or ill or off-color but sick. And moreover, he thought she looked sicklier than the last time. He greeted her with a warm smile and said, 'Dr Sujata! What are you doing out in this oppressive heat?'

Dr Sujata apparently hadn't noticed Vishnu come in through the gate and gave a small jump at Vishnu's greeting. 'Oh, Vishnu! You scared me there. Is it time already? Please let us go in,' and she directed Vishnu to their inner sanctuary. Vishnu immediately noticed that the air-conditioning wasn't on full blast as required in Chennai. Also, he felt like Dr Sujata gave a slight shiver before she sat down and couldn't contain herself.

'Are you cold?' he asked.

'Just a bit. Nothing serious really,' Dr Sujata replied without conviction.

'Odd. It is sweltering outside!' Vishnu exclaimed.

'Is it? I hadn't really noticed. You can turn the air-con to full if you like. Make yourself comfortable. I will send for coffee,' Sujata said.

Vishnu was slightly shocked at that statement. Typically, Dr Sujata would herself get water for both of them, and she would do it with great gusto. Today, she was going to ask her maid to get them coffee. Something was up with Dr Sujata, he could sense it, but not quite put a finger on it. He thought about asking Dr Sujata about her well-being, but thought against it. 'Yeah, coffee would be nice,' he said instead.

'So, what have you been up to? By the way, did you find out about Vignesh?' Dr Sujata asked.

More warning bells! Dr Sujata would seldom lead their conversation in the past, but recently she had done just that on two occasions. Vishnu also noted Dr Sujata's obsession with Vignesh during their past two meets. He couldn't rein in his frustration and asked slightly haughtily, 'No, why?'

'Well, that is the crux isn't it? Once you make peace with the fact that Vignesh does not exist, you can begin the journey of forgiving and repair,' Dr Sujata said in a soothing tone.

Vishnu's head was swimming. Did that mean Dr Sujata believed in the Prosecutor's theory that Vishnu suffered from split-personality disorder? It surely sounded like it. But Vishnu pushed these thoughts aside and said, 'I just found out that Arya died in an accident. It seems he suffered a stroke.'

Vishnu watched Dr Sujata quite keenly and thought he saw a quick but recognizable change in her entire body. It was as if her whole body tensed up for a moment and then went limp. Even her face contorted to show an emotion that Vishnu couldn't really put a name to, before it smoothened out to her normal serene façade. It was pain, but not just pain. Was it discomfort, he thought. But it wasn't that mild either. 'Are you alright Dr Sujata? Is the air-con too much?' he asked.

'What? Oh yes,' Dr Sujata said hurriedly, as if coming out of a trance. 'It is just that Arya seemed to have such a promising life ahead. I feel sad when I hear young ones dying.'

So that was it, Vishnu realized. It was the reaction to a young death.

'You said Arya died in an accident?' Dr Sujata probed.

'Well, it looks like he had a stroke while driving his motorcycle and met with an accident that killed him. No real mystery there,' Vishnu elaborated. 'I wonder what Sita might be up to, poor girl.'

'Then it doesn't have anything to do with Gopika or you or Vignesh, or does it?' Dr Sujata asked.

'No, not at all. You had asked me to follow-up all the cases we had taken on, but most cases had amicable results and I don't think they will crop up as complications. I thought it was prudent to follow up only those cases where something seemed astray,' Vishnu answered.

'Well then, what else?' Dr Sujata asked as she offered Vishnu the coffee cup that the maid had just set down in front of them. The maid made another trip to set down a jug of cold water and two glass tumblers just as Dr Sujata prodded Vishnu further by saying, 'That doesn't help you in any way.'

'I traced back the Thank You card to its sender.' Vishnu disclosed and paused to see if Dr Sujata was interested in that line of the story. She was absentmindedly sipping her coffee when she realized the silence that hung about the room and looked up to see Vishnu gazing at her expectantly and said, 'Yes . . . sorry, I was thinking of something else.'

'Gopika donated blood to a woman who had undergone an emergency C-section and had saved the lives of the mother and the baby in the process. The woman sent the Thank You card after she had recovered.' Vishnu finished the sentence with no real understanding of the importance of this chain of events.

'Hmm,' was the only reply he could elicit out of Dr Sujata and that didn't satisfy him. He looked at Dr Sujata quizzically.

Dr Sujata could easily interpret the confusion in Vishnu's eyes and said, 'So she donated blood? Didn't you say she was scared of needles?'

'She did. The lady's Mom said it was Gopika's first time,' Vishnu explained.

'Then how was Gopika called on to donate blood? She would not have been a registered blood donor,' Dr Sujata's question exploded like a bomb in Vishnu's head. He wondered why he had not thought of it earlier. Why was Gopika there at the hospital in the first place? And how was she roped into donating blood?

'Well, the lady's Mom who saw Gopika donating blood said something I cannot really understand,' Vishnu said, visibly perturbed. 'She told me that throughout the entire blood-donation, Gopika was more interested in how the needle was inserted, how the blood flow was established, the amount of blood that could be extracted, how the bleeding could be stopped after getting the needle out and so on.'

'Oh? Well, those are all the questions anyone would have isn't it? Especially someone who was scared of needles,' Dr Sujata said.

'No, not really!' Vishnu exclaimed. How was it that Dr Sujata had missed it completely? A first-timer scared of needles would rather avoid any mention of needles, pricking, piercing or blood. 'A first-timer would ask how the blood is stored. What the shelf-life is? And more importantly, how often could you donate blood.'

Dr Sujata's looked at Vishnu with intent. She had just realized something. Vishnu looked at Dr Sujata expectantly as she said, 'You are right. So what does that prove?'

'I don't know yet,' Vishnu said. 'But I am going to find out. I also took the hint you gave me last time, about Gopika possibly duping me of money. It turns out she was skimming a fixed amount of cash each month from the agency's account.'

'And doing what with it?' Dr Sujata asked.

'I haven't figured it out yet, but I will,' Vishnu said with conviction.

Dr Sujata seemed like being taken aback by the resolve Vishnu showed in his statement. 'I wonder what you are looking for and what you will find. More importantly, I wonder what you will do when you find whatever you are looking for.'

Vishnu noticed that something had suddenly changed. It seemed that Dr Sujata was not sure of Vishnu's innocence.

'I will have to somehow track down Vignesh and that will absolve me of the crime,' Vishnu said with sincerity.

'Fine. Let us go over everything that we know about the case and everything that you have gathered so far. Maybe that should give us a way ahead,' Dr Sujata said helpfully.

'Good. That is exactly what I had in mind. I think that will point us in the right direction!' Vishnu exclaimed.

'So, I am going to just spell out the incidences. No judgement here, just hear me out and correct me if I go wrong or miss something,' Dr Sujata said and continued. 'On that night, Gopika asked you to stay back and meet with the new recruit you call Vignesh.'

'That was his name,' Vishnu interrupted.

'I am just stating facts here, Vishnu. Except for your claim that Gopika asked you to stay back and meet this Vignesh, we have no other way of corroborating the fact.' Vishnu was stunned into silence. After all his efforts, that was still true. 'Furthermore,' Dr Sujata continued, 'I don't think Gopika ever gave you his name, did she?'

'Y-yes. I met the guy and he said his name was Vignesh,' Vishnu said honestly.

'Right, moving on. You waited for Vignesh. He was late and called you up informing you of the delay. You waited. He arrived and somehow drugged you as you do not remember anything after the meeting till the next morning when you were woken up by the shopkeeper, Ganesh,' Dr Sujata narrated with almost no emotion. Vishnu simply nodded.

'Police records indicate that the cell-phone call was made from within the vicinity of your office and that very cell-phone was found with Gopika's body in the storage freezer. Also, there was a couple of hours' gap between the phone call and the time you supposedly met Vignesh.' Vishnu nodded again. His eyes were fixed wide-open and his fists were clenched so tight that his knuckles had turned white.

'It is also noted that there was a gap of about ninety minutes give or take between the time you supposedly met Vignesh and the time Gopika was allegedly murdered. The freezing of the body made it difficult for the coroner to fix the time of death.' Vishnu sat motionless, but Dr Sujata's long pause made him look up. He nodded again. Everything that Dr Sujata had said so far was what was proved during his trial.

'The next morning you were woken up by Ganesh and you called Gopika's phone multiple times – twenty-three times to be exact! You even visited her hostel. The hostel watchman informed you that she had actually gone out the night before to meet you for dinner, something you claim never happened.' That part was also true, Vishnu thought.

'In fact, the watchman was told by Gopika that she was going to have dinner with you and start a new life and so was vacating the hostel. When you went back to your office, you saw that the police were already on the scene. Ganesh had called them after shockingly finding Gopika's corpse in the storage freezer. Police investigators also found Vignesh's alleged cell phone in the same freezer, along with Gopika's frozen corpse.' Vishnu could hear his heart thumping.

'With the available evidence, you were sentenced to jail for willful manslaughter and were incarcerated for close to eight years. You also attempted suicide on three occasions and were put on suicide watch. Dr Prakash was assigned to you as a psychiatrist and after your release; you followed up with him as advised by the Court. He then referred you to me.' Vishnu was thankful for Dr Sujata's kindness. She had missed narrating the part where he had pleaded in court about the existence of Vignesh, but no shred of evidence to that effect was ever found. She had also missed out the part where Vishnu's father had pooled in all his resources to hire the best possible team of defense lawyers and was successful in saving Vishnu's neck from the hangman's noose. More importantly, Dr Sujata had missed how Vishnu's father was a sad and broken man to see his only son being convicted of the crime he hadn't committed and how within a matter of months, he had died, unable to bear the sorrow of Vishnu's incarceration. Dr Sujata continued further.

'We started off by looking at the cases you had investigated, which could potentially give someone the motive to murder Gopika. This was assuming that if Vignesh existed, we need to find a reason for why he would murder Gopika. We tried to find who she had wronged, enough to be murdered,' Dr Sujata paused a bit and continued further, 'I guess, the most she wronged was her parents and they basically had written her out of their lives. And for that, we began following up on all the cases you had ever handled, where revenge could be a motive.' She looked at Vishnu for a minute when a long spell of dry, bone-jarring cough wracked through her entire body. It was a sickly sound, hollow, like a kid's cheap plastic rattle, but Vishnu was so engrossed to get to the end of this that it didn't register with him. Instead, his impatience had the better of him and he continued the narrative instead.

'I followed up all the cases of consequence that we looked into and found a few things.' Dr Sujata hurriedly tried to suppress her coughing and focused on what Vishnu had to say.

'I found that none of my past clients had any motive to wish us any harm; at least not to the extent of murdering Gopika. The only sad story so far is that of Arya, but then accidents do happen and young software engineers had recently shown a propensity to suddenly drop dead due to strokes and heart-attacks; a direct result of the high-rewards high-pressure work-environment they lived in.' Vishnu looked at Dr Sujata and she had a hint of a smile on her face, or was it a wince, Vishnu thought.

'On the aside, I did find that Gopika was more concerned about making money,' Vishnu said, but the euphemism wasn't lost on Dr Sujata.

'Say it straight,' Dr Sujata said. Vishnu had never heard Dr Sujata in that tone. It was a snarl more than anything else.

'It seems Gopika was never in love with me. Rather she used me to make money and money she did make. She was also skimming our business of a decently large fixed sum of money every month. What she was doing with the money needs to be traced,' Vishnu concluded.

'And there is still no sign of Vignesh!' Dr Sujata said. It was a statement which reeked of finality. It was as if she meant to indicate that they had come to a conclusion. Vishnu, obviously was not ready to accept that. His face was defiant and Dr Sujata recognized the look. 'Did I tell you that my main area of expertise and study has been the split-personality syndrome. In technical terms, it is also known as multiple personality disorder or dissociative personality disorder. They don't mean exactly the same thing, but they do go hand-in-hand in most cases.'

'I don't have split-personality disorder,' Vishnu said relatively angrily. He couldn't believe that Dr Sujata would come to that conclusion.

'I am not saying you do. I am simply saying, we have to also consider it. In any case, why does it matter, those who are dead are dead and you have borne the punishment you were decreed.' Dr Sujata tried to use a consoling tone but it was futile.

'It matters. You, of all people, should know this. I don't care if the world sees me as a murderer. I want to face a mirror and say I am not! And one day, I will,' Vishnu's conviction was getting stronger.

'So then, are you any closer to finding Vignesh's whereabouts?' Dr Sujata asked but Vishnu was already thinking out loud.

'Gopika told the watchman that she was going to have dinner with me. She had made plans for a late dinner with me before she went to the hostel. But she never told me anything about starting a new life. Something she told the watchman. And with the money she stole from the agency's account, she could definitely have a head start someplace else. And why did she go to the hospital? Looks like she went just to learn about how to draw blood. But why? There are all these questions that need answering. And that can lead me to something.' His tone was full of excitement and his breathing was rapid.

'True. It is something to look into,' Dr Sujata said but with an air of being not fully convinced.

'And then there is Sanjana and Mrs. Devi!' Vishnu said.

'Well, what about them? I thought you said you were unable to trace Mrs. Devi or Sanjana,' Dr Sujata said with a confused look on her face.

'Well, yes. But I did find John and Shalini married. So, what happened to Sanjana and Mrs. Devi? After all, that is where it all started for us!' Vishnu's eyes sparkled as if he had realized something he hadn't before.

'What started? What are you saying? You have totally lost me now,' Dr Sujata said.

'It was Mrs. Devi who had come to us with another job that might have involved murder. It was where I disagreed with Gopika and she proposed hiring Vignesh in the first place,' Vishnu seemed like a man who had seen the light at the end of the tunnel. Dr Sujata though looked at Vishnu as if she was seeing someone enticed by a mirage.

'I think it will be a good idea to first figure out what Gopika was up to. Why the scheming, why the theft of money and why the vacating of her hostel? What was her end game? And did someone find it out, not approve of it and kill her?' The hint in her question was too obvious.

'Maybe,' Vishnu said hastily and once I find who that was, I will be able to put this to rest.

Dr Sujata looked at Vishnu like a person totally oblivious to the truth staring him right in his face. And Vishnu looked like he had just stepped on unsettled ground!

'There is another scenario to consider,' Dr Sujata said hesitantly and Vishnu had a gut-feeling he was not going to like it. 'Let us look at the facts we know and try to connect them to form a story.' She picked up the notepad on the table, something she had seldom done during their numerous chat sessions, and began writing down some pointer.

'Gopika seemed to be more interested in making money one way or the other, rather than solving any cases. If we factor in the money she stole from her parents, the doctored tape, the scribbled notes as well as the money she had been skimming from the agency's account, we could conclude that she did not have too many moral convictions where money-making was involved, correct?' Vishnu realized it was a rhetoric question, because Dr Sujata didn't stop for an answer. She just wrote a succinct version of this argument on the notepad and continued with her reasoning.

'Due to some differences between you and Gopika, she was acting a bit distant and had also initiated the recruitment of a new partner you call Vignesh. Apparently, Vignesh had a moral compass similar to Gopika's and you were getting the impression that Vignesh was being brought in to replace you. In fact, transcripts of the voicemails you had left on Gopika's cell-phone the day following her murder has no mention of Vignesh; only *Vishnu*. But, you did argue during the trial that you meant *Vignesh* every time you said *Your Vishnu*, just out of spite. Obviously, you were hurt and angry at being replaced so casually by Gopika as you had invested so much in her. Can I safely conclude that you had feelings for Gopika?' Vishnu nodded. Again, the question was just to emphasize the point and nothing more. Dr Sujata wrote on the notepad.

'The differences between you and Gopika started because you thought the *solution you proposed* to Mrs. Devi's problem was not to be taken seriously, while Gopika thought the idea of murdering one person and blaming it on someone else was perfectly alright.' Vishnu had not missed the emphasis Dr Sujata had put on the phrase *solution you proposed*. Vishnu realized that he was destined to rue that moment for all eternity. But he nodded in agreement. Dr Sujata's assessment was quite correct and he watched her write it down in the notepad.

'Gopika seemed to be planning something that you did not know of.' Dr Sujata paused and looked intently at Vishnu and saw that the statement had made the impact she thought it would. For a brief moment, something that looked like satisfaction flashed over her face and then she was back to her calm neutral expression.

Vishnu's head jerked up, his eyes were wide open with what seemed to be a mixture of shock and fear and said, 'What do you mean?' The confusion on his face was genuine and so was his query.

'Well, you have yourself emphasized the aversion Gopika had towards blood donations or needle pricks in general.' Dr Sujata paused to see Vishnu nod in consent and continued, 'Yet, she did donate blood to a complete stranger!'

'That doesn't prove anything, really. There is always a first time for everything. Maybe Gopika wanted to get over her fear of needles and do something good.' But even as he completed the sentence, Vishnu realized that his conviction in the veracity of his statement had left him.

'Not quite. As you pointed out yourself, it seemed that Gopika was more interested in how blood can be drawn from a body rather than the actual act of blood donation and saving life. Add to that the fact that she had funneled a substantial amount of cash from the agency and the fact that she had vacated her hostel that very night; letting the watchman know that she was starting a new life. And to top it all, she hadn't shared any of these plans with you. It seems like Gopika was going to go through the same routine with you that she went through with her parents. Take whatever money she can lay her hands on and disappear.' Dr Sujata was simply stating the facts, albeit in a connected fashion but Vishnu thought a sort of cruel look had come over her usually kind face. It was his imagination purely, for Dr Sujata's statements ripped through the veil of decency and camaraderie that he had draped Gopika's memory in for all these years. Dr Sujata wrote something down in the notepad, but for Vishnu, it felt like she was hammering a nail in the coffin; and the coffin contained his version of Gopika.

'Have I missed something?' Dr Sujata asked.

'W-well . . .' Vishnu stammered. He almost saw where this was going, but still, the end of this path that Dr Sujata had led him on was foggy.

'Yes?' Dr Sujata prompted and bent forward when another of her rib-cage wracking coughing episodes erupted.

Vishnu stood up to offer her a glass of water, but Dr Sujata waved him to sit back down and managed to get control of her coughing.

'Remember the needle prick that was found on Gopika's inner left arm during the post-mortem?' Vishnu asked Dr Sujata. 'The one that the Prosecutor argued was where I supposedly injected her with an air-bubble.' Dr Sujata nodded.

'Well, couldn't it be that Gopika realized how good it felt to donate blood and save lives that she wanted to do so regularly? She left me that evening saying that she was going to address some *women issues*. Wouldn't it be possible that she was called in to donate blood to save some other woman's life?' Vishnu had found a thin line of gossamer silk and clung to it, unable to accept the fact that Gopika was a cold-hearted gold-digging schemer who had just been using him all along.

'So wasn't this the same needle prick due to the blood she donated to the lady who had the emergency C-section?' Dr Sujata asked confusedly.

'No, this wound was fresh and according to the post-mortem had been inflicted somewhere between the previous twenty-four hours. The blood-donation for which Gopika received a Thank You card happened close to two weeks ago.' Vishnu set the timeline straight and Dr Sujata seemed to have a faint smile on her face.

'Well, no blood bank would allow blood to be donated within three months of the previous donation, unless Gopika was donating blood for money. But the money isn't that great unless you bleed gold!' Dr Sujata said.

'I don't think she did it for the money. The lady's Mom had offered money in the first instance but Gopika had refused,' Vishnu noted.

'But then, why would Gopika skim money from the agency to build a nest egg and why would she vacate the hostel on her own accord and why would she let the watchman know that she was starting a new life?' Dr Sujata fired away a series of questions. 'These questions are still unanswered unless . . .'

'Unless?' Vishnu asked.

'Well, it looks like for Gopika, you had outlived your usefulness and she wanted to move on. She had a nice little sum of money stashed away to start a new life away from you. And the night she was murdered was also the night she was going away from you,' Dr Sujata said. 'I don't understand why . . .' and she trailed off.

'What is it Dr Sujata?' Vishnu asked. His mind was already busy in assimilating all that Dr Sujata had presented so cogently.

'I don't understand why she had to learn how to draw blood in the first instance and secondly, I don't understand why she came back to the office that night.' Dr Sujata looked quite confused, but no more so than Vishnu.

Why indeed, he asked himself. Gopika had never ever given as much as half a hint that she was bored of him. So why did she plan on leaving him so suddenly and in such secrecy. And why did she come back that night? She had the money stashed away. She had vacated the hostel. She could have just vanished and no one would be the wiser. Of course, he would have tried to locate her; maybe he would have put his substantial financial power in tracking her and might even have succeeded. And what then, Vishnu thought. His investigations would have led to her financial fraud. And yet, he would have begged her to take him back and Gopika would have said no and they would have argued. And then . . . Vishnu's heart was thumping so loud, he could feel it in his eardrums. Just the thought horrified him more than anything ever had in his life. Why had she come to the office that night, he wondered. And how did the blood donation fit into all this? And where was Vignesh during all this? Vishnu's head was spinning. He looked at Dr Sujata, hoping to find solace but couldn't stop himself from the very thought that had been growing in his mind, 'Maybe Gopika came back to tell me that she was leaving?' he said.

'And maybe you came to know about her skimming from the agency's account?' Dr Sujata continued with a query. 'What might your reaction have been then? Would you harm her?'

'N-no! Absolutely not! I loved Gopika,' Vishnu said but again realized that it wasn't very accurate. Yes, he did like her – a lot, but something had always prevented him from going all the way. Something he couldn't quite put his finger on had always stopped him just short of being in love with Gopika. But Dr Sujata now had a very understanding expression spread across her face.

'You wouldn't harm Gopika, I know,' Dr Sujata said and paused ever so slightly and said, 'But *Vignesh* would!'

CHAPTER ELEVEN

Vishnu left Dr Sujata's home with a question that had only two possible solutions, and he had answers to neither one. Either Vignesh killed Gopika, in which case he had to delve deeper into the past to see who would have the motive to kill Gopika. The other possibility was just too horrifying to even think of. That Vignesh was Vishnu! With that conundrum in mind, he sat in his car and his trusty driver drove him straight home. Vishnu also realized that Dr Sujata had slowly weaned him out of their chat sessions. Initially, they had been every week and then they were held every ten days for quite some time. But now, he was only going to meet her after four weeks. That seemed to be a long time to be away from therapy. Vishnu was on slightly shaky ground, for he had always found solace and direction at these chat sessions with Dr Sujata. It was also quite unlike her to not give him a fixed day and time for the next appointment. But this time around, she had just indicated that they could meet in about a month's time, but the exact time and day would be confirmed via a call by her closer to the date. She had noticed the slight crease of concern on Vishnu's face and had offered to talk over the phone if Vishnu had anything to discuss urgently. That too was out of character for her, for in their first meet Dr Sujata had emphasized on the face-to-face chat sessions and the bodily ticks, facial expressions and other markers that were so important to get the complete picture regarding a person's psyche. But Vishnu had not protested any of it. A month was a long time. He resolved to get to the bottom of the mystery that surrounded Vignesh. Did Vignesh really exist?!

He greeted his old housekeeper absentmindedly and headed straight to the storeroom that held his past. The room full of boxes. He was just thinking about what to do next when a soft tap was accompanied by the door opening and Aiyya standing there with a mug of hot coffee. In his frustration, he asked, 'Aiyya, who would kill a girl like Gopika?' The answer that his housekeeper gave was as unexpected as it was impactful. Aiyya in a soft voice filled with emotion looked at Vishnu meaningfully and said, 'Who would blame you for her murder?' It was like a bright flashlight had just turned on in Vishnu's head. He had been looking at this wrong the entire time. So far he was just thinking of trying to find someone in Gopika's past who had the motive to kill her. And he had tried to comb her past starting from their time together and he was fast running out of places to look. He had already known from her parent's testimonial during his trial that Gopika had a pretty ordinary life with them and there was no one holding a grudge against her strong enough to kill her. Thus, he deduced, the clues lay in their time together at the detective agency. Someone with a grudge had not just murdered Gopika but ensured that Vishnu would take the fall for it. He realized that he had to look back at all the cases with a finer comb, with more meticulous detail. He needed to find that end of the string and yank it hard to unravel the web of murder and intrigue that had tangled up his life for almost a decade. But what did Gopika do with the money she stole from the agency's account? And what role did the unexpected blood-donation and the needle prick found on Gopika's corpse during the post-mortem play? Vishnu realized that he had stepped over a boundary. For the first time ever, he thought of it as Gopika's *corpse*! Aiyya had given him a new sense of direction and confidence and made him totally outgrow Gopika's unwarranted hold over his psyche.

He looked at Aiyya and thought how his wizened eyes still sparkled with intelligence gained from years of dealing with a plethora of people and situations. Maybe he should confide in Aiyya and use his intellect in all this. But he thought against it. The sparkling eyes were deep set in a wrinkled, weather-beaten face, fixed atop an old, frail body. Vishnu didn't want Aiyya to go through the same trauma all over. He didn't want Aiyya to once again experience Vishnu's failed pleas of innocence. But Vishnu had given Aiyya's power of reading people much less credit than it deserved.

'Just ask me what you are thinking, Thambi. I will not ask you what you don't want me to,' Aiyya said in the same soothing voice, but the context was clear. Vishnu realized that his father's trust in this old sack of bones was absolutely well-placed. He understood that any insincere excuses he might think of offering would only insult Aiyya's intellect and trust and so he just asked what popped in his mind first.

'What would a middle-class person do with that amount money?' Vishnu asked, expecting a direct answer.

'How much exactly?' Aiyya asked.

Vishnu could see why Aiyya was his father's most trusted lieutenant. He remembered his father talk about Aiyya. 'Remember this, my dear boy – Opinions are like arseholes, everybody has one!' It was the typical earthly wit that made his father the shrewd and successful businessman that he was. 'For me, this man is priceless for he never has an opinion. He either has the correct answer or he doesn't, but he does not give me opinions,' his father had said. 'Opinions come from incomplete information and false intelligence. Answers come from complete information, exact calculations and careful analysis.'

And Aiyya needed all the information before he could give an answer, Vishnu thought. And Vishnu told him the amount. 'Each month for about two years,' Vishnu added.

Aiyya smiled and asked, 'Past two years? Or two years from now?'

'Two years starting about ten years ago,' Vishnu said and looked at Aiyya.

Aiyya nodded in understanding and said, 'If she was not too wise in the ways of the world, I would say it all went in a safety deposit box or some such saving scheme. If she was intelligent, however, then the best would be to invest in property.'

'Obviously!' Vishnu said out loud. 'How did I not think of that?'

'We all get farsighted at times and we lose sight of things close to us,' Aiyya replied with a sly smile. Vishnu realized then that Aiyya had used the feminine pronoun in his earlier answer. He didn't have to tell Aiyya everything, he already knew.

'Could you find if at all Gopika bought a property?' Vishnu asked Aiyya.

'In the whole wide world! Oh Thambi! That is impossible,' Aiyya said without any apology and continued, 'But if you give me a locality, I might be able to find something. Most likely, if she bought it using her own name.'

'Oh, alright then.' Vishnu's sudden enthusiasm seemed to have ebbed away, but Aiyya was still there.

'You have come this far, Thambi. I am sure you will find something.' He took the coffee mug from Vishnu's hand and retreated closing the door behind him, leaving Vishnu to go back into his past; the past that lay in front of him in the room full of boxes. In this past, Vishnu was going to find who had the motive for this heinous crime that had ruined so many lives.

He sat down for a minute to collect his thoughts but something inside him stirred. Why had Gopika visited him that night? And why did he not remember anything after his meeting with Vignesh? What did he remember about Vignesh, he thought. Vignesh was a person of average built and about Vishnu's own height. He had no visible scars or bodily quirks. He spoke without any specific accent. He had a very normal voice, just as unique as every other person. He wore normal clothes. He came in, and he woke me up. He greeted me and he sat down. He handed me a glass of water from the jar on my table, to moisten my throat. I drank it. And then I was woken up by the ice-cream parlor helper and it was morning. Did Vignesh drug me with something that messed with my memory? It was the same question that had cropped up in Vishnu's mind all those years ago. But a forensic analysis on the jar or the glass had revealed no evidence of a drug being administered. And Vishnu hadn't tasted anything peculiar either; might have been the effect of the cold water. But then all those blood and urine tests the police conducted on him didn't turn up anything suspicious either. And that evidence or lack thereof, combined with the Prosecutor's arguments and his own inability to remember anything new from that night had frustrated him ever since. 'He handed me a glass of water!' Vishnu said softly. Vishnu closed his eyes and said it again, 'He handed me a glass of water.' And after a few repetitions, the entire scene floated in front of him as if it was happening right then and there. Vishnu had been so repulsed and angry at the idea of a new partner that he hadn't even bothered to look up to Vignesh's face. All he could see was a hand offering him a glass of water. All of a sudden, something had gleamed! It was a ring. Vishnu blinked and the apparition was gone.

His heart was pounding. After all these years, he had remembered something. Vignesh wore a ring. And it had a peculiar design. It was what is popularly known as the *Navaratna Ring*, studded with the nine precious stones as per the Hindu culture, typically worn by someone to bring good luck. He wondered if the ring had brought any luck to Vignesh. Why had he not remembered this during the trial? Why did this pop up now? And how was it going to help him in finding Vignesh? Why did Gopika visit the office that night? And why didn't he recall meeting her that night? Why would Vignesh want to murder Gopika and blame it on me? Why did Gopika steal money? What did she do with it? And why did she vacate her hostel and also tell the watchman that she is starting a new life that very night? And what role did the blood-donation and the needle prick play?

When he woke up, it was already morning and his back was sore. He was huddled uncomfortably on the floor, crouched between a few boxes. What had happened? Had he blacked out, he thought. But he could clearly remember everything that he had thought of the night before and how his mind was full of the entire quiver of unanswered questions. He clearly remembered being in the storeroom having a chat with Aiyya, sipping his coffee. He remembered the new insight Aiyya's question had given him and his heart slowed down. He hadn't suffered a blackout now. 'And I didn't suffer a blackout then,' he said out loud in an adamant tone. He knew what he had to do and realized that this was just meticulous, menial work. He decided that he would use the substantial workforce he already had at his disposal to sift through the boxes that lay scattered in the room. He called up Aiyya and asked for three capable men who would do this. Aiyya arranged for three able-minded men with an eye for detail who could find the smallest snippet in a ream of papers. Vishnu's instructions to them were quite clear. They had to look at each and every piece of paper in each and every box and any major financial transactions, real-estate related or otherwise, were brought to him for approval.

It was a relatively nice day where the typical Chennai humidity was not exacerbated by the oppressive temperatures. Vishnu decided to walk around his bungalow to get some fresh air and clear his mind. His estate was exactly what Vishnu had always wanted; in fact his Dad had purposefully built it to match the description of a *Dream Home* Vishnu had given him when he was young. It was a sincere attempt by a misunderstood father to find place back in his only son's life, Vishnu realized – a bit too late. But Vishnu was thankful for it now. It was the perfect home, a quiet, private and well-appointed property. The estate was a large, naturally contoured piece of land with some densely wooded area as well as a substantially large manicured garden, something that would sooth the wild as well as the cultured side of a man. The house was a three structure affair with the main dwelling area which was designed to mimic an old colonial bungalow, slanting tiled roof and everything, an outhouse combined with a four-car garage and a row of houses some distance away that were the servants' quarters. The plan was such that from any point within the property, only one structure was ever visible. That led to a feeling of solitude and privacy. Vishnu had a look at the garden and saw a couple of people tending to it. He wanted total solitude that morning and decided to take a walk along the wild corridor. The serene tranquility of it all washed over his mind and body and he felt more refreshed than any bath had ever made him feel. He thanked his Dad for this wonderful gift and reiterated his promise of unravelling this mystery and absolving himself of all criminal blame. His pace quickened and so did his thought process.

Why would Gopika possibly invest in a property without ever letting him know, he wondered. He had always thought that Gopika was equally in love with him as he was with her, but that her less than privileged upbringing had made her more materialistic. During the trial, a different picture emerged which was confirmed through his recent findings. Gopika, for some reason unknown to him, had just grown up with the notion of financial independence. In fact, she was ready to sacrifice his familial ties to ensure that she had money for herself and to that effect, had stolen from her own parents and never contacted them or her elder sister ever again. The hostel's watchman had made a sworn statement during his trial that Gopika had clearly told him of her intentions of meeting Vishnu that fateful night. She had also vacated her hostel room insisting that she was going to start a new life that very same night. And yet, Vishnu had no inkling about any of her plans. 'Had she just planned on leaving me altogether and start fresh?' he asked no one in particular. 'And had Vignesh decided to backstab Gopika for some monetary gain?' he continued. 'But why would Vignesh do that? Moreover, how did Vignesh know anything about Gopika's plan? In fact, what was Gopika's plan?' Vishnu mused.

By the time he had returned, it was just time for lunch. He couldn't believe that he had been roaming around the woods for almost four hours. As expected, Aiyya was there to welcome him to the dining table. Vishnu sat down and looked expectantly at Aiyya. Aiyya gave a nod of understanding and said, 'Years of memories will need some time to sift through. Don't worry Thambi, something will turn up.'

It was the soothing yet confident tone of Aiyya's voice that reassured Vishnu instantaneously and he started his meal. It was a delicious one as always, not heavy but rich and tastefully prepared. For the first time in many years, Vishnu really savored the flavors and aromas the food gave away and they were appetizing, to say the least. He had his fill and had just done washing his hands when one of the men came and waited by the dining room door. Aiyya walked briskly towards him and the man bent down and said something in Aiyya's ear. Aiyya nodded in understanding, smiled at the man and extended an open palm. The man put a few sheets of paper on the palm and left without saying a word. Aiyya met Vishnu's enquiring gaze and smiled. Vishnu knew what the smile meant in an instant and walked hurriedly towards Aiyya.

'Do you recognize any of these leaflets, Thambi?' Aiyya said thrusting the bunch of papers he had just received.

Vishnu had a look at them. There were about seven of them. They were leaflets advertising various properties. Two were advertising for apartment complexes, two were advertising for resale of built vacation homes and another three were advertising for empty lots. Vishnu realized that Aiyya's hunch was spot on. Gopika was looking to invest in some sort of real-estate. He looked at Aiyya with an expression of amazement and gratefulness. Aiyya understood.

'I will send people to enquire at all places,' Aiyya said.

Vishnu stopped him. 'No, wait. We don't have to go looking everywhere. We must prioritize. Save some time and effort.'

Aiyya looked at him quizzically.

'Well, I think we can rule out the apartment complexes as they should have been a lot dearer than the money she swindled,' Vishnu declared. If Gopika really wanted to get away from me, she would choose a more secluded locale to live in, probably a bit more distant from Chennai, he thought. And in the same vein, even one of the vacation properties was ruled out as it was in quite a well-known area on the outskirts of Chennai. 'And this bungalow is also out, I think.' Vishnu then looked at the remaining three leaflets in his hand and then handed them back to Aiyya. 'To start with, please find out about these three,' he said.

Aiyya nodded and went away to organize the search. It should be quite an easy one Vishnu thought and how correct he was. It wouldn't be easy for any average joe, he knew. But his family had been in the real-estate business for three generations now. They knew how to search out ownership lines for almost any property, no matter how many shadow buyers occluded the reality. And Aiyya being the trusted lieutenant who had been in the business for almost all his life, would know exactly what key to turn and what locks to open to trace down the real owner of the properties he had indicated. Now it was just a waiting game. But he did not want any outside influence on the property and so had asked Aiyya to warn his men not to enter or even go near the property. If Vignesh was using any of these properties, Vishnu did not want Vignesh to get suspicious. He personally wanted to confront Vignesh and let the edge of surprise work its magic.

The rest of the day and almost all night were spent by Vishnu in a restless state, envisioning scenarios of what he would do when he confronted Vignesh. Would he just ask Vignesh to come clean to the police? Or would he first beat up Vignesh to a pulp for the years of torture and shame he made Vishnu endure? Maybe he would first ask Vignesh about how he managed to kill Gopika, frame Vishnu and vanish. Even before that, he would want to know why he killed Gopika in the first place. But his seething anger knew no bounds. He realized that none of those answers would change anything. Gopika was dead and he had lost almost a decade of his youth to an unfair prison term. Vignesh was anyway non-existent. 'And he will remain so!' Vishnu resolved. He had made up his mind. Vignesh had to die. He remembered the conversation they had with Mrs. Devi all those years ago. When asked if Vishnu would kill the person who had killed Gopika, Vishnu had given a very roundabout answer of first finding why the person had killed Gopika and so on. Gopika had bristled at Vishnu's apparent lack of passion. But now, when the situation was about to present itself, Vishnu had vowed to kill the person who had killed Gopika. But he shuddered at the thought, for he had never thought of killing anyone; the actual act of killing was a far scarier and distant proposition. It was a conundrum that kept his pulse rate high and his mouth tasteless and dry for almost the entire next day. Late in the evening, the same man who had given Aiyya the leaflets regarding the various properties came back to see Aiyya. Vishnu almost thought of talking to the man directly, but thought against it and let the man finish his conversation with Aiyya. The man again whispered into Aiyya's ear and walked away without so much as a glance at Vishnu. Aiyya walked to Vishnu and in soft clipped tones told Vishnu what he had eagerly been waiting to hear for more than twenty-four hours. His men had found a property that was registered in Gopika's name!

'Do nothing rash, Thambi. The property has been there for the past so many years and it will still be there tomorrow. Night is for sleeping and resting. The day is for working hard.' Aiyya had telepathically read Vishnu's eagerness to get to the property that very night, that very instant. Vishnu was about to put up an argument but looked at Aiyya's calm face. This man has brought me so close to the heart of the mystery, Vishnu thought. Surely his words of wisdom were worth listening to. 'What is one more restless night, Aiyya!' Vishnu exclaimed and started towards his bedroom when he swung around and asked, 'When was the property bought?'

Aiyya looked at Vishnu with a smile that Vishnu thought hid pity and said, 'Looks like it was bought about a couple of months before her death.'

Vishnu nodded and slowly walked to his bedroom. He then turned around and shut the door quite deliberately. He knew fully well that sleep was never entering his room that night.

The next morning, he was surprised to realize that he actually woke up, which meant he had indeed slept. He hastily took a shower and got out of his bedroom to see Aiyya holding an omelet sandwich in one hand and a cup of hot coffee in another. 'There is no escaping this man,' Vishnu thought and scarfed down the sandwich and with equal haste gulped down the coffee. It was scalding hot and he realized that he was not going to taste anything for the next few days. Didn't matter, he said to himself for he was about to taste success.

'Your jeep is waiting outside. I have given directions, so the driver will take you to the property,' Aiyya said and read the question on Vishnu's face.

'Some part of the road is unpaved and a jeep will do better than the car,' Aiyya explained. 'It is quite a distance away from the city. In fact, it is quite a distance away from the countryside too. It is in the middle of nowhere really,' Aiyya elaborated.

Instead of deepening the mystery any further, it actually made Vishnu confident that this was the very property he was looking for. But why did Gopika want to buy some inconsequential piece of land far from the city in the middle of nowhere. He looked at Aiyya a bit bewildered and Aiyya explained further, 'It seems it was one of those hill-station resort type development projects that never took off. Something to do with improper zoning and building permissions it seems. The entire project went bust years ago and I will be surprised if the jungle hasn't taken over what was left.'

Vishnu thanked Aiyya for the information and the arrangement and the breakfast until he realized that he would never be able to thank Aiyya adequately for everything that he had done for the family. With that thought in mind, he proceeded with a grateful heart, straight to the jeep. Vishnu sat in the passenger seat at the front and immediately recognized the burly driver. The man was clean-shaven and wore a tan-colored safari suit. He was somewhere in his early forties with a physique that would rival many of the young generation lead actors with their chiseled bodies. He was tall, clearly above six feet and had the air of a man confident and well-aware of his own power and limitations. Vishnu had seen him around the bungalow from time to time and had always thought he was one of the security personnel. He was surprised to note that he was just one of the many drivers used by their company. Little did he know that Aiyya had specifically asked for this particular person to accompany Vishnu on his little outing to the middle-of-nowhere. Though Aiyya did not have any clear knowledge as to why Vishnu wanted to visit this property so eagerly, he cared for Vishnu sincerely and didn't want

Vishnu to get into any kind of trouble anymore. The person accompanying Vishnu was capable of taking care of any kind of trouble that would dare come their way and his loyalty was unquestionable.

It took them almost an hour to drive right across Chennai traffic to get to the highway they had to travel on. Then another hour to find the right turn where they entered state-designated forest area and about forty-five minutes of unpaved road to get to the dilapidated development. Aiyya was very correct in his assessment. The jungle had truly reclaimed the uncared-for developmental site. Skeletons of construction warehouses and worker settlements were overrun by wild vines and bushes. Pathways were overrun by trees with trunks the size of a grown man's wrist. On some crumbling walls, survey numbers were barely visible, but mostly, there was no way of exactly finding where a particular plot of land began or ended. Vishnu saw the futility of it all. Some poor soul would have bought a plot here aiming to get away from the hustle and bustle of the metropolis and the entire development had gone bust killing the dreams of tranquility. Poor Gopika, he thought. Stole money to buy land and was killed even before she could do anything with it and finally, the land too was useless. It was as if nature had conspired to erase all existence of Gopika. 'Surely, I am not going to bump into Vignesh here,' Vishnu thought to himself as he got out of the jeep. He looked around and noticed that his driver was a much bigger man than he had given him credit for. The kind that is generally described as *a mountain of a man*, he thought to himself and felt an uncanny sense of security in the presence of the *Mountain*!

The question now was to find the exact plot of land that Gopika had bought. Unfortunately, the dense bush had obliterated any identification markers and searching for a specific piece of land was going to prove next to impossible. 'And what am I going to do even if I did find the plot?' Vishnu asked himself. Surely, finding Vignesh living here was out of the question. So what was this exercise going to uncover? Simply that Gopika had bought a piece of land by embezzling from their business accounts. That much was already clear from the property registration details Aiyya had managed to procure. Vishnu's heart sank and all that enthusiasm he was feeling about confronting Vignesh the other day had suddenly ebbed out. He was about to turn around and get back to his jeep when he felt a heavy hand on his shoulder. He jumped and turned around to see who the assailant was when he saw the expressionless face of the *Mountain* staring back at him, as if to say, 'With me around, who else can touch you?'

'Board,' the *Mountain* spoke and pointed to a rusting piece of iron sheet welded to angle-beams on either side.

Vishnu followed the direction being pointed at and saw a very familiar contraption. It was what would usually be used for as a nameplate for a street, only larger. Vishnu had seen such boards when he used to accompany his father on various construction sites. Some used to be advertising the development; some had the project and contractor details, some had survey number details and some had a sort of a rough map with plot numbers. These contraptions would be used by people ferrying construction material to the site as not all would have a blue print and not all could read maps. It would be taken off once the construction was finished and the residents moved in, but during the construction period, this board served as the handy *map*, directing visitors to the right plot. Vishnu stared at the piece of metal, wondering what this might be. In the meantime, the *Mountain* had already started clearing out the foliage and the mud that caked parts of the board. Vishnu stepped in closer and found faint lines and numbers filling up the board. There were splotches where the lines and numbers had rusted away and there were some close to being unreadable, but many were still readable, barely. He hurried to the board and started clearing away the foliage too, but the *Mountain* with his hands as big as dinner plates had already managed to clear most of it. Vishnu looked at the *map* and his heart jumped! The plot number he was looking for was staring back at him. It was hazy and rust had eaten away at the borders and some of the paint had peeled away but it was there, right in front of him. He made up his mind. Now that he was here, he was going to see what Gopika had invested in. He pointed out the number to the *Mountain* and the *Mountain* understood. He stood on his toes to look around as if to get his bearings calibrated and then walked towards the jeep. Vishnu was bewildered, but his bewilderment turned to calm understanding when he saw the *Mountain* walk back with a long machete. Without saying much, the *Mountain* walked up to what looked like a wall of dense green bush and started hacking away. The strength of his swing was such that no branch dared stand in his way and he never had to hack at a branch twice. Soon, he had carved a walkable path through the bush and called out for Vishnu to follow at a distance. Vishnu understood the warning. He didn't want to come within the arc of the *Mountain's* machete swing and be decapitated! After about thirty yards of hacking through, the *Mountain* stopped abruptly and stepped aside to give Vishnu a clear look ahead.

There was a small clearing where the bush hadn't fully taken over and looking down Vishnu realized why it was so. He could clearly see the scattered heaps of sand and old cement pits that had probably made it unwelcome for seeds to germinate. And right ahead was what looked like a crumbling, half-built house. A small piece of granite painted with the plot number, similar to the road-side milestones common all over India. Vishnu couldn't understand how that relatively small amount of money could have bought Gopika this piece of land and financed this incompletely built house. He looked quizzically at the *Mountain* and asked him the same question, half expecting the *Mountain* to just say he didn't know how; but the *Mountain* surprised him. 'Looks like it was bought as a second-hand property from someone with financial trouble,' the *Mountain* said.

Vishnu looked a bit confused and couldn't quite fathom what that meant. 'What do you mean?' he asked.

'Well, think of this, sir. Say you bought the land and started building and then you ran into some financial trouble, you would stop the construction and want to sell the whole thing off. But because it is an incomplete build, no one would want to buy it. And those who would; will be asking for a much lower price, for the incomplete build has to be demolished to build the house they want.'

Vishnu looked at the *Mountain* in awe; not of the *Mountain* but his father. 'You did know how to pick the right people,' Vishnu said looking towards the sky. The *Mountain* was not just muscle. He also possessed a decently sound analytical brain.

'That is quite a stretch of imagination,' Vishnu said.

'What does it matter, sir? It is here and that is that!' came a matter-of-fact reply. Vishnu realized that though it sounded like the reply of a thoughtless bum; it could also be interpreted as having a deep philosophical meaning. Reasons could exist but finding those reasons were not going to change the reality of what was in front of him. It was better to deal with what he had in front of him, rather than waste time arguing over why or how!

'Well, let us go in and see what waits for us inside,' Vishnu said and the *Mountain* led the way.

By the looks of it, this was going to be a quaint little guesthouse. An open plan living room and what looked like a kitchen made up the entire floor and an incompletely built staircase was supposed to house a small toilet and give access to the first-floor, but that had never materialized. Some of the walls were covered with the first coat of plaster while most of the walls were naked brick. Iron rods and bars protruded in various twisted angles all over, making it difficult to walk through, mounds of sand and hardened cement lay scattered and banyan and peepal trees, also known as Sacred Fig trees had already started establishing roots through the bricks and part of a wall had already collapsed. Vishnu started looking around and the *Mountain* also started to carefully traverse every nook and corner of this derelict ruin. A thought popped into Vishnu's mind and he gave a wry smile. It seemed that everything associated with Gopika was fated to be ruined! What a twist of fate, he wondered. Such a dream location and an absolute dream house by the looks of it, but ruined. And suddenly he thought about something else. He had found the property that Gopika owned, but how did that help him. And just then, he heard the *Mountain* call out, 'Sir, I think this is what you are looking for!'

Vishnu hurried to where the call came from. The half-built staircase obstructed his view and so Vishnu went around and saw the *Mountain* stare at a spot on the ground. The flooring wasn't yet done and the soil was exposed, slightly discolored due to constant shade. Vishnu saw nothing peculiar and stared back at the *Mountain*. 'Something has either been buried here or dug out,' he said calmly.

'What? Where? I don't see anything!' Vishnu's pulse raced.

'You see where the ground looks a bit sunken,' the *Mountain* pointed with his finger and Vishnu could barely see the outline of an almost oval pit about three feet wide and five feet long. 'That happens only when you bury something dead that has decomposed over the years or when you dig something out and fill it up with soil that is loosely packed back in. I know sir, I have seen it quite often.'

Vishnu shuddered to think why the *Mountain* would know such a thing, but at the same time was thankful he did, cause he himself would never have found this pit. It had never crossed Vishnu's mind that he would have to look for something buried. Now that he thought of it and the explanation the *Mountain* had provided, he realized how plausible it all was. He looked around and said, 'Well, I don't see anything to dig it up with, but I have to.'

The *Mountain* pulled the machete he had slung at his hips and with the broad face of the blade, began digging. Vishnu could not contain his excitement and started to claw his way into the pit. He immediately realized that the soil was not as soft as he thought it would be and bare hands were not going to get anywhere. He pulled his slightly bruised hands away sheepishly and waited for the *Mountain* to uncover something. After digging about two feet deep, the *Mountain* stopped and started digging in a way that kind of isolated an oval mound from the rest of the ground. Vishnu was again confused with this approach. He just wanted to see what was buried underneath but it looked like the *Mountain* was more interested in an archaeological excavation. 'That will take too much time! Here, let me do it,' Vishnu said and extended an arm asking the *Mountain* to hand over the machete.

'If we want to keep what has been buried here intact, this is how we have to do it. If we just dig from the top, the machete will destroy whatever had been buried. The pit wasn't dug too deep, I found its bottom, so it shouldn't take us much time, sir,' the *Mountain* said.

Vishnu marveled at the *Mountain's* intelligence. It almost seemed like he was the perfect forensic investigator and bodyguard rolled into one! But Vishnu's mind moved on and was busy thinking what would have been buried here. And if at all they would find it or whether it was buried for a time and then removed. He also wondered if whatever was buried was pertinent to solving the mystery of Gopika's murder. He half expected it to be some sort of a sewer or an incomplete column or some such innocuous structure. 'Don't get your hopes up,' he murmured to himself, all the while observing the care and efficiency with which the *Mountain* was trying to unearth, literally, what was buried.

Once the entire perimeter was dug up, the *Mountain* headed back to one end of the oval mound he had separated and started carefully scraping off the soil. After what looked like almost an hour but what were in reality just about ten long minutes, the *Mountain* stopped scraping and gingerly tried to tug at something. Then suddenly, he looked up to Vishnu, as always with an expression that gave nothing away. 'What is it?' Vishnu asked, unable to bear the suspense any longer.

'It is a shoe with a foot in it,' the *Mountain* stated calmly.

'What?!' Vishnu thought he had not heard it correctly; a foot in a shoe is what it had sounded like. Surely, that wasn't right, he thought.

'Someone has been buried here, sir. From the shoe, it looks like a man.' Again, Vishnu couldn't help but notice the calmness in the *Mountain's* demeanor. And it made the hair on the back of his neck stand up in awe and shock.

'Dig it out. See what else is buried with him,' Vishnu said, as his voice cracked with excitement.

After about a real hour of careful scraping, the complete horror lay bare for both of them to see. It was a human skeleton, decomposed right to the bone. Just the leather shoes, belt and blackened bones were all that remained of what once would have been a man almost the same size as Vishnu. He was curled up in a loosely fetal position. Vishnu's head was spinning. He didn't understand what to make out of this find. On a property secretly purchased by Gopika, they had found a decomposed skeleton of an as yet unidentified man! 'I wonder who he is and how long this man has been dead!' Vishnu queried himself loudly enough for the *Mountain* to hear.

'I cannot tell you who he is, but definitely murdered. As for how long, it definitely has been some time. Maybe years,' came the dispassionate reply.

The answer created more questions in Vishnu's mind and the *Mountain* was proving to be a treasure-trove of macabre knowledge. Maybe I should have partnered with him instead of Gopika, Vishnu imagined and the thought amused him quite a bit. 'The *Reed* and the *Mountain* Detective Agency' he thought to himself and chuckled. The *Mountain* looked at him but as always without any expression or emotion betraying his thoughts and then looked back at the skeleton. 'How can you conclude that?' Vishnu asked.

'That he was murdered is straightforward, sir. He was carelessly bundled and buried in a shallow grave in a crumbling house in the middle of nowhere. Why else would he be disposed like this, unless he was murdered.' The *Mountain's* reasoning made perfect sense. Vishnu had guessed as much. It was the time the poor sod was buried for that was more confusing. But the *Mountain* continued. 'For people he knows, he has just vanished without trace and will remain so for all time. Poor bugger.' And just then, a wild thought crossed Vishnu's mind. Did Gopika actually murder this guy?! But the *Mountain* wasn't done talking yet. 'The soil is damp but not really soggy and the ground has been shaded from the elements and yet all that remains of the poor soul are a set of bones, his belt and shoes. So, it looks like this body has been buried here for a number of years.' Practice beats theory, Vishnu thought with a smile on his face. He might have the college degree in Forensic Science, but it was the *Mountain* who had seen it; recognized it.

Vishnu carefully looked at the pile of bones lying in front of him. A man seemed to be of a similar height as him, he could judge that from the femur bone of the skeleton, had been murdered and buried in this shallow grave a number of years ago. How was this person murdered? Vishnu saw no immediate way of answering this. His heart raced. Vignesh!? But then, with this rate of decomposition, how was he going to prove it? He just had to be certain for himself and started to carefully scan every inch of the skeleton when suddenly, he noticed something odd. There seemed to be a bulbous piece of mud clinging to the right hand ring finger. Vishnu pointed to that and said, 'Can you see what that is?'

The *Mountain* delicately picked up the skeletal hand and picked at the finger and lo! The finger simply broke off! The *Mountain* looked at Vishnu sheepishly, picked up the skeletal finger and rubbed off the mud to reveal a ring. The *Mountain* rubbed off the dirt that clung to it and handed it over to Vishnu and Vishnu almost fainted! It was the *Navaratna Ring* he had seen on Vignesh's finger all those years ago. 'Vignesh!' Vishnu cried out loud.

'Yes sir!' came the reply; the *Mountain* was looking at Vishnu expectantly.

Vishnu's eyes were still open wide with excitement and his heart was thumping ever so fast that he had totally missed the connotation and said, 'It is Vignesh!'

'Really, sir? I am Vignesh too!' the *Mountain* replied.

Vishnu was stunned! 'What?!' he asked again, not quite believing what games fate was playing with him.

'My name is Vignesh, sir. You said this skeleton is also Vignesh?' the *Mountain* said pointing to the skeleton.

'Yes, at least that was the name he told me when he met me all those years ago! He is real! He exists!' Vishnu said elated. He felt lighter, as if a ton of weight has suddenly been lifted off his shoulders. He could in fact feel that his shoulders no longer stooped.

'I DID NOT KILL GOPIKA!' Vishnu shouted.

He had not gone crazy either. Vignesh was not a figment of his imagination after all! He had existed and he had called him that night and he had met him that night and . . ., Vishnu's train of thought came to an abrupt halt. And what? What happened then, he wondered. Gopika was murdered and now he had also uncovered that Vignesh too had been murdered; and buried in a property Gopika had secretly purchased. That was a lot to take in, but he had finally uncovered something of use. He had believed all these years that if he could prove Vignesh's existence, he can absolve himself of the crime and today, after eight years, he could!

'What do we do with this, sir?' the question came in the same calm, unwavering tone. It seemed that more than *Vignesh*, The *Mountain* was an apt name for this behemoth Aiyya had sent with Vishnu. The *Mountain* was simply immovable. Nothing seemed to bother him. He was asking Vishnu what to do with the skeleton in the same calm tone someone would ask where to dispose of a banana peel.

'You know, I don't think I will call you Vignesh. I think *Malai* sounds apt for you, the Mountain!' Vishnu said. 'I hope you are not offended by that. I honestly wouldn't dare to offend you,' Vishnu said with a twinkle in his eye and a sly smile.

'No, sir. Malai is fine. So, what do you want to do with this?' The *Mountain* hadn't wavered. A quick acknowledgement and back to business at hand.

'I guess we can just bury it all up the way it was. I will ask Aiyya to pull some strings and buy this entire property if still possible. Else, we will come back and get rid of it for good. What say?' Vishnu asked.

'As you see fit, sir,' Malai replied. 'If this is of no use, I suggest we destroy it right away. Now that we have dug it up, there is no point of this reaching the wrong hands.'

It made perfect sense, Vishnu thought. If the police find the skeleton and trace the property back to Gopika, they would once again pin this murder also on him. And he will have no proof to the contrary. The best course of action was to get rid of this skeleton once and for all. But something didn't feel right. His intuition still said that his original plan to buy the property was a better one. He asked Malai to get the scene reorganized exactly as they had found it and went out to call Aiyya. He told Aiyya that he had found the property and instructed him to buy and fence off the entire property as soon as possible using one of their shadow companies. No one was to trespass into the property unless explicitly permitted by Vishnu himself. Aiyya assured Vishnu that all that would get done and asked him to be home soon. Vishnu looked at the watch and was astonished to see that it was well past noon and for the first time, he felt hungry, really hungry in a long time. He started to walk back to where Malai was working. 'Gopika was murdered by someone and I had always thought Vignesh did it,' Vishnu thought out loud. 'But now I found that even Vignesh was murdered, probably at the same time or thereabouts. But who did this? And why?' And then he remembered Aiyya's words and the complete puzzle was in front of him for the first time ever, 'And who framed me for the crime?'

A flurry of thoughts started reorganizing themselves in Vishnu's brain. Finding Vignesh's body here proved two things. First, he had killed neither Gopika nor Vignesh, for if he had, why would he bury Vignesh's body here and keep Gopika's in their Romantic Corner's storage freezer. Vishnu could have easily buried both the bodies in this isolated property and no one would have ever found any bodies, meaning no one could ever prosecute him for any crime. It also told him that he had no knowledge of this property till Aiyya found it for him; which evidently Gopika had bought by siphoning money from their detective agency's account. Secondly, he realized that there was someone out there who wanted Gopika dead and had probably used Vignesh to get the job done and later, disposed of him as well. But the crux of the matter was that the whole crime was planned and committed such that Vishnu was convicted of Gopika's murder. And that was the new thread he now had to pull. Vishnu had to find someone from his past who would want to ruin his life. Gopika could basically have been collateral damage and so was Vignesh. Had this something to do with his Dad's business, he wondered. Such sagas of murder and vengeance were quite common among the old landlords and business rivals. But Vishnu quickly set that thought aside. If that was the case, surely his Dad, with Aiyya by his side, would have unmasked and duly punished the culprit. Yet, he made it a point to ask Aiyya about this once he got home.

When Vishnu walked up to the site of the grave, he was astonished to see that Malai was just applying finishing touches to his job, scattering dried leaves and twigs haphazardly. Then he went out of the house and came back with a leafy branch and swept off all their footprints as they exited the ruin. It was all very professional. 'If I ever want to murder someone, I am definitely going to take you along, Malai,' he said.

'Whom do you want to blame the murder on, sir?!' Malai retorted and that set off a chain reaction in Vishnu's mind. As he walked towards the jeep a deep sense of purpose was starting to take root. He knew that what he had to do next. As he sat in the passenger seat, he felt something poking from the front pocket of his pants. He slid his hand to see what this offending article was and when he pulled out his hand it contained the skeletal finger and the *Navaratna Ring*!

CHAPTER TWELVE

Malai had illuminated a path that Vishnu had never seen before. He knew exactly what he had to do. With a rejuvenated sense of purpose, he stepped out of the Jeep as it stopped smoothly at the porch and was happy to see Aiyya standing at the door. He looked back at Malai and thanked him for the help. Malai, for the first time, seemed flustered and acknowledged with a deep bow of his head. 'What Thambi? Looks like you have found what you were looking for,' Aiyya said.

'Looks like it, Aiyya. By the way, I think Malai is a helpful character. I will want to keep him around and from now on, he will be my companion on all my trips,' Vishnu said.

'Malai? . . . Oh! I get it,' Aiyya said with full comprehension. 'Good choice Thambi. He is perfect to take my place and carry on helping you and the business.'

Vishnu was shocked! 'I never meant replacing you, Aiyya. Don't misund. . .' But Aiyya raised a hand to silence Vishnu.

'No Thambi. He was personally groomed by me from a very young age for exactly this purpose. I am old now and seldom get out of the house. And one day, I too shall be dust. I will like to leave you in capable hands. Malai,' Aiyya chuckled, 'has proved worthy to take my place, once I retire. And that doesn't look like it is happening any time soon!' Aiyya had a twinkle in his eye and a naughty smile on his lips.

Vishnu was appeased. 'Thanks Aiyya. I am famished. Lunch ready?' he asked and he already knew that it was. The aroma of freshly made Sambar was inescapable. He headed immediately towards the dining room and then suddenly stopped to speak to

Aiyya. 'Should I invite Malai to have lunch with me?' he asked.

Aiyya smiled. 'All in good time, Thambi. But I will let him know that you were very happy with his services. Need to feed the lion slowly, else the lion gets lazy and will not roar!'

'What Lion?' Vishnu asked.

'The lion of ego!' Aiyya said and saw the look on Vishnu's face. 'Something else you wanted to ask me, Thambi?' Aiyya queried.

Vishnu started, 'I was wondering if this had anything to do with our family business. I mean my . . .,' and stopped when Aiyya raised his hand indicating he had understood the context.

'Your Appa spent every minute of every day for the short time he was alive after you were wrongly convicted by the Court, trying to answer that question. That is what ultimately killed him. I saw him wither away and I hope I helped delay his death by shouldering some of his burden. The answer is NO! Your father was a scrupulous and moral businessman, as was your grandfather. They cheated the system at times, but they never cheated a human being of his due. That is what makes the name of your business command the trust and respect that it does today. He didn't even entertain the thought of buying a patsy to take the fall in your place. Your father did not want an innocent human being to be unfairly punished and he firmly believed in your innocence till the day he breathed his last.' Aiyya's voice softened while he spoke of his Master and the love and loyalty was clear for Vishnu to see. Aiyya looked at Vishnu and put an arm on his shoulder and said, 'Whatever happened must have happened as a consequence of what you were involved with. It has nothing to do with the business or anyone else from your family.'

Aiyya led Vishnu to his seat at the table. Vishnu ate to his heart's content. He asked Aiyya for some fresh piping hot coffee to be brought up to the storeroom and marched on to his room for a quick bath and a change of clothing. He felt refreshed as he headed into the storeroom. In his hand, he had a piece of paper and his Mont Blanc fountain pen. The room welcomed him with the refreshing aroma of freshly brewed filter coffee. Aiyya never missed anything. Vishnu looked around and saw the thermos and the coffee mug placed precariously over a stack of files. He picked them up and looked around the room as he poured the elixir into the mug. He headed out towards the balcony. It was just past five in the evening and perhaps due to the lush greenery surrounding his bungalow, it was relatively cool. He placed his mug on the coffee table on the balcony and slid around a chair made of Malacca cane. And then, he began writing.

When he finished, he looked intently at the document trying to recall if he had missed out on any pertinent details. The document looked something like this:

Gopika was killed? By Vignesh?

Vignesh was killed? By whom?

I was framed and convicted of Gopika's murder. So someone who had a grudge against the both of us did this. That means something from our past cases came back to haunt us. How does Vignesh feature into all this? Did someone use Vignesh to get to me and Gopika and then kill him? And how did they convince Gopika of *hiring* Vignesh? Why did Gopika tell the hostel watchman that she was starting a new life that night? Why did she buy that godforsaken piece of land by stealing money from our agency?

Cases that needed looking into:

Case	Resolution
Arya – Sita – Mr. Narayanan	Arya dead – accident. Sita? Mr. Narayanan?
Sujay – Kamal – Mr. Kamat	Both married to different partners. Both living happily. Gopika doctored evidence but seems like both Sujay and Kamal are oblivious to the fact. **Resolved**
Sanjana – John – Shalini – Mrs. Devi	John married to Shalini! Sanjana? Mrs. Devi?
Mrs. Devi – Murder? – Gopika – Vignesh???	????

And he had a clear lead. It had all started with Mrs. Devi asking them if they could get her business rivals out of competition. But she breached that topic only when they had satisfactorily resolved the background search regarding Mrs. Devi's daughter Sanjana and her boyfriend John. And in an astonishing development, he had also discovered that John had married Shalini, the girl he was fooling around with when he was having an love-affair with Sanjana.

Also, there were Sita and Mr. Narayanan. What had transpired after Arya's death? Did Sita or Mr. Narayanan blame him and Gopika for Arya's death by some warped connectivity? He simply had to find out how Sita and Mr. Narayanan were doing now.

Vishnu read through what he had written again and again. He had found Vignesh, though not the way he had expected. He had found Vignesh dead, murdered! And rather than solve everything, it had almost complicated everything. But it had done one good thing. It gave Vishnu confidence that he had not murdered Gopika. And once that realization had sunk in, it gave him the sense of relief that he hadn't experienced for the past eight years. With that ungainly burden of confused guilt gone, he was more focused on solving the mystery of who had come up with this diabolical scheme of ruining three lives in one fell swoop and why. Vishnu decided that he will have to quicken the pace and the scope of his investigations if he wanted to keep his recently lost insanity at bay. He decided that he was going to pursue Mrs. Devi and Sanjana. He had tried this earlier the easy way and found it hard. So, he decided that he was going to reverse the process. He was going to find Sanjana through John and then find Mrs. Devi through Sanjana. At the same time he was going to ask Malai to locate Sita and Mr. Narayanan. Once their whereabouts were known, he would personally look into the finer nuances of the investigation and try to find out how they were doing. With that thought, he called out for Malai to be sent in.

Within a few sentences, Vishnu gave Malai the details he had of Arya, Sita and Mr. Narayanan. Vishnu had already told Malai to concentrate on Sita and Mr. Narayanan as Arya was dead. Malai did not speak a single word and when Vishnu was done talking, he just nodded and walked out. A man of few words, Vishnu recalled. With one loose end being taken care of, Vishnu concentrated on the other loose end – Sanjana and Mrs. Devi. Vishnu vividly remembered John's office building and the vivacious receptionist. He didn't really look forward to chatting up the receptionist, but it looked like he absolutely had to, to get to John. He wondered how he was going to track down Sanjana and Mrs. Devi via John. Mrs. Devi, he reminisced, the repeat client. She had come back with a weird request. After successfully concluding a background search on her daughter's boyfriend, she wanted us to help her get rid of her business rivals. And that had sowed the seeds of a rift between him and Gopika. 'How could we have done it at all?' Vishnu thought. 'All Mrs. Devi wanted was to find some dirt on each of the business rivals that she could use for blackmailing the two out of competition.' Vishnu answered himself. It was just another background search, only this time; it would have been for a different reason. He had flippantly suggested that one business rival could be killed and the murder be blamed on the other, almost something that had happened to himself. He smiled forlornly as he slowly fathomed the irony of it all. Someone had murdered Gopika and framed him for the murder!

Had Mrs. Devi played a part in all this? She definitely had the resources. She was rich, she claimed then. 'But why would she? She was all happy with the background search we had conducted,' he said to himself. 'John is not married to Sanjana and that is what Mrs. Devi had clearly indicated as her preference,' Vishnu was trying to recall the incidence. 'Did Sanjana find it all out and react badly to that?' he wondered. 'But then why were John and Shalini living a happy married life?' he argued. 'If Sanjana had a grudge, she would have been mad at John the most, then her own mother and truly speaking, she had no reason to hold a grudge against Gopika or myself. We didn't forge anything. From the pictures I took, it seemed like John might have been two-timing Sanjana and having an affair with Shalini! Well, now that John and Shalini are married, it looks like my suspicion was quite justified.' Vishnu's excitement had ebbed quite as suddenly as it had peaked. Sanjana looked like the perfect suspect for just a minute but then she didn't look as promising at all. He wondered what Sanjana looked like. Mrs. Devi had come in with John's photo and details and they just had to dig into his activities. Vishnu had taken pictures of John with Shalini, but he had never seen John spend any time with Sanjana, so the opportunity to see Sanjana had never presented itself. But there was something not quite right with it all, Vishnu felt. 'I hope so,' he said to himself. He realized that with Vignesh dead, the only two viable leads were Sita and Mrs. Devi. With Sita's follow-up safely delegated to Malai and his enormous hands, he was now left only with Sanjana and Mrs. Devi, he reminded himself.

The next day, Vishnu was back in his casual attire, heading into John's office. The high quality linen, the hand-stitched crocodile-skin shoes and the Patek Phillipe watch all oozed understated elegance. For a casual observer, he was well-dressed but to a discerning viewer, he was a class above everyone else. The receptionist, in spite of her seemingly low stature in the company's hierarchy, was a discerning viewer. What better way to pass all that time than to look at online catalogues for the latest, trendiest and classiest fashion accessories. Though not many around would notice anything particularly impressive in Vishnu, the receptionist noticed every minute detail of his expensive apparel. Her face had already lit up with the most enticing of smiles. 'So, you did finally come to take me out for coffee!' she said coyly as Vishnu approached her workbench.

'Well, . . .' Vishnu was at a loss for words and was trying to come up with a quick way out.

'Just kidding, sir. Did you meet up with your friend finally? Or are you meeting him here?' the receptionist asked.

Vishnu had to think on the fly and started, 'Actually, I was caught up in something else and couldn't quite get to him that day. And I just couldn't come in the very next day, so I didn't have the address to visit him at his home either.' He looked at the receptionist to check whether she believed him so far. Little did he know that she was so enamored with him that he could have said he had been to Mars in the meanwhile and she wouldn't have batted an eyelid! 'Could you get me his address please?' he pushed his advantage further.

'Our company has strict policy against giving confidential employee information to strangers. I am also new to this job and really need it. You know with all the market downturn and the competition, it is really difficult to find a job, no matter how boring this one might be, at least . . .' and on she would have continued, had Vishnu not interrupted her.

'Alright then,' he said dejectedly and was about to turn around when the receptionist called out in a slightly louder voice, 'But if you take me out for a coffee, we wouldn't be strangers, would we? We would be friends and I could then give Mr. D'Souza's details to a friend, can't I?!'

Vishnu turned around stunned! Life had surely passed him by! He would never have envisioned such a flirtatious girl in Chennai a decade earlier. But, what the receptionist said made complete sense, he thought amusedly. And it was just a coffee, he thought. He looked up to the young woman, probably in her mid-twenties if at all that and said, 'Well, friends call each other by their first names! I am Vishnu.'

'My name is Nisha. As you can tell, I am not from Chennai or even Tamilnadu for that matter,' she replied.

'So, let us get some coffee,' Vishnu said. He wanted this to be over with as soon as possible, having no interest whatsoever in this gorgeous young lass who was literally throwing herself at him.

'Ahem! Sorry, I am working now. And there aren't any good coffee shops around here. All the places will be full of the stiff-necked professionals around here. Pick me up at half past five in the evening and I will take you to a proper coffee place,' Nisha said. He had left the office with a weird feeling as Nisha's gaze followed him right up to the very end when he got into his car.

Vishnu had no other go but to agree with Nisha. He thought he would take a nap in the quiet air-conditioned backseat of his car and then come pick this girl up for coffee, but then thought against it. Instead, he asked the driver to head back home where he could collect his thoughts about approaching John. He still hadn't figured it out. If Nisha did give him John's address, of what use would that be? How was he going to ask John about Sanjana and Mrs. Devi? That needed some thinking and the best place to think was his balcony with a mug of piping hot filter coffee.

His decision had been wise, but it hadn't made any difference. After close to three hours of intense deliberation, the conundrum persisted. Once Nisha gave him John's address, he was still unsure how he was going to approach John. He had thought of various scenarios; an ex-classmate of Sanjana's emerged as the most plausible one. But even that wasn't a very viable option. Why would John, a married man want to accept knowing Sanjana, especially if he had cheated on her. For that meant John had cheated on his current wife Shalini as well. With all that confusion, Vishnu downed his fourth mug of strong coffee and was wondering if coffee really was what he wanted again with Nisha. But then, he realized that coffee was just an innocent excuse, and all Nisha wanted was to get to know him better. Would the girl really like to know a convicted murderer, he thought. That was the ace up his sleeve really. If Nisha got too clingy, he would just tell her the truth and that was it. He also wondered if Nisha was just another gold-digger, like Gopika was and the thought made his bile rise up. He sincerely hoped not. 'I am not sure whether Nisha could tell I am rich,' he said out loud. 'And if she does, it is worth knowing her,' he concluded. Someone with that keen an eye and those exquisite tastes must definitely be worth knowing, he realized. He also realized something else. It had been two weeks since he had met Dr Sujata and their chat sessions were already a habit for Vishnu. But this time, that habit was about to be broken. He still had two weeks to go without meeting Dr Sujata. He thought it would be a great idea to call her up and update her on all that he had uncovered. After all, a lot had come to light in these past few days. The finding of Vignesh's skeleton buried in an abandoned property secretly bought by Gopika had all but absolved Vishnu of any crime. It was something Vishnu wanted to share with Dr Sujata, for she seemed to have questioned his innocence the last time they had spoken. Vishnu dialed Dr Sujata's number and waited for an answer. After several rings, the phone automatically switched to a voicemail and Vishnu hung up dejectedly. 'I could get to the bottom of this whole mess in the next few days,' he thought to himself. 'And then, I can go to Dr Sujata and let her know everything.'

Vishnu headed back to his car and as always, Aiyya was there to see him off. Vishnu asked the driver to take him to the same office building they had been to a few hours ago. The driver nodded and the car headed out. On route, Vishnu also let the driver know that once they picked up the girl from their first destination, Vishnu and the girl would sit in the backseat and the girl would give further instructions. Vishnu apologized profusely to the driver for his rudeness and the driver assured him that Vishnu's usual practice of sitting in the front with the driver was a practice unheard of in the rich circles of India. The rest of the drive was quiet. Vishnu liked that in the driver. He had driven him to so many destinations on a number of occasions, but he never had any small talk, never had any comment on anything happening around him, was very steady and safe with the car and never seemed to be in a hurry; the silent but efficient type. His father and then Aiyya had surrounded themselves with this particular type of people; who spoke only when it mattered and for all other time were happy in doing their jobs to perfection.

Vishnu alighted from the car and opened the door to the entrance lounge. Directly in front of him, he could see the reception desk and Nisha seemingly tidying up her table for the day. She looked up and beamed in appreciation. 'You are here and on time,' she said. 'What a gentleman!'

Vishnu muttered something that was as meaningless as it was inaudible and Nisha rightly recognized it as a man blushing. She picked up her dainty little sack that was currently the in-fashion purse and followed Vishnu to the car. She promptly stepped close to the front passenger seat and was about to open it when Vishnu said, 'Please, we can sit at the back. That way, we will have more time to talk and I will not be distracted by the driving,' and he opened one of the back doors.

'Oh . . . ok,' Nisha stuttered. Vishnu realized that having a driver in the car was not what she had expected. 'Impossible expectations,' Vishnu thought. This girl expected the first formal meeting to be a romantic drive and dinner date!

Nisha slid into the backseat and Vishnu followed suit from the other side. It was immediately clear that she had never been in a car of this quality. The plush calf-leather and teak interior had clearly impressed her. 'Where to?' Vishnu asked.

Nisha mentioned a coffee house which was really a café at one of the top five star hotels in Chennai. Vishnu had never been there, but his driver knew exactly where it was. Vishnu then broached the subject, 'So, about John.'

Nisha looked a bit annoyed as well as a bit crestfallen and said, 'Obviously straight to the point. But as I said, let us have coffee first. Right now, you could just be kidnapping me! I need to be friends with you first, before I give away any confidential information.'

Vishnu realized his mistake. In his eagerness to get information, he had forgotten basic etiquette. 'My apologies, Nisha,' he said. 'So tell me, what is so special about this coffee shop?'

Nisha was visibly taken aback and Vishnu noticed it. 'What did I do wrong this time?' he asked.

'Nothing,' she said. 'You just surprised me, that's all. Generally, someone would start with a generic question like, tell me about yourself or some such thing.'

'Oh, right. But you haven't answered my question,' Vishnu said with a smile. 'Why do you want to go to this coffee place?'

'To be honest, I have never been there!' Nisha confessed. 'I just overheard some top guy from our company say that this place served the world's most expensive coffee and I wanted to taste it. I will pay for my own coffee, mind you,' she said adamantly.

'Oh, you mean Kopi Luwak! I have tried it once,' Vishnu lied. He was something of a coffee connoisseur and his own house stocked probably as much Kopi Luwak as the hotel! 'You do know how it is made though, right?' Vishnu asked with a sly smile.

'Yes, I did google it,' Nisha admitted.

'And why did you pick me to go to this café? You have the money to pay for your own cup, so you could have visited it on your own at any time?' Vishnu queried.

'True,' she said. 'But I thought you are the right person to have this experience with,' she said it with all the honesty of a young child and then continued, 'So what is your story? Are you one of those Millennium Millionaires?'

'I don't understand,' said Vishnu flatly.

'This car, your pure linen clothing, the Mont Blanc, that Patek Phillipe,' she said. 'Where did all that money come from?'

'Oh, you noticed! You are probably the first one to do so,' Vishnu said and at the same time was quite impressed with this young girl's keen eye for class as well as with how well-informed she was with all things manly. 'I was born with a silver spoon in my mouth, or rather a gold spoon really,' he spoke the truth unabashedly.

'And you don't really know Mr. D'Souza, do you?' Nisha had let the cat out of the bag.

'Not personally, no.' Vishnu admitted, realizing that there was no fooling this very perceptive young lady. 'But I need to get some information from him and so I need to find the right place where I can ask him what I want to.'

'This isn't about any company secrets, right?' Nisha asked quite sternly.

'No, not at all,' Vishnu replied. 'It is more of a personal nature.' He was half expecting follow-up questions but was surprised at Nisha's next question.

'So where is your bachelor pad?' she asked. And just then, they had pulled into the porch of the hotel. As is customary at such establishments, two immaculately dressed attendants opened the car doors for both Vishnu and Nisha to get out. Vishnu asked Nisha to go ahead to the table while he gave some instructions to the driver. He then discretely called up Aiyya who confirmed what Vishnu was already suspecting. His own company had sourced the land for this lavish hotel and as a token of good-will, the hotel owners had also gifted a prestigious VIP Card to be used by anyone nominated by Vishnu's company. Aiyya gave Vishnu the card number. Vishnu went through the usual metal detector and welcome drink routine and headed straight for the Reception Desk. An attendant saw this and let Vishnu know that Nisha had been seated at one of the café's most sought-after table, overlooking the posh manicured gardens and the fountain. Vishnu had a quick exchange of words and gave the VIP card number to the attendant. The attendant quickly excused himself and went straight to a bossy looking chap in an ill-fitting but tailor-made suit and whispered in his ear pointing at Vishnu. The chap was the floor's shift-manager and he immediately spoke a few words into his hand-held walkie-talkie, waited for the response from the other end, nodded when it came about and then hurried over to Vishnu. 'Right this way, sir. It is a pleasure to be of your service,' he said in the most welcoming of tones as he led Vishnu to the table where Nisha was seated. 'Please peruse through the menu, sir. As always, whatever you want is on the house, of course!' And with that he walked away to give them privacy.

Nisha looked at Vishnu aghast! 'What did you do? Buy the hotel?!' she asked with shock clearly audible in her voice.

'No, nothing of that sort,' he said 'My company will take care of the bill. Let us order that coffee. Do you want any cakes or biscuits with that?'

'No, just the coffee will do, thank you,' came Nisha's polite reply.

Vishnu called the server and ordered two Kopi Luwak, and then he looked around the place taking in all that rich opulence the entire café and lobby exuded. 'It seems that you have never been here,' Nisha said.

'Would it surprise you if I said I have never been inside a five star hotel ever?!' Vishnu asked and the reaction was exactly as he had expected.

'What? Never!' Nisha exclaimed. 'I don't believe it. But spin whatever story you want to. I will not question it.'

'So, do you live alone?' Vishnu asked.

'Alone as in away from my family, yes,' Nisha explained, 'But I share an apartment with two other girls.'

'Right. And have you been doing this for long?' Vishnu asked.

'Not really,' Nisha said. 'I told you, I am quite new to this job and I have only recently started living on my own too.'

'How about you?' she asked. 'You haven't answered my question yet. Where is your bachelor pad?'

'It isn't one really,' Vishnu spoke the truth. He had never thought of it as a bachelor pad. And with Aiyya and the numerous maids and servants and business employees constantly around, Vishnu never thought he lived alone. Yet, he realized, he never had to see anyone if he didn't want to. That was some ingenuity on his father's part who had designed the estate and on Aiyya's part, who ran it that way. 'I live on a small estate just outside the city. I have some good people there who help out with the upkeep and smooth functioning.'

Just then, two attendants came up to the table, each carrying an ornate silver-plated serving tray that shone as new. One attendant set down a set of two fine bone china cups and saucers, a coffee-pot, a milk kettle and a sugar bowl all decorated with the finest gold filigree. The other attendant set down a matching dish full of neatly arranged white biscuits that looked oddly like Scottish shortbread and a second one with a neatly arranged set of some sort of grilled sandwiches. Just as Vishnu was about to voice his objection, the shift-manager hurried to the table and said, 'Our warm, fresh-off-the-oven Shrewsbury biscuits and grilled chutney and cheese sandwiches are extremely famous, sir. Compliments of the Hotel.'

Vishnu looked quite content. Come to think of it, he was feeling a bit hungry anyways. 'Please let us know once you are finished and I will get you some Black Velvet cake as well. I am sure the lady will love it,' the shift-manager said before he ushered himself and the two attendants off the table.

Vishnu was famished. Before even pouring the coffee, he grabbed a sandwich and took a bite. It was exquisite. The spicy chutney perfectly complemented the tartness of the cheese and the mint cooled it all down nicely. Nisha first looked as if she was in a trance. Then she saw Vishnu moving for the sandwich and came out of it. She then looked at the coffee set and the food spread on the table and then at Vishnu. Probably, the attendant saw her predicament and came up to the table. 'Shall I serve, madam?' he asked politely and Nisha nodded. Vishnu realized his mistake, but it was too late already, so he continued munching on his sandwich. The attendant poured the hot, thick decoction of Kopi Luwak and then added a dash of milk. Finally, he put in a rough-cut cube of brown sugar. He then carefully picked up a sandwich in a fork and spoon, something typically seen only in India, and placed it on a small side plate next to Nisha's coffee cup. With that, he retired back to a distance, just beyond the eardrop. Vishnu looked at Nisha sheepishly and said, 'Sorry, I was starving!'

'Well, it really does seem like you have never been to a five star hotel before!' Nisha said with a peal of laughter.

'I told you so. I wasn't lying,' Vishnu reaffirmed.

'So, here is Mr. D'Souza's address, at least what is recorded on file,' Nisha said as she passed Vishnu a neatly folded piece of paper.

'T-thank you,' Vishnu stammered not knowing what he was going to do with it.

'You know, Mr. D'Souza comes into the office at ten past nine exactly, like clockwork. And from twelve thirty right up to one thirty, he sits at the same table he has reserved at a restaurant close to our office having lunch and sipping his coffee,' Nisha said.

Vishnu took it all in, but he still had no idea of what Nisha was hinting at. 'So John comes in at a particular time and he sits at a table at a restaurant, so what?' Vishnu wondered. That wasn't helping him and his face clearly elaborated that.

'Well, if you want, we could have lunch together at that restaurant so that Mr. D'Souza can see you with me,' Nisha added as she sipped her coffee contently.

Vishnu understood, 'But of course! I will be happy to take you to lunch,' he said.

'This is really good coffee! And the biscuits are nothing like I have ever tasted before!' Nisha exclaimed.

'Glad you like it. But don't scarf them all down just yet,' Vishnu kidded. 'You still have a luxuriously decadent piece of cake coming your way!'

'Oh that's right, isn't it!' Nisha said and put back the fourth biscuit she had just picked up.

And they chatted. There was enough coffee to last almost three refills each and they finished it all. Slowly but surely, the biscuits vanished, as did the sandwiches and unbeknownst to them, so did the hours of the day. When finally, the attendant came in to clear the plates and set up the scrumptious cake slices in front of them, Vishnu glanced at his watch and was suddenly shocked to see that they had been sipping coffee and chatting for the better part of three hours. 'It is past dinner time!' he exclaimed. 'Do you want to spoil your appetite with cake or do we skip this and head out for a proper meal?'

'More food after all this?!' Nisha asked mockingly. 'No way! Plus, it would be a sin to return this delicious looking cake. I would rather have the cake and skip dinner.'

'Alright then. Once you are done, I can drop you home,' Vishnu offered.

Nisha looked at him quite quizzically and asked, 'What do you do really? You are obviously rich and well connected, but you seem to have all the time in the world and your phone hasn't rung once in all this time!'

'So?' Vishnu asked, not understanding where this was going.

'Well, I don't know of any businessman who can be kept away

from his phone for longer than a few minutes!' Nisha said matter-of-factly.

'I come from old money,' Vishnu said 'Real estate, to be specific. It is a slow moving business. So, phones are not that necessary.'

With that, Vishnu and Nisha were back in some more pointless conversation about cakes and the weather and suchlike. Once they were both done, they stood up. The shift-manager hurried to their table and thanked Vishnu repeatedly and also apologized profusely for any inconvenience or oversight he or his staff would have caused Vishnu and his lovely companion. Vishnu assured them all that the service was perfect and that there was nothing to complain about. He didn't have to pay for the coffee, the sandwiches, the biscuits or the cake, but he had left a generous tip on the table. No sooner had they stepped out did they see Vishnu's car already parked and the doors open. They were politely ushered in and once the car doors were shut the driver asked, 'Where to, sir?'

Vishnu looked at Nisha and she immediately gave the driver the name of a decently famous shopping mall. Vishnu realized that Nisha was not going to lead him directly to her place of living. He didn't press the point either. After about three quarters of an hour, the car stopped in front of the mall where Nisha thanked the driver for the drop off and also thanked Vishnu for the wonderful evening. The car sped away without a pause. Nisha waited for the car to drive away out of sight, smiled to herself and started walking. Vishnu came home to see Aiyya waiting in the living room.

A quick call to the hotel reception had informed Aiyya that Vishnu had been adequately fed and watered. A glass of cold coffee was waiting on the dining table that Vishnu gratefully picked up and headed to his room. He had quite a few scenarios to run through his head. Nisha had given him an opening and now he had to follow it through. He wondered how Malai was getting along with his search for Sita and Mr. Narayanan. He also recalled fondly that the three odd hours spent with Nisha was the longest period of time he had spent happily in someone else's company in the past few years. It gave him a sense of calm and he went to sleep, content.

CHAPTER THIRTEEN

Vishnu woke up the next day and headed down for his breakfast. He thought something was different today and basically associated it with the true happiness he felt. He looked at the breakfast table and instead of seeing Aiyya there, waiting to direct the servers, he saw a plate covered carefully and a glass of juice with a lid placed on top. As he slid the chair to sit, one of the men Vishnu recognized as a regular kitchen help in the household hurried out and blurted, 'You are here Anna. Will you be having breakfast this late? I will get your coffee first.' With that, he hurried back into the kitchen as fast as he had appeared. Vishnu was puzzled. 'What did the man mean by *this late?*' he thought and looked up to the clock on the wall. He was stunned! He had basically slept for almost eleven hours! And it wasn't out of tiredness but rather out of bliss. He uncovered the plate to see it contained nothing! But just as he was about to call for some food, the same man came running with a cup of piping hot coffee and said, 'Idli coming right away, Anna.' A good breakfast assured a good start for the day Vishnu realized and ate his Idli, Sambar, Chutney and bowl of fruit and yoghurt. He washed it all down with a good cup of coffee and headed up for his daily ablutions. Though all this sounded quite elaborate, it didn't take him too long to be out; dressed expensively but casually as he always was. He had missed catching John during his morning entry into the office, but he definitely had to make it for the lunch appointment.

When he came out fully dressed, Aiyya was there to see him off and his driver was waiting by the car for instructions. Vishnu sat in his usual front seat and after greeting the driver asked him to drive to Nisha's office. Just as they had exited the property, Vishnu realized that he hadn't heard anything from Malai. He called Malai but all he could reach was his voicemail. Vishnu left a short message on his voicemail to call back and focused on the task ahead. He already had a plan in mind and he was going to need a few lunches with Nisha to get it to work. And he had to make sure that Nisha introduces him to John and that John sees them together for a few times before he could approach John on his own. As if on cue, Vishnu's driver stopped the car in front of Nisha's office just when the clock struck lunchtime. When Vishnu walked in, Nisha was just tidying her desk and was about to open her lunchbox when Vishnu's approach made her look up and she gave a slight start, 'You!' she said.

'Of course, who else were you expecting?' Vishnu said. 'We have a lunch date, remember?'

'Oh-h-h, right! Well, today will not work,' came Nisha's flustered and terse reply.

Vishnu could feel something was wrong but couldn't quite guess what it was and asked, 'Why? You are here, I am here and the restaurant is here, I checked.'

'N-no, I mean it is of no use today as Mr. D'Souza has not come in today,' Nisha clarified.

'Oh,' Vishnu exclaimed crestfallen, but recovered almost immediately and said, 'So what? A promise is a promise. I told you I will take you out for lunch and I will.'

'N-no. That is not necessary at all. Come in some other day and when Mr. D'Souza is in and we shall see,' Nisha said. Vishnu was bewildered. The same girl who was swooning over him a few hours ago was suddenly giving him the cold shoulder and couldn't figure out why. He looked at Nisha carefully and realized that she wasn't even raising her head to have eye contact and that's when it hit him. She wasn't giving him the cold shoulder at all. She was afraid of him! She knew! How much, he couldn't judge, but she knew. She was a bright girl; that much he had judged for himself during their past encounters. And after their quite open conversation, how difficult would it have been to dig up some past news snippets, he thought.

'I guess Google did give away some of my history. I haven't lied to you so far and I don't want to ever after. All the questions you have asked, I have answered truthfully and I will here onwards as well. Just hear me out,' Vishnu said, and his sincerity was quite apparent.

Nisha hesitated and Vishnu could see it. 'Let us go someplace to talk. You already know who I am. If you want, you can call one of your roommates and let her know who you are with, if you are worried I may harm you,' Vishnu assured her.

'That's fair. Let us go,' Nisha said with some resolve and picked up her sack-purse.

'Where do you want to go? Do we drive there or is it a walking distance?' Vishnu asked.

'Wait here . . . I will be back in ten,' she said and ducked in through the wooden door next to her desk.

Vishnu waited patiently and Nisha came out through the same door about ten minutes later as she had said she would. He looked up at her expectantly and she said, 'Ok, let us go!'

'Where?' Vishnu asked, not really sure what Nisha had in mind.

'Well, let us have some lunch first and then you can tell me all about your past and what do you want with Mr. D'Souza. I just took an hour off for an extended lunch,' Nisha said and started walking towards the door.

'Are we . . .' Vishnu had just started the sentence when Nisha cut in, 'It is just a ten minute walk to a decent eatery. They have some booths that will give us a bit of privacy.'

And so Vishnu and Nisha had a chat as they sipped their lemon sodas and ordered food. Vishnu spoke and Nisha listened. Vishnu told her all the salient points of his life for the past decade and a half. He told her how he met Gopika and how they had started a detective agency. He told her the kind of cases they typically encountered and how life, though not as exciting as they had envisioned was still good. Then, Vishnu's voice took on a somber tone as he gravely told Nisha how Gopika's dead body was found in the freezer and how he was convicted of her murder. He quietly refrained from mentioning his suicide attempts but he mentioned his psychological evaluation, the split-personality argument, his incarceration and early release from jail for good behavior as well as his follow-up treatment regimen first with Dr Prakash and then with Dr Sujata. He filled her in on his findings in the past few months leading up to Gopika's property purchase and Vignesh's dead body. Finally, he told Nisha about his last ditch effort on finding who would have had a reason for vengeance and how that had led him to pursue John. By the end of it, the lemon sodas were empty, the food was cold and Vishnu was drained of all energy. Yet, he felt lighter than ever. He had actually shared all he had gone through with an almost complete stranger. It was a scary thought, but it was also liberating in a sense. Once done, he looked up expectantly at Nisha who looked deep in thought, trying to process the warped plot.

Finally, she looked up and said, 'That you were incarcerated was already mentioned in the news clipping. That you are rich is abundantly clear from the way you dress. Do you have any proof that everything else you have said is true? I mean finding Vignesh's body after all these years sounds like quite a stretch.'

'Body? Huh, skeleton really. Well, here is my address,' Vishnu said as he laid down a card on the table. 'I still have all the case files stored if you want to have a look.' Vishnu's mind drifted back to the storeroom and then to the long hours he had spent pouring over each and every one of them. He still saw no movement in Nisha and was disheartened that he couldn't yet make one other person trust his story. He made a futile gesture of rubbing his palms on his thighs just to get up when something pricked him through his trouser pocket. He smiled but was surprised as well, as he slid his hand through the pocket and the touch immediately reminded him of what he was touching. He pulled it out and put it on the table and said, 'This is all I have to show for all I have said.' Nisha stared at the skeletal finger and the *Navaratna Ring* that dangled on it. Her eyes and mouth were wide open in shock and she had suddenly lost her appetite. Vishnu left money on the table to cover for the bill and stood up. He picked the ghastly relic and pocketed it in one smooth motion, then tapped on the card he had placed on the table and said, 'Well, you know where to find me.' He left Nisha at the table, still in trance, unable to move a single muscle. And yet, her mind was whirring frenetically.

Vishnu went up to his car and dejectedly asked his driver to drive him home. He was totally drained due to the effort of retelling his horrendous past to Nisha who could potentially help him unlock a part of the mystery – Sanjana and Mrs. Devi. The car stopped at the porch as always and Vishnu absentmindedly walked up the steps to head into the living room. At the final step, instead of seeing the plush Iranian carpet adorning the entrance, he saw two huge mud-caked leather shoes and as he raised his gaze upwards, he could make out two enormous legs, almost like two thick teak trees growing out of them. The legs terminated in a torso that was almost devoid of any excess fat and then a huge head with an expressionless face – Malai! 'Do you want to talk here sir, or should I come in?' Malai asked in his usual gruff straight-to-business voice.

Vishnu looked at Malai and wondered if anything ever moved him. 'What moves a mountain?!' he asked himself and smiled. He was happy that Malai was here and that meant that he had found something about Sita and Mr. Narayanan. 'Let us talk in the balcony,' he said. Malai stepped aside and followed Vishnu as he led the way. On the way, he asked one of the kitchen staff to send up some coffee. He then asked Malai to wait in the balcony as he had a quick change of clothing. By the time he was in the balcony, sitting in his favorite chair, piping hot coffee was already served on the table. 'Aiyya is asking if you will be having lunch up here,' the kitchen-hand asked.

'N-no. I don't need lunch right now,' Vishnu dismissed the man and sipped his coffee. He saw that Malai was still standing almost entirely obstructing his view to the estate. Vishnu motioned Malai to sit and handed him a mug of the steaming brew. Malai accepted it with a light bow of his head and took a sip. Vishnu had half expected Malai to show signs of a sudden refreshment or burst of energy, but he had no such luck. Malai was stoic as ever. He looked at Vishnu as if asking for permission to begin. Vishnu was also eager to get Malai talking and said, 'So, it looks like you have found something. About Sita? About Mr. Narayanan?'

'They are dead, . . . all three of them,' Malai said this without any hint of emotion. Vishnu almost fell off his chair!

'What?!' Vishnu's voice was loud and brimming with disbelief.

'They are all dead. Arya died in a freak road accident. Sita committed suicide, most likely due to the grief over Arya's death and Mr. Narayanan died a few months later of a heart-attack.' Again, it was the calm even tone. It was as if he was reporting that he had a flat tire on the way over. No, not even that, Vishnu thought. It was as if he was saying I woke up and brushed my teeth! Vishnu looked at Malai. It seemed like Malai was still having something more to say, but he had paused just to give time for Vishnu to take in what he had already conveyed.

Vishnu's mood was somber. Death of a loved one. How differently it affects people, he wondered. In his case . . . well his case was complicated, he concluded. In Sita's case, the death of her beloved Arya had driven her to commit suicide. And her death, in turn, had led to Mr. Narayanan die of grief. He shook himself out of it and asked Malai, 'And? There is something more you want to say?'

'Oh, I am sure you know but; Arya was adopted,' Malai said in his usual nonchalant way.

Vishnu jumped up from his chair. The shock was too much to bear! How come they hadn't known this, he wondered. 'Arya was adopted,' Vishnu said it out loud as if that was going to make him believe it. It had never come up during their investigation. All Vishnu had ever focused on was Arya's social schedule, people he interacted with etc., especially women. It had never occurred to them to check Arya's parental lineage. 'Who in their right mind ever does that? Question someone's parental lineage?' he asked himself. But he was also ashamed of the fact that they were really poor detectives and had not done a good job at background searching in a number of their cases. It needed a murder, a seven-year jail term and two psychiatrists to tell him that follow-up on cases was vital and now this brute had found something that he had failed to. Arya was an adopted child. Not that it mattered now. He was dead. In fact, they were all dead. Vishnu thanked Malai for his efforts and bid him adieu. Overall, it had been a bad day for him. He had lost his only way forward in Nisha and the other viable strand had turned out to be a dead end. But then, he remembered his father's last words as he bid him farewell from behind the bars – This too shall pass!

A number of thoughts whirled in Vishnu's mind as he lay wide awake in his bed. His entire life sped past him, from the young carefree days of his childhood spent in the idyllic countryside to the adolescent days of his youth spent at the posh boarding school. He reminisced on the time he decided to live life on his own terms and how he had spent his college days, living alone, free of all the familial and financial bonds that his uber-rich family came with. He remembered meeting Gopika for the first time, only instead of feeling a deep sense of loss; he now felt a deep sense of hurt lined with betrayal. He then recalled how he had almost single-handedly set up the Romantic Corner and the detective agency and once again realized that he had done almost everything. Well, not quite, Vishnu realized. Recently, he had found out through Aiyya that it was his father who had coaxed one of his business contacts to offer Vishnu the loan amount he needed without any collateral. Gopika had done very little in terms of hedging the financial risks; neither had she done any major fieldwork. She did however steal money from their agency's account; that's something, Vishnu thought. He then remembered that fateful night when he met Vignesh and the morning after when he had searched for Gopika. With a feeling of nausea and a lump in his throat, he remembered Gopika's lifeless, frozen body being stretchered out of their office, the trial, his Dad's pleas and his as well. He recalled how the circumstance had been manipulated to entrap him as the murderer. The news of his Dad's death, the years of isolated incarceration, the suicide attempts and his ultimate release; all flashed by. He could feel his throat being parched but something had him paralyzed and he couldn't move a muscle. The flashback he was going through was equally horrifying and mesmerizing. His heart thumped away loud enough that he could feel his eardrums vibrate; any louder and they would burst, he thought. And just as the crescendo had reached its zenith, it slowly began to ebb away. He now felt the excitement he hadn't felt in a long time. He recalled how he had eliminated each of his past cases to find someone with a motive; a motive to kill Gopika and devastate his life. And Vignesh's too, he added as an afterthought. He remembered how he had discovered Gopika's treachery and how he had found Vignesh's skeleton. He fondly remembered Dr Sujata for all her help, but for some reason, he couldn't remember Dr Sujata's face as it looked like the first time they had met. Somehow, the recent, sickly looking Dr Sujata's persona had eroded the memory of an earlier more vivacious Dr Sujata. And then he remembered Nisha and smiled unknowingly. Something had tugged at his heartstrings, not in a romantic way, but in a way they had never been tugged ever before. And then there was Aiyya who had helped him all along without ever once questioning his innocence or his motives. And finally he thought of the Mountain – Malai. In him, Vishnu had found a Djinn! All Malai needed was a command from Vishnu and he would get it done; at least that is what it looked like.

Vishnu was suddenly disturbed by the sounds of the morning; birds chirping, doves cooing and the sound of raindrops falling. He had not slept a wink! It hadn't helped make headway in his case, but for some unknown reason, it hadn't drained him of energy. He got out of the bed and walked out to the balcony to greet the early rays of the Sun. He asked for his usual mug of coffee and ducked into the washroom for a while. By the time he had come out, the coffee was on the balcony table and the aroma had wafted all the way to his room, refreshing everything it touched. He sipped his coffee leisurely, but with a sense of nothingness filling his mind. 'There is nothing more to do,' he said to himself and finished his coffee. He pulled on his white linen walking trousers and shirt and headed out to walk among the woods on his estate. The morning rains had stopped and everything was wet, dripping and buggy. Mosquitoes and insects of all kinds were up and about, but couldn't keep up with his brisk pace. He lost track of time and started to circle back to his bungalow once the rays of the Sun started pricking his neck. He felt like a change in his coffee would do him good and as he entered the house, he asked one of the housemaids to make him a pot of Kopi Luwak. He was just at the bottom of the stairs heading to his room when he heard Aiyya call out for him. 'Thambi, a girl is here to see you. I have asked her to wait in the front balcony.'

Vishnu hurried over to the balcony and his heart fluttered! It was Nisha; he could still make out her comely figure, though she was standing with her back at him and the Sun shone brightly in the background. 'You are here!' Vishnu exclaimed. He hadn't fully recovered from this unexpected stroke of good luck and those were the only words he could put together!

'You own a piece of heaven!' she said turning around. And just then, the maid brought in the coffee pot and the accompaniments. He poured a mug and offered it to her.

'It is Kopi Luwak!' she said in amazement after a sip. 'That was fast!'

'A coincidence really,' he said. 'I specifically asked for this after my morning walk and here you are to share it with me.'

'Well . . .,' Nisha too hadn't fully thought out why she was here and what she was going to say.

'Please come with me,' Vishnu said as he led Nisha to the storeroom where he had kept all the boxes. He opened it and ushered her in. 'This is everything,' he said gesturing at the boxes, papers, files, computer screen and other office material strewn around. 'That box contains John's case file. I think it could lead to something.' He looked at her as she scanned the room and rested her gaze on the box he had indicated. 'I will leave you with this while I have a quick shower,' he said and with that, he left the room.

When he came back into the room, he was back in his all-linen casuals and looked suave as ever. He found Nisha holding a piece of paper which he recognized as the one he had tabulated his potential leads on to. 'You think Mr. D'Souza is somehow involved in all this?' Nisha asked incredulously.

'Not really,' he said. 'But his case is the only one left to look at. All other avenues have dried up.'

'What happened to the other case?' Nisha asked as peeped back into the paper she was holding and said, 'Right, Arya's case. What about that one?'

'That is literally a dead end!' Vishnu said and chuckled at the irony. And then, he proceeded to fill in the details of what Malai had found. Nisha nodded in understanding and then squinted back at the paper she was holding.

'I cannot believe that Mr. D'Souza could ever cheat on his wife,' she said adamantly. 'Their love-affair is the stuff of legend in our company!'

'Well, as you can see, we did investigate him for infidelity at the behest of Mrs. Devi whose daughter Sanjana was in love with him,' Vishnu said. 'We were hired by Mrs. Devi to look into John and we found that he was also romancing Shalini; seems like Sanjana was beyond his means.'

'I still don't believe it!' Nisha said. 'And even if he did, how does that have anything to do with what you went through?'

'That I don't know yet,' Vishnu said honestly. 'But I do know this; a lot that I have learned recently came from seemingly unconnected events. In any case, I don't want to trouble your Mr. D'Souza too much. I just want to know if he has any current information about Sanjana and Mrs. Devi.'

'Well, in that case, I will look into it,' Nisha said. It was not a request or an offer, Vishnu realized. It was a statement with a ring of finality.

'What are you . . .?' Vishnu started but was cut short by Nisha.

'I will find what Mr. D'Souza knows about Sanjana or Mrs. Devi,' she said and then there was a slightly uncomfortable silence.

'Well, how about a spot of breakfast then? I assure you, our kitchen is the best in Chennai!' Vishnu said to ease the tension hanging in the air.

'Your kitchen, you mean?' Nisha said pointedly.

'What?' Vishnu asked confusedly.

'Well, this is your house. It is your kitchen. They are your servants. They all work for you, isn't it?' Nisha clarified.

'Ha! Not at all. In fact, I know nothing about the business. Aiyya takes care of it all. And there are probably others who oversee every aspect of the running of the house and the business. Without them, nothing would function, not the house, nor the business and not me either!' Vishnu spoke with all honesty. 'They all work with me. You can say they work for me as well, but I definitely cannot repay them for their kindness and I absolutely do not own them!' After he let all that sink in, he said, 'Now, are you ok for breakfast?' Nisha nodded.

Breakfast was a slightly unexpected affair, Puttu and egg curry. Vishnu quizzically looked up at Aiyya who said, 'Kerala staple, Thambi; just for a change.'

Both Vishnu and Nisha had a hearty breakfast and then Nisha headed for the door. 'So, you are no longer afraid of me?' he asked.

'Well, I am here, aren't I?' she said matter-of-factly and then walked down the porch. She had almost reached the car and Vishnu's driver was just opening the car door when she paused and looked up to Vishnu. The look on her face was enough to make Vishnu understand the import of whatever was going through her mind and he hurriedly climbed down the porch.

'What is it?' he asked.

'Well, I was thinking about all that you told me earlier and I was just wondering . . .,' she let it hang.

'What is it, Nisha? What are you wondering?' Vishnu couldn't keep his inquisitiveness in check any longer.

'Well, who were Arya's real parents? Biological ones, I mean,' she made a face that Vishnu couldn't decipher and with a shake of her head she said, 'Well, it doesn't matter after all these years. But, I wonder how their life shaped up.' And with that, she got in the car and was gone. But she had done what Vishnu had never expected. She had given him yet another string to tug at; another line of investigation to follow. He quickly went back into his room to fetch his cell-phone. He dialed and heard someone pick up at the other end and said, 'Malai, find out who Arya's real parents are.'

CHAPTER FOURTEEN

It was well past evening when Vishnu heard Aiyya's voice at the door. 'Nisha madam has come back, Thambi. Should I send her up?'

'Nisha is here? Yeah, send her up, Aiyya,' Vishnu said, his voice jangling with excitement.

'Will you both be having dinner anytime soon?' Aiyya asked.

'We will have dinner for sure, but not soon, I don't think,' Vishnu said. 'But I will ask Nisha when she comes up. In any case, send us some coffee.' Aiyya nodded in understanding and headed back down. In a minute or two, Nisha was walking up to his room. Vishnu indicated that they go to the front balcony to chat.

'Are you hungry?' Vishnu asked. 'We could have dinner first and then you can tell me what you found.'

Nisha looked at her watch and said, 'It is too early for me for dinner. I can wait for an hour or so. It will be good to have lemonade or a glass of juice though.'

'No worries,' Vishnu said. 'I have already asked for coffee, if you fancy that.'

'Coffee! At this hour and in this hot humid weather! No way!' Nisha said, 'Cold water if there isn't any juice.'

Just then, the maid brought in the coffee and Vishnu asked the maid to organize lemonade for Nisha. 'So, did you talk to John?' Vishnu asked.

'I was right!' Nisha said with an air of victory. 'Mr. D'Souza has never been in love with anyone else except Shalini madam. In fact, he didn't even know of any Sanjana. He comes from such a humble background; it is nothing short of a miracle that he has made it this big in his area. Of course, Shalini madam has also done her bit and this angel . . .' Nisha seemed to veer off the point and Vishnu interrupted.

'Slow down, Nisha. Tell me everything exactly as your conversation took place. Don't leave out anything. John did not even acknowledge that he knew Sanjana?' Vishnu exclaimed, 'That big fat liar!'

'Wait a minute!' Nisha said adamantly, 'Let me finish! First of all, Mr. D'Souza was very polite and patient with my questioning. I asked him about their legendary love-affair and he was so humble about it, even though their love really is the stuff of legend,' Nisha was clearly in awe of John, Vishnu thought. 'You know Mr. D'Souza and Shalini madam have known each other since they were school kids? They finished school together, they went to college together and then they joined the company together. And on numerous occasions, they have given up lucrative offers and promotions from our company and other companies, just to be together. And trust me when I say this, cause women can immediately make out if a man is lying about this, but Mr. D'Souza has never cheated on his wife.' Nisha's eyes were blazing as she wound down her diatribe and glared at Vishnu.

Vishnu was both shell-shocked and disheartened. All this was for nothing, he thought. He had accomplished nothing. He looked at Nisha dejectedly, hoping that something worth saying will come to him, but nothing did. Just then Nisha said, 'He did however agree that he knew a Devi.'

Vishnu's heart skipped a beat! 'What?! He accepted that he knew Mrs. Devi?'

'No. Not a Mrs. Devi. A Ms. Devi really; *Devi madam* according to Mr. D'Souza,' Nisha clarified and continued. 'It seems that Mr. D'Souza's father was an ordinary driver for Devi madam's father who owned a decently large forge. Mr. D'Souza came to know through his father that Devi madam was studying in some other city at the time and then she was about to be married, but something happened that even Mr. D'Souza doesn't know and she never married. She again went away for studies or something and Mr. D'Souza's father never saw her again. Mr. D'Souza himself has never met her. All he knows is that she started a trust-fund to finance education and other start-of-the-life ventures for all the forge workers' kids. Mr. D'Souza was supposedly one of the benefactors. His entire education and that of Shalini madam was fully funded by that trust-fund.'

'What about Mrs. Devi's daughter, Sanjana?' Vishnu asked impatiently. 'Did he not have a romantic fling with her?'

'I told you, the Devi madam that Mr. D'Souza mentioned was never married and so there is no point of a daughter at all.' Nisha shouted and then looked crookedly at Vishnu and said slyly. 'When I looked into your files today morning, I could see there are photos of Mr. D'Souza and Shalini madam.' Nisha looked at Vishnu.

'Yes, and . . .?' Vishnu was not sure where this was leading.

'But there is no photo of Mr. D'Souza with this Sanjana,' Nisha said pointedly.

'Great, so now we are playing, state the obvious!' Vishnu blurted incredulously. 'Of course there isn't! We were paid to investigate *your* Mr. D'Souza and his other romantic liaisons!'

'Well,' Nisha said with a slight pause, 'how come there isn't a single photo of Mr. D'Souza with this Sanjana?'

'Again! That was the whole point!' Vishnu was fast losing patience with this seemingly thick-headed girl. 'He never spent any time with Sanjana! I only ever saw him spend time with Shalini.'

'Right!' Nisha said mockingly, 'So you did see Sanjana at some point of time during your investigation?'

Vishnu was stunned! It seemed that the whole world was spinning and his lips were suddenly dry! His eyes widened as reality dawned and he opened his mouth but no words would come out.

'Huh?' Nisha prodded, 'What did you say?'

'No,' Vishnu said in a voice so thin, he himself couldn't hear that he had said it.

'I am sorry, what?' Nisha asked mockingly.

'I never saw Sanjana!' Vishnu said it more for himself rather than Nisha. That realization stung him like a slap in the face. In their greed for excitement and their lethargy for not being very particular about the veracity of what the client told them, they had made a fatal flaw, him and Gopika. They had blindly believed the story that Mrs. Devi had fed them and had only focused on getting John caught with some girl other than Sanjana. They had never checked if Mrs. Devi's story had any truth in it. If at all that was Mrs. Devi in the first place, Vishnu mused.

Nisha's look was more of incredulity than anything else as she said, 'So basically, you are saying that you dug up Mr. D'Souza and his wife's actions at the behest of someone totally unknown to you.' It sounded like a question to Vishnu but it really wasn't. Nisha was dispassionately stating the facts as they had now presented themselves. 'You don't know who this Mrs. Devi is and you don't know if Sanjana ever existed. And on top of that, we don't know if the *Ms. Devi* Mr. D'Souza is talking about is the same *Mrs. Devi* you encountered all those years ago.' And she paused and let all that she had said sink in and then asked quite pointedly, 'So what *do* you know?'

Vishnu thought about it hard. What did he really know, he thought. A middle-aged lady had come to their office, claiming to be a Mrs. Devi and had fed them a convincing story about her daughter Sanjana being the apple of her eye and being madly in love with John. She was also quite forceful about wanting to break their relationship within twelve days, the deadline Sanjana had purportedly set, and wanted Vishnu and Gopika to find or fabricate some evidence to that effect. Vishnu had followed John and quite easily was able to photograph him with Shalini. Those candid photos were enough evidence for Mrs. Devi to be satisfied and she had paid handsomely for them. In fact, she was so impressed with the quick turnaround that she had come back to them with an even more challenging problem. She had talked about how she would love to get rid of her business rivals and how Vishnu had joked about murdering one and blaming it on the other.

'What?! You said that to her?' Nisha's voice boomed and Vishnu realized he wasn't thinking of the past. He was actually narrating the past loudly enough for Nisha to hear. 'Don't you get it?! You gave away an idea that was used against you!' Nisha's excitement was clear as she jumped off the swing she was sitting in and started pacing through the balcony. 'We just have to find this Mrs. Devi or Ms. Devi or whoever she is!'

'And Ms. or Mrs., somehow this lady is connected to John. We need to find everything that your Mr. D'Souza knows about his Devi madam,' Vishnu said. 'Can you manage that? Or do we need to think of how to go about it?'

'I can do one better actually!' Nisha said haughtily. 'I have already found out all there is to know about Ms. Devi, or at least everything that Mr. D'Souza knows about her.'

Vishnu looked at Nisha and suddenly found himself quite inadequate. This girl had really conducted a thorough background search during what could possibly be her first ever attempt at it. And he had basically botched up almost all of them during his stint as a detective. 'What did he tell you about her?' Vishnu asked in a voice loaded with expectation.

'Well, I have already told you how Ms. Devi started a trust-fund that supported Mr. D'Souza's and Shalini madam's education and all that,' Nisha said and continued 'Mr. D'Souza and Shalini madam tried to pay back to the trust-fund once they were settled but it seems that in the meantime, Ms. Devi's Dad had passed away and she supposedly had some other mishaps in her life. So, about a decade ago, she wound down the business and just vanished, probably left the country or something.'

Vishnu thought carefully about all he had heard for a while and then asked, 'Did you find out what those mishaps were?'

'I asked Mr. D'Souza, but he didn't know any more and moreover, too many questions were making him suspicious,' Nisha said matter-of-factly.

'Obviously,' Vishnu thought. 'A passing inquisitiveness is one thing, but a full-fledged interrogation is something entirely different.' Mrs. Devi had mentioned something about a business when she had approached them for the second time all those years ago, Vishnu recalled. And she had spoken with confidence and sounded like a businesswoman, he remembered further. 'I somehow need to track down this Mrs. Devi or whoever she really is,' Vishnu said hoping that the despair in his voice was not too apparent.

'We have to track her down if we want to get to the bottom of this,' Nisha said with conviction and asked, 'The only question is how?'

Vishnu heard a faint sound of footsteps as Aiyya approached them and said, 'Ok for you Thambi, but it is not good manners to let a guest starve.' Vishnu understood. Aiyya had cloaked his request for dinner in such a way that Vishnu couldn't refuse. He ushered Nisha on to the dinner table downstairs. The food was light and delicious as always, but Vishnu didn't really have his mind in it. Nisha on the other hand ate with great gusto and generously complimented the cook. To her surprise, the entire team of two cooks and two helpers were there at their table to receive her compliments and smiled in contentment. She then nudged Vishnu and said, 'Isn't this Meen Kozhumbu simply the best?!' to which Vishnu nodded absentmindedly and muttered something. Nisha nudged him again and said, 'No, honestly! I have never tasted this delicate balance of spice, sourness and fishiness in a curry, have you?' And that is when Vishnu realized that his entire cooking staff was waiting for him to say something nice about the food. He felt ashamed at being so self-centered. He apologized for the oversight and helped himself to an extra serving of the Meen Kozhumbu. As he looked up to Nisha, he saw that her face had gone ashen and her eyes had widened to an extent that couldn't widen any more. At the same time, a huge shadow seemed to loom over both of them and the dining table. 'Malai!' Vishnu exclaimed and heard a muted, 'Humph,' in response.

'Have a seat Malai. Have you had your dinner?' Vishnu enquired.

'No,' Malai said as he pulled out a chair and sat on it. As soon as he did, the entire chair seemed to have vanished behind the bulk of this human mountain.

'Have some dinner with me,' Vishnu pressed.

'I have something to tell you,' Malai said.

'It can wait,' Vishnu said with a dismissive gesture, 'Have dinner with us.' And then as he realized, Vishnu said, 'Oh! By the way, she is Nisha, a friend of mine.' And then he looked at Nisha and said, 'This is Malai.' Vishnu did not want to put Malai or the rest of his staff in a troubled situation by calling him a friend and he didn't know what else to call him. Both Malai and Nisha exchanged guarded looks and nodded their heads ever so slightly to acknowledge each other and went back to being guarded strangers. Vishnu was engrossed in savoring the Meen Kozhumbu when he noted one of the maids set up another plate for Malai. Malai's uneasiness was apparent as he was being stared and smirked at by all the staff serving the food. Aiyya, who had just come in, took a quick look at the entire scene and said, 'Malai? You are back already? Your food is ready. Follow me.'

Malai made a slight move to get up when Vishnu said, 'No Aiyya. Malai has something to tell me and I asked him to join us for dinner.'

Aiyya nodded in comprehension and said, 'But you guys are almost done, while Malai hasn't even started. Why don't you finish and go upstairs and I will send Malai once he is done?'

At that thought, Malai's eyes lit up and he smiled thankfully at Aiyya. Unfortunately, Vishnu missed that subtle gesture and pressed on, 'No worries at all Aiyya. Malai will eat with us. We can wait a while.'

Aiyya shrugged at Malai as if to say, 'I tried,' and ushered the servers to bring up Malai's dinner. It too was a simple affair, but something that quite surprised both Vishnu and Nisha. A full roast chicken, a large pot of fiery reddish-brown spicy Vatha Kozhumbu and a pot of rice that seemed sufficient to serve any five average South Indians, were neatly arranged around his plate. A generous serving of Rassam was poured in after every few mouthfuls and a large jug of spiced buttermilk was provided to wash everything down. Malai tried to hurry it up as both Vishnu and Nisha were done and it seemed like they were smirking, unable to avoid their amusement. But Vishnu noticed his discomfort and said, 'Don't be hasty Malai. Take your time.'

After a good twenty minutes, they were all well-fed and Vishnu asked Aiyya to send up some coffee to the balcony. Nisha immediately voiced her objection and asked for lemonade instead. Malai was stoic as usual. Vishnu ushered Nisha and Malai followed. Once they were all occupying their favorite perches, Vishnu in his chair, Nisha on the swing and Malai standing ramrod straight next to the railing, the pin-drop silence accentuated the air already heavy with anticipation. Vishnu looked up to Malai and said, 'First sit down, Malai! It pains my neck to look up to you when you speak!'

Malai gave a shy glance, bowed his head and looked around for a place to sit. Vishnu understood his conundrum and motioned Malai to sit on one of the chairs such that all three of them were almost located at the corners of an equilateral triangle with the coffee table in the middle. Vishnu poured coffee and handed one to Malai and then gave Nisha her glass of frosty cool lemonade. 'So, what do you have to tell me?' he asked.

Malai looked at Vishnu then at Nisha and then again at Vishnu hesitantly. 'Don't worry, Malai. Nisha is also helping me with this. It is ok for you to tell what you want to in her presence.'

Malai quickly recounted how he had approached Arya's (foster) parents as an insurance agent with some cooked up story regarding a life insurance policy. He told Vishnu and Nisha how he had asked the parents to provide evidence that they are the sole next of kin for Arya, at which the parents had flown of their handle. He told them how Arya's parents had cursed him and basically driven him out of the house; all the while shouting that this was another one of those tricks by the wretched lady who had visited them some time just after Arya's death. Finally, he assured Vishnu that he will go back soon and use some *other methods* to find out more about Arya's adoption.

Vishnu and Nisha took a moment to assimilate all of what Malai had just narrated. Vishnu noticed the peculiar tone Malai had used when he said *other methods* and was immediately concerned. 'No need to use force with these people, Malai. They have already suffered quite a lot,' Vishnu said sympathetically.

'Did you get the name of the lady who had visited these poor people after their son's death?' Nisha asked.

Malai looked at her and then at Vishnu. 'Well, did you?' Vishnu prodded.

'Devi,' Malai said. 'I will also start to look for her tomorrow onwards, but just thought I should tell you what has happened in the meantime.'

But both Vishnu and Nisha gave no heed to Malai's very last sentence. At the mention of **Devi**, both Vishnu and Nisha stood up and looked at each other with excitement. The strand that could unravel the case wide open or in this instance connect everything was finally there! *Devi*! She had been the common strand in all the stories. She featured in Vishnu and Gopika's life, she also was difficult to track down and now it seemed that she had come to their detective agency under false pretense and furthermore, Malai had just connected Mrs. Devi to Arya! Surely all this couldn't be just coincidence. It all pointed to one thing. Mrs. Devi was deeply involved in all that had happened so far and Vishnu also had developed a plausible theory as to why it all happened. What remained was to confirm his suspicion and track down Mrs. Devi's whereabouts, if possible, Vishnu added as an afterthought. Vishnu looked at Malai with a thankful gaze. 'Once again, you have helped me in a way no one has Malai!' Vishnu stated and could see Malai's chest swell with pride, but only for a moment.

'Just give me a bit more time sir, and I will get you all the details of Arya's adoption.' It was the cold resolve in Malai's voice that scared Vishnu, not for Malai's sake but for the safety and well-being of Arya's foster parents. Vishnu knew how unflinchingly loyal Malai was to him and for that he knew Malai could move mountains if it were required. Breaking a couple of bones or putting the fear of God in the hearts of two old sad souls wasn't something Malai would have a second thought about. But Vishnu knew that Arya's parents had already suffered enough and anymore pain was just not what they deserved. He had to find another way. 'We will have to find this Devi, Malai,' Vishnu said calmly. 'But not by troubling or threatening Arya's parents. We will have to think of another way.'

As always, Malai nodded in obedience. Vishnu remembered something and smiled, 'A Djinn only obeys his master's command but never ever questions it.' Vishnu looked at Malai and said, 'You still need to try and find something more about Arya. Start with his adoption details; something that possibly connects Arya to this mysterious Devi.'

Malai nodded, downed his mug of coffee, stood up and walked away; as always, a man of few words and economy in action. Vishnu was impressed by how succinct Malai was in almost everything he did. He then looked meaningfully at Nisha. 'We will have to go back to John,' he said.

Nisha nodded pensively. She understood what Vishnu meant. With Vishnu's background of being a convicted murderer, it was going to be counter-productive for Vishnu to come face-to-face with John. Which meant she had to go back to John and without giving away too much, convince John to give away whatever information he might possess regarding Devi madam that he had missed during their first encounter. It was going to be a tricky business. 'I need to handle this very carefully for this to work,' she said.

'True,' Vishnu said and then added, 'Sorry, you have to do this.'

He fully understood the difficult position he was putting Nisha into. Nisha would have to delicately navigate a minefield to extract whatever information John might still have regarding Mrs. Devi. One wrong word and John might clam up and that would mean an end to ever solving this mystery – at least for the time-being. But Vishnu somehow felt confident. With both Malai and Nisha engaged in their respective tasks, he only had one thing to do – Dr Sujata.

CHAPTER FIFTEEN

Vishnu had asked one of the drivers to drop Nisha home and as a courtesy had accompanied Nisha in the car, lest she feel lonely or insecure during the night-time. By the time he got back, it was way past midnight and when he hit the bed, he slept like a log. As was his habit, he woke up relatively early, after his usual six hours of sleep and felt quite fresh and charged up. He was surprised that he had slept that quickly and soundly. He got out of the bed and after his short but rigorous routine combining calisthenics, yoga and aerobics; he headed down for his morning cup of coffee. As always, the coffee was on the table and he savored it. Immediately after, he ducked out of the bungalow and headed for a walk around the estate. An hour later, he was back; fully refreshed and sharp as always. His breakfast was ready and he was visibly overjoyed to see that it was Idiaapam and Aatukaal Paya. A hearty breakfast and a hot shower later, Vishnu was back in his signature linen and heading towards the porch. He had tried calling Dr Sujata a couple of times earlier, but each time there was no answer. During those calls, he had not left any real message for Dr Sujata. But now, he had so many things he wanted to discuss with her that he just couldn't keep himself from not visiting her. He sat in the car and his driver already knew where he had to go. Vishnu absentmindedly stared at the sparse traffic on the road. It was past the office-hour rush and he was still on the outskirts of the bustling metropolis. Soon, the Sun would be up on the head blazing its wrath down upon everyone below, and the smoke, the bellowing dust, the cacophony of horns and sirens and hawker calls would drown out all the fun of city-dwelling. He wondered how Nisha was faring in her conversation with John.

Vishnu was eager to meet Dr Sujata to let her know how far he had progressed in terms of the investigation and in terms of life and companionship. From a recluse, he now had two companions he could confide in; Malai and Nisha. He now had two people who were actively helping him in finding answers he sought. Surely, Dr Sujata would welcome this change in Vishnu's life. Vishnu was looking forward for words of solace and guidance from Dr Sujata and when he rang the doorbell, he was half-expecting the surprisingly energetic Dr Sujata to answer the door. When that did not happen after three bells and about five minutes of waiting, Vishnu was a bit worried. But just then he heard the locks being turned, and the maid Vishnu had seen a couple of times during his earlier visits answered the door. 'Hello, is Dr Sujata home? I am here to meet her.'

'Do you have an appointment, sir?' the maid asked without budging even a little from her position barring the small crack in the doorway that she had opened.

'N-no, but Dr Sujata knows me. Tell her Vishnu is here,' Vishnu said.

'Madam is not in. I will let her know when she comes home,' and before Vishnu could say anything further, the maid ducked in the house and shut the door in Vishnu's face.

Vishnu was taken aback. Dr Sujata hadn't called him though it had been four weeks and she wasn't at home either. He was almost about to ring the bell and barge in as soon as the maid opened the door, but thought against it. Instead, he dialed Dr Sujata's number and could faintly hear the phone ringing inside the house. After quite a few rings, the line switched to an automatic answering machine and Vishnu left a message. He wondered how he could get to Dr Sujata. Though he had made substantial progress in unravelling the mystery, something Dr Sujata had facilitated by at times being supportive and at others, playing the devil's advocate. When he got back to his car, his mind was still caught up with Dr Sujata and he wondered how he could meet her again. A thought suddenly flashed in his mind but something distracted him and no matter how hard he tried, he couldn't recall what that flash was. By the time he reached home, it was just a bit after lunchtime and as expected, the table was already set. As he sat down, he thought if calling Nisha would be a good idea, but then decided against it. If she had found something to tell him, she would call on her own, he reasoned. The same reason stopped him from calling Malai as well. No information about either's progress had wrecked his hunger and he had his lunch without his mind in it. Yet, he remembered to compliment the cook as a token of gratitude. Nisha had taught him that, he reminded himself.

After the lunch, he decided to take a stroll around his estate but the afternoon heat and humidity was too oppressive to entertain that thought for long. He decided against it and instead sat in his favorite chair on the balcony sipping a frosty glass of cold coffee. His mind wandered and he started recalling Nisha and her mannerisms and he couldn't quite remember when that memory morphed into one about Gopika! Vishnu smiled wryly. It had been long since he had thought about her. With all the forgery and the stealing and the lies and deceit, Vishnu no longer felt a tug at his heartstrings when he remembered her and he acknowledged that. At last, he was at peace with the fact that Gopika was dead, murdered in cold blood by someone. That he had taken the fall for her murder was still stinging and the reason still eluded him, but he was sure this mysterious Mrs. Devi had all the answers. 'And *we* will find it!' he said out loud. And that is when he realized he was going to be ok. So far, he only had himself, all alone with no aims, no friends and no confidants. But now he had a friend in Nisha, a confidant in Aiyya . . . and Malai. What was Malai? He asked himself. He wasn't a friend and he wasn't a confidant either. Malai didn't ask any questions ever and he always maintained a formal distance. Malai just did as he was told. Yet, Vishnu had been with him enough to recognize that Malai was not just a heap of muscle; he also possessed a sharp mind and that combination was a very useful asset. He wondered what Gopika ever gave him and just one word came to mind – tasks! She had always relied on him to do things and when he didn't do them to her satisfaction, she would pout and throw a tantrum. He wondered if things would have been different if he had disclosed his vast family fortune to Gopika, but then realized that would be cheating fate. Gopika was more in love with herself than with anyone else and all she cared for was money. Was Nisha any different? He asked himself and somehow, it seemed that Nisha recognized wealth but valued human relationships more. And Malai, well, he seemed to care about nothing except what Vishnu wanted done.

'I don't think chatting with Mr. D'Souza helped much.' Vishnu craned his neck as he came out of his thoughts with that sentence and saw Nisha half smiling apologetically.

'What do you mean? Did John not help you?' Vishnu enquired, disappointment tinged his query.

'Well, Mr. D'Souza was very kind and patiently listened to what I had to say,' Nisha explained. 'He was quite sympathetic to your plight and wanted to help, but he really had almost nothing of note that could help us track Mrs. Devi.'

Vishnu heard each word carefully and then suddenly looked up and said, 'Almost?'

'He sent me a copy of the scholarship letter he received from the trust-fund Devi madam was associated with,' she said handing Vishnu a piece of folded paper that he opened and scanned carefully. 'There is nothing there regarding her. No name or address; just nothing!' she said dejectedly.

Vishnu looked at the sheet and then at Nisha. She was telling the truth. Except for the amount of money being awarded to John and the name of the College it was going to and the name of the trust-fund organization, there was nothing there. He suddenly squinted and Nisha as if on cue said, 'I did a basic Google search for the organization. It looks like it has been defunct for quite some time; just like Mr. D'Souza had mentioned.'

Vishnu gave a sigh and said, 'We still have Arya's parents and adoption to look into. Malai is on to them, so let us see.' He looked at Nisha who was standing there with her head bowed down and said appreciatively, 'Don't beat yourself up over this, Nisha. You did quite well. You could convince a third person about my innocence!'

Nisha looked up and smiled. 'We have some time before it is dinnertime. What would you like to do?' he asked and noticed her hesitation. 'Unless you have any other plans, of course,' he offered.

'No, I don't have any plans as such,' Nisha said. 'How about you show me around your estate?' she asked.

'Splendid idea!' Vishnu exclaimed and said, 'I was thinking of taking a walk earlier but it was too muggy. It should be perfect now.'

And with that they both headed downstairs. Aiyya greeted them on their way out and asked them if they would like to have dinner at home. Before Vishnu could answer, Nisha said, 'That would be fantastic! I don't want to eat a second-best meal at some restaurant when I can have the best here for free!' Both Aiyya and Vishnu were visibly happy at her response.

Vishnu and Nisha spent close to two hours around the estate. Vishnu regaled her with the history of his family. He told her how his forefathers were business-savvy and people-savvy at the same time. He filled her in on how he lost his mother at a young age and was put up in one of the top boarding schools in India and how he decided to make a life on his own as a private investigator, without his family's substantial wealth to support him. Nisha listened to Vishnu's autobiography with keen interest and also commented on many things. Sometime later, it was Vishnu's turn to probe Nisha about her past which was quite simple. She was the only child of a military family. Her father retired as a Major in the army and had died a few years ago due to cancer. Her mother, she had lost just a couple years ago. As she was a military brat, her childhood and youth was spent shuttling through beautiful but far-flung destinations all around the country and so, she had not made any lasting friendships. Due to her father's impromptu holiday schedule and his strict, somewhat quirky army nature, there weren't any close relatives either; they were there, but on the fringes. After her Mom's death, she basically had no place to call home and so she had decided to start her life afresh. She had initially thought of Mumbai or Delhi but for a lone young woman, it seemed that South India was a more welcoming place. She wanted to try her luck at Bangalore but found it a bit too pacey and expensive for her taste and so she settled for Chennai; and so far, the city had treated her well. They were just returning back to the bungalow when Nisha giggled and said, 'My life is like a boring short story while as yours is like a fairy tale and a murder mystery combined into one!' They both laughed heartily at that and Vishnu really felt the shackles of his past break away as he heard himself laugh. He had finally gotten over his past and whether or not he could completely solve the mystery surrounding Mrs. Devi, who and why, he understood that life here onwards will be alright. At the same time, Nisha looked at Vishnu with his open laugh, his expensive casuals and no airs persona and realized that she had found a friend in this world. It was a liberating moment for both!

As they entered the house the aroma of fresh spices and the warm wafting scent of Mughlai biryani welcomed them. The dinner was a simple but royal affair; Mughlai mutton biryani, spicy chicken roast, onion raita and salad. Vishnu and Nisha had their fill and noted that the cooks had really outdone themselves this time. Vishnu enquired if there was enough biryani made for the entire household and was satisfied when shown the large pot steaming in the kitchen. They had their usual lemonade for her and coffee for him in the balcony and then Vishnu asked Aiyya to arrange for a car and a driver. He accompanied her on her way home and this time, she let the car stop right outside her apartment. As she got out of the car, she said, 'See that window with the yellow light on the third floor? That's my apartment – Flat 302.' Vishnu nodded in acknowledgement and waited for Nisha to go to her apartment and wave through the window and then asked the driver to take him home. As he drove away he thought when he was going to see Nisha again and as she

Body in the Freezer

waved him goodnight, she was wondering the same.

As Vishnu lay in bed waiting for sleep to take away his senses for a few hours, his mind was a bit unsettled. He recalled his brief encounter with Dr Sujata's maid and suddenly Dr Prakash's face flashed in front of his eyes. He immediately sat up remembering this was what had flashed in his mind just as he got the door slammed in his face at Dr Sujata's home! To ensure he didn't forget it again the next morning, he wrote it down on a piece of paper and placed the paper on his dresser. He recalled that Dr Prakash was the one who had directed him to Dr Sujata and it was likely that Dr Prakash had more knowledge about her and possibly knew more of her whereabouts. He was also a bit ashamed that he hadn't kept in touch with Dr Prakash that often; for Dr Prakash was his well-wisher too and had been his primary care-giver for a major part of his incarceration and immediately thereafter. Dr Prakash was instrumental in weaning Vishnu off his addiction to anti-depressants and Vishnu was forever thankful to him. Remembering Dr Prakash made Vishnu happy, for now he had a plan; a chore to occupy him for tomorrow.

Next morning, Vishnu woke up as usual and after his morning rituals wondered if it would be a good idea to visit Dr Prakash unannounced. He thought against it and called up Dr Prakash at his clinic. After a few rings, he realized that it was too early for anyone to be at the clinic and hung up. He remembered that Dr Prakash had given Vishnu his personal cell number and had asked Vishnu to call him whenever he felt like it. Vishnu tried the number and after a couple of rings, Dr Prakash's mellow voice answered. Vishnu was relieved to hear the soft comforting voice from the elderly doctor. Vishnu asked if Dr Prakash would have some time to meet him today. Dr Prakash hesitated for a minute but immediately gave Vishnu a time slot in the early afternoon. Vishnu made a note in his mind that the agreed meeting time called for a heavy breakfast and a late lunch. As he hung up, he wondered if he should call up Malai and ask for an update but then remembered what he had realized about Malai. If he had something important to convey, Malai himself would have called up. He went down and told Aiyya about his plans for the day and Aiyya ensured that necessary arrangements would be made. With that, he headed out for his usual walk around his estate. The Sun wasn't fully up yet, but the air had already started getting warm and humid. He realized that he would have to make it a short stroll unless he wanted to risk being roasted in the Sun, soaked in sweat and bitten to death by the mosquitoes. His assumption proved correct and within half an hour, the atmosphere was unbearable to sustain his brisk walk. He quickly headed back to the bungalow for a cold shower. As he stepped down the stairs, he noticed that the breakfast table was already set. He had a heavy breakfast which was delicious as usual and headed out to the car. It felt weird for every time he had visited Dr Prakash, it was by bus. But today, he was going to use his car. His driver listened to the destination instructions and though it wasn't one of the usual places he had taken Vishnu to in the past few months, he didn't show any surprise. They were on the way when Vishnu's phone rang. It took some time for Vishnu to realize it was his phone ringing and he only picked it up when the driver pointed it out to him. It was Malai. 'Yes Malai, did you find anything?' Vishnu asked.

'I found where Arya was adopted from, but the orphanage says that he was an abandoned child, left in the orphanage's collection basket soon after birth,' Malai explained, but the pause seemed like he had something else to add.

'So that is a dead end. Anything else?' Vishnu asked without any real hope of hearing something useful.

'Well, it seems this Devi had visited Arya's parents just after his death and claimed to be his birth mother,' Malai offered.

Vishnu was stunned! A plot started forming in his mind. He slowly had an inkling of how Mrs. Devi was linked to all this, but there were still some gaps that needed filling; some pieces of the puzzle missing.

'Sir?' Malai again.

Body in the Freezer

'Thanks Malai. I will talk to you later,' and with that the conversation was over. Vishnu still couldn't understand why Mrs. Devi would hatch such a devious plan to kill Gopika and ruin him. He also realized that the only person who could answer this question with certainty was Mrs. Devi herself; and she was nowhere to be found. He filed all that information in his mind's filing cabinet to be recalled later, and started looking forward to meet Dr Prakash. His driver stopped the car right in front of the gate and Vishnu entered the small reception area of Dr Prakash's clinic. He told the receptionist about his arrival and she relayed it over the phone to Dr Prakash. She then asked Vishnu to take a seat as Dr Prakash was in a sitting with another patient. Vishnu took the seat pointed out to him and started thumbing through one of the many old National Geographic magazines haphazardly strewn across the table. In a few minutes, the door opened and a young twenty-something youth scurried out with his head bowed down. Psychological help was still a taboo in India, Vishnu realized. A small bulb on the receptionist's console glowed and she politely asked Vishnu to go in.

Vishnu remembered Dr Prakash's clinic. It was not the comfy, homely environment that Dr Sujata had created in her living room. This was a proper clinic. Dr Prakash was old-school and when someone entered the clinic they knew they were here as a patient and they were going to be treated as such. Dr Prakash had his trademark warm smile out in no time. It seemed like he was genuinely happy to see Vishnu. Vishnu remembered that Dr Prakash truly cared for his patients and had grown somewhat fond of him. 'Hello, Dr Prakash. Hope you are doing well,' Vishnu greeted him.

'You know how it is; I am getting older by the minute!' Dr Prakash joked and said, 'But you are looking quite well yourself. That's wonderful!'

'Sorry for not visiting you earlier. I was busy with a few things actually,' Vishnu said apologetically. 'I have been meeting with Dr Sujata quite regularly,' he paused and then added, 'Had been.'

Dr Prakash looked at Vishnu's forlorn look and said, 'I know, quite sad really,' and it seemed like his eyes were damp. 'It looks like Sujata has made a positive change in yet another life.'

'I cannot agree more, Doctor. She definitely helped me with my issues,' Vishnu said honestly. 'I have been unable to reach her for the past few weeks.'

'Oh! So you don't know. Poor soul. I wonder why someone so good has to endure so much in life,' Dr Prakash's voice was heavy with emotion.

'Know what Doctor?' Vishnu asked with concern. 'Has there been anything wrong with her?'

'Ha,' came a short sarcastic laugh, 'I wonder if she ever had any good moments to savor.'

'Really? But she seems to be comfortably well-off. Is well-educated and totally devoted to her cause,' Vishnu was confused. In the past months, he had visited and chatted with Dr Sujata a number of times and it never ever occurred to him that she had lived a difficult life. He did remember that she was looking a bit sickly during his recent visits, but he had attributed it to some random bug she might have caught, the flu or some exhaustion.

'She really is well-off. You know she is the sole inheritor of a tidy fortune left to her by her father. I have known her since her undergraduate days when I taught Human Physiology . . .' And so Dr Prakash narrated the entire story. He told Vishnu how she had been in love with a classmate of hers and was engaged to be married. He told how the classmate and his entire family had perished in a railway accident plunging Sujata into deep depression. How she had broken all ties with the world and gone into reclusion. How she had reinitiated contact with Dr Prakash, finished her studies and devoted her life to serving humanity. He described how she had actively started and promoted charities that helped the poor and the downtrodden and just when she was back to normal; fate had delivered her another blow. Her father had died leaving the substantial business empire to her. He narrated how about a year later; she had suffered a debilitating accident that had left her scarred to the extent where extensive reconstructive surgery and physiotherapy were needed to get her back to normal. 'I remember the day our paths crossed again and I didn't even recognize her. Her face and her posture had changed drastically,' he recalled. And then he elaborated her journey from a simple MBBS doctor to a psychiatrist, with a doctorate in multiple-personality disorders from a reputed foreign university. He told Vishnu how she had been keenly interested in Vishnu's case ever since she had heard of it and when Dr Prakash offered to handover Vishnu's future treatment direction to her, Dr Sujata had immediately accepted the challenge. 'And now that she has the opportunity to look at your astonishing recovery and transformation and gloat at her own skills and success, she is being strangled by the cruelest of diseases!'

Vishnu looked at Dr Prakash with a look that was a combination of rage and sorrow and astonishment and revelation.

'Yes, my dear boy. She was diagnosed with leukemia, aggressive, stage-three,' Dr Prakash said with finality. 'They have given her probably a month at the very best.' His eyes were filled to the brim with tears and he swiftly dabbed them with a tissue before a single tear spilled over.

Vishnu sat in his chair motionless. His mind was a complete blank for a while and then he looked at Dr Prakash as if asking for forgiveness for making Dr Prakash recall the sorrowful story. 'Could you tell me where I can find her?' he asked.

'She is back in her home now,' Dr Prakash said. 'It is funny actually. She called me today just after you did, to tell me that she will have to hand over your follow-up treatment to me for obvious reasons.'

'I must visit her,' Vishnu said.

'Surprising! She said she had called you too but you didn't answer,' Dr Prakash said.

Vishnu frenetically patted his pockets and dug out his cell phone and of course, there was a notification, *1 missed call* flashing. He unlocked his phone and saw another notification about a new voicemail. He listened to it intently and hung up. 'She has asked me to visit her today if possible, Doctor. I have to go,' Vishnu said as he stood up.

'Of course. Please give her my regards too. I am too old to face her and give her any words of solace. It is a pity. Old bones like me keep on clinging to life when good people like Sujata are mercilessly mowed down so early.' There was real emotion in his voice and he bowed his head down as if to hide his sorrow.

Vishnu left the clinic with a heavy heart. A huge part of his life was coming to an end. As he sat in his car, he asked his driver to drive to Dr Sujata's home. 'No need to stop a few blocks away this time,' he said. 'Drive right up to her home. This is probably the last time we get to do it.'

CHAPTER SIXTEEN

Vishnu was quite sad and apprehensive to even ring the door-bell, fully aware that this might be the last time he would do it. With all that Dr Prakash had disclosed about Dr Sujata, it was almost certain that she wouldn't survive the month. Vishnu wondered how he was going to face her and what he was going to say. Yet, his inner-self yearned to talk to her face-to-face. He had discovered so much during these past weeks, all in Dr Sujata's absence; or rather in her ever-guiding presence. He had almost reached the end of his quest . . . for inner peace. He now knew what had happened and why it had happened and what he had to do with it and more importantly, he had realized that some mysteries never fully resolve themselves. Just like the grand mystery of life and death. With a slight tremble in his hand, he rang the door-bell and was expecting the curt maid to open the door. At first, there was nothing; no motion at the door and no sound from the inside either. Vishnu waited a whole minute before he rang again. It is weird how long a minute really feels like when you have to wait for something and how short it is when you are enjoying something. Vishnu was well into his second minute of waiting when he heard the inner bolt of the door being undone and the door cracked open slowly. What greeted him was horrifying and he was clearly taken aback.

A frail woman, a husk of what once was Dr Sujata, was standing almost propped up by the door. Her lips moved trying to imitate a smile, but the pain that wracked her body made the expression more grotesque than anything Vishnu had ever witnessed. He averted his eyes for a moment, but realized that it was quite a rude gesture on his part and looked back into the almost lifeless face of Dr Sujata. With all the flesh from her face melted away by the aggressive treatment she had just endured, her bare-bone structure was evident and that quietly gave away a bit of her past life. The high cheek-bones, the unchanged jawline; it all made Vishnu cringe a bit. 'How . . . Hello, Dr Sujata,' he said.

Dr Sujata motioned him inside and said, 'Please close the door behind you.'

Vishnu could see that though she tried to stand erect and walk as gracefully as ever before, her body couldn't do it. The room too had changed. The curtains were closed and the room had a somewhat sickly feel to it; almost like the dark corner he used to spend most of his time in. Vishnu waited for her to take a seat and he noticed that rather than her usually favored sofa, she had a slightly tall, ergonomically designed chair she sat in. Vishnu tried to find a seat that would face her, but that one was in the dark. He hesitated and Dr Sujata sensed it. 'You can open one of the curtains. The sunlight hurts me now,' and she covered her eyes with a pair of dark shades, the kind seen on people who have just had their cataract removed. Vishnu opened the curtain to let a sliver of light into the gloom.

'You spoke to Dr Prakash.' It was a statement and not a question.

'Yes,' Vishnu nodded. He understood what her statement had meant. She didn't want them to talk about her illness. 'Why didn't you . . .,' Vishnu started and stopped mid-sentence. He looked at her and it seemed like she too was looking at him through her shades, but no one spoke. 'Is there anything . . .,' Vishnu started again, and again he stopped. There was no good way to start the conversation. 'I need a glass of water. Can I get you one too?' Vishnu asked as he got up and he realized that the air-conditioning was on full-blast and the room was quite cold. He usually loved the comfortably cool room during his previous visits but today, it was positively chilly.

'Just bring me the thermos you see on the kitchen counter. The glasses are on the top-left shelf next to the refrigerator,' she directed.

'There must be a couple of cold water bottles in the refrigerator's door-rack.'

Vishnu did as told and had to make two trips to the kitchen. He was amazed to note that the refrigerator was almost devoid of any food and the kitchen seemed to have been unused for quite a while. Sanitized was the word that popped into his mind. He handed Dr Sujata the thermos and poured himself a glass of cold water. She carefully poured a golden-yellow colored liquid into a cup and sipped it. Vishnu looked at it with suspicion and Dr Sujata said, 'It is an ayurvedic tea infused with medicinal herbs and spices, supposed to ease the pain.'

Vishnu grasped the subtle connotation in that statement. Dr Sujata had accepted the fatality of her situation. The tea was not a cure or a delayer of things to come. It was just a momentary relief. He had a long drink and the cold water combined with the cold room gave him Goosebumps. He was just fidgeting around in his mind about how to start the conversation when Dr Sujata came to his rescue and asked, 'So, you seem to have uncovered quite a bit about the mystery surrounding Gopika's murder?'

With that query, all the cobwebs Vishnu had in his head disappeared and the clear path of how this conversation was going to proceed illuminated itself. 'Yes! Let me tell you everything I have uncovered so far. I still haven't connected all the dots.'

'Let us hear it then,' she said feebly.

Vishnu took a deep breath and began, 'Incredibly, the events that led to Gopika's murder and my incarceration, were initiated a generation ago. A rich girl named Devi delivered a child out of wedlock. By the look of it, the baby was abandoned at an orphanage. That baby was adopted by a childless couple and named Arya!' Vishnu stopped for a sip of water and couldn't help but notice an almost inaudible gasp from Dr Sujata. But that was it. She didn't speak or show any further reaction. Probably, it pained her to show anymore, Vishnu thought.

'Arya grew up to be a decent boy and upcoming software

professional. He met Sita and soon, the two fell in love, contemplating marriage and a life together. Sita's Dad, Mr. Narayanan, like most responsible single parents, wanted the best for his only daughter. He wanted to make sure that Sita, in her blind love lust, wasn't making a mistake in choosing Arya as her life-partner. So he hired us, me and Gopika, to do a thorough background search on Arya. We were idiots and bored of routine background searches and Gopika was only looking for ways to make more money; something that I have come to know only recently. She presented Mr. Narayanan with an email in a way that seemed to have convinced him that Arya was not worthy of his daughter.' Vishnu paused for a moment. Though the room was cold, he felt his earlobes go warm. He looked at the floor quite ashamed of the blind trust he had put in Gopika. But then, he rectified himself. It wasn't blind trust, he reminded himself. It was something more complex. It was fear of offending or losing the one he loved combined with the shrugging away of responsibility for convenience. Maybe it was also a cry for attention. With his mother snatched away from him too early and his father being distant, Gopika was the only person with whom Vishnu had managed to establish any kind of closeness or intimacy. It wasn't as if he was looking to replace the lack of parental love; it was more like trying to hold on to some form of human intimacy. It was complicated.

'This is what any shrewd businessman would do, isn't it? Look to make more money?' Dr Sujata asked. 'There is nothing idiotic about that, really.'

'Even I thought so for quite a while, but over the past few months, thanks to your guidance, I have realized that we were not selling candy. We were playing with people's lives,' Vishnu's voice trembled. 'We were oblivious to the fact that our actions, our findings might have an enormous impact on people's lives. We should not have been that cavalier in attitude.'

'So Arya didn't get to marry Sita, so what? Many people go through that,' Dr Sujata prodded.

'True,' said Vishnu, 'But I think somehow, our incomplete investigation and Gopika's approach to Mr. Narayanan for money resulted in three deaths; Arya, Sita and Mr. Narayanan.'

'Four deaths really, if you count Gopika!' she said.

'Well, five if you count Vignesh too!' he said and looked at Dr Sujata. Her eyes were shaded and so it was difficult to read anything, but Vishnu saw Dr Sujata's lip twitch and she gave a sudden start. But as soon as she did that, her body seemed to have complained and she winced in pain.

'V-Vignesh? Dead? How?' she stammered.

'It is a long story. That is what I wanted to tell you so eagerly and that is why I had called you a couple of times in the past few weeks.' Vishnu looked at Dr Sujata as his heart filled with a sense of relief. 'Thanks to you, I am able to convince myself that I really did not kill Gopika. We found Vignesh's decomposing corpse, skeleton really, buried on an abandoned piece of property, a few hours' drive from the city.'

'Oh?! So if Vignesh killed Gopika, who killed Vignesh?' she asked.

'We shall come to that. There is more. I found that the property was registered to Gopika. In fact, it was bought by her without my knowledge; kind of a nest egg.' Bitterness filled his mouth at the mention of Gopika's treachery. 'Can you believe it?! I trusted Gopika with everything I had and she was stealing money from our agency's account right from the very beginning. And all the while, she had shown her greed and I had turned a blind eye.' Repentance and shame tinged his voice.

'Well, who did you go with, to find Vignesh's body?' Dr Sujata asked.

Vishnu looked at her quizzically and she said, 'You said, *We* found Vignesh's decomposing corpse, didn't you?'

'Oh, I was with Malai,' Vishnu added and now it was Dr Sujata's turn to be quizzical, but Vishnu had already started narrating more of what he had uncovered. 'I should have just let Gopika go, but I was totally blinded by something. Now that I think of it, I know it wasn't love for I liked her, but we were never overly romantic. I don't quite know what it was, but I never questioned her, never opposed her; and that was my downfall.'

Dr Sujata sat in silence for a while and then said, 'So, what does Arya's death have to do with what you endured? Who killed Vignesh?'

'Right. Well, it all goes back to Mrs. Devi. She is the same woman who hired us to do a background search for John who was the love-interest of her non-existing daughter Sanjana. She also approached us for another job soon after. She is the same woman who visited Arya's parents just after his death. In fact, she is also the same woman who John calls Devi madam. I have thought about all this quite a bit and this is what I think happened,' Vishnu said and had a drink of water from his glass.

'So, it seems you have unraveled the entire mystery,' Dr Sujata said.

'There are gaps in what I know, but then that's where you have always helped me; filling the gaps and pointing me in the right direction,' Vishnu said. He took a moment to collect his thoughts. He had all these loose threads that he had to weave into a web of deceit, revenge and murder and then he would have to untangle each knot to get the mystery out in the open.

'So, it all started with me stealing a seemingly scandalous email from Arya's desk. Gopika tried to use it to leverage some more money out of Mr. Narayanan, but her plan failed and we lost the client. Mr. Narayanan, in his protective Dad-mode, probably called off Arya's engagement with Sita. That shock, compounded with the typically stressful lifestyle of young software professionals, resulted in Arya suffering an untimely stroke which ultimately led to his death in a road accident.' Vishnu paused and let Dr Sujata take in every word. Dr Sujata sat in her chair motionless, her eyes shaded by her dark glasses.

'Arya's accidental death was a pebble in the ocean. It set off a series of ripples that morphed into a tsunami by the time they reached us, me and Gopika.' Vishnu noted that as he spoke out loud, he also started understanding new facets of the story he had hitherto not yet grasped.

'Mrs. Devi, if what I understand is correct, had an unlucky life. She was all alone once her father died but somehow, the only hope she had was to get back in touch with her long-lost son. And just when her search for him led to Arya, Arya was taken away once and for all from her, by a cruel twist of fate. She had lost him once somehow and now that she had found him after all those years, she had lost him to a freak road accident. She would clearly have been distraught.' Vishnu paused to see if Dr Sujata had followed what he had said, but she showed no reaction whatsoever and he continued.

'She dug up the circumstances surrounding Arya's death and found that it all started with our botched investigation in to his background; the job Mr. Narayanan hired us for. She decided to teach us a lesson. She posed as Mrs. Devi and hired us to conduct a background search for John as her daughter Sanjana was in love with him. And we were such idiots that we took her words for granted and didn't even check if Mrs. Devi really had a daughter!' Vishnu paused, this time to appreciate the stupidity they had shown in their dealings with their clients.

'Seems quite diabolical of this Mrs. Devi. She should have been scorched by the loss of her only living heir,' Dr Sujata said it with feeling. It was a statement.

'The degree of our abject ineptitude outstrips her diabolical nature really. In fact, I wonder what her plan would have been, had we found out that she was lying about having a daughter named Sanjana. But that doesn't really matter now. What happened is for everyone to see. We fell for her ruse, took some pictures of John and his *real* girlfriend Shalini and gave it to Mrs. Devi. It is funny because John and Shalini are married to this day and are living together quite happily. In fact, both John's and Shalini's educations were sponsored by Mrs. Devi and John knows of her as Devi madam!' Vishnu couldn't quite believe the enormity of their oversight while handling the John-Sanjana case.

'So John knows of her. That must be quite easy then to finally track her down. But then what? How does that help you with Gopika's murder?' Dr Sujata's breath came in gasps now, but Vishnu wasn't sure if that was due to exhaustion or excitement.

'Stupidity was our quality, mine and Gopika's. Mrs. Devi was quite intelligent. John only remembers the name as his father used to work as a driver for Mrs. Devi's Dad. John has never met Mrs. Devi and has no clue about her current whereabouts. He couldn't help us in tracing her,' Vishnu elaborated.

'So where does that leave you? I mean, it seems like only this Mrs. Devi can . . .' and Dr Sujata trailed off, but Vishnu had already started talking, as if he couldn't hear what Dr Sujata was saying.

'Mrs. Devi came back to us with a risky job to offer. It was to get her two business rivals out of competition. I wonder if any of this is true now. It was clearly a job way above our league. But you know how it went. I made an off-hand comment that we could kill one of her business rivals and make it look like the other rival has done it. It was a joke obviously, but Mrs. Devi egged us on and Gopika in her greed for big bucks, wanted to go ahead with it. I tried to stop this insanity right then, but I failed! I should have totally distanced myself from Gopika and called it quits with the partnership in the investigative agency, but I was too tangled up with Gopika to do that either.' As he said these words, he realized fully, how his inability to stand his ground against Gopika's whim, had led to a catastrophe for so many people.

'And what happened then? How did Gopika die? And who is this Vignesh? Did he kill Gopika? If yes, then who killed him? How is Mrs. Devi involved in all this?' Dr Sujata let go a series of questions and Vishnu thought she was just losing her patience. His story was just winding around without ever reaching the heart of the mystery.

'I am really not sure what exactly happened then. It is something that only Mrs. Devi can reveal,' Vishnu said pointedly. I will tell you what I think might have happened. 'It seems like, Gopika in all her avarice had decided that she had enough of me and was looking to start out on her own, or rather with someone who shared her morals; someone who had no qualms about committing murder and blaming it on an innocent person. Where she found Vignesh from, I don't know for I couldn't find his identity, but she definitely had something in mind that night. Whether it was to get rid of me, I have no clue; but I wouldn't be surprised if she did. And how Mrs. Devi came to know about all this is also unclear but she did, and she used Gopika's plan to her own advantage. She killed Gopika with Vignesh's help and framed me for her murder. Then, she got rid of Vignesh and thus destroyed all links that connected her to me and Gopika. And she did this in a way that if ever his body was found, it would again be blamed on me!' The brilliance and nimbleness of Mrs. Devi's mind was clear to Vishnu and he was in awe. It was a fluid situation and Mrs. Devi seemed to have used it perfectly to suit her aim – a horrendous vengeance against those who had wronged her.

'How do you know Mrs. Devi was helped by Vignesh in Gopika's murder? And how could she then dispose Vignesh's body at the property Gopika had bought; a property no one knew about?' Dr Sujata asked instantly.

Vishnu thought about all possibilities and the only logical explanation was the one that further strengthened what he has suspected for quite some time now. But rather than think about it, he decided to say it out loud. 'It seems that the only one who was oblivious to Gopika's plan was me! But Gopika had somehow decided to dump me and put me in some sort of trouble. What she had planned for me, she took to her grave, but Mrs. Devi used it perfectly to manipulate the circumstances. I think Mrs. Devi never intended to kill anyone really. But what circumstances led to the deaths of both Gopika and Vignesh, I cannot fathom.'

Dr Sujata twitched a little and sipped a bit of that golden-yellow liquid she had poured for herself. She removed her shades and Vishnu could see the large black circles she had around her eyes. All their lively twinkle and radiance was gone. 'How do you know

Gopika had something planned for you?'

Vishnu had almost expected this question and began with gusto. 'Once I put all the connected things together, a pattern emerged. Gopika stole from the agency and bought a piece of property without my knowledge. Then Gopika and I had a misunderstanding of sorts and instead of talking it over with me, she went ahead and found this Vignesh who supposedly was ok with the whole murder-one-blame-the-other plan. Then, she told the hostel watchman that she was starting her new life and vacated her room; but I was told nothing of this. Add to this the fact that she went out for a blood-donation, something she absolutely hated, but probably did it to have a learning experience. So, she was thinking of something that involved her own blood-letting. She then sent Vignesh to meet me and he probably slipped something in my drink, for I passed out with no recollection of what ensued that night.' Vishnu paused to recollect if he had missed anything and then remembered his time in court. Evidence had been stacked up against him since the word go!

'Vignesh must have been observing me from a near-by location that night; for he called me to say he was running late, but the police found that the phone-call came from close vicinity of our office. Moreover, it came from a SIM that was bought using my own identity documents; looks like this was Gopika's design too. Without the existence of Vignesh corroborated at that time, the police found it quite easy to prove that I had made up the entire scenario, just to murder Gopika and get away with it.' Vishnu paused and then added, 'That Mrs. Devi came to know about all this is shocking, but I must commend her on the way she used this information to set me up.'

'So, once Mrs. Devi is found, you can be absolved of all wrong-doing!' Dr Sujata exclaimed. 'That is wonderful news. I think you should just concentrate on finding her.'

Vishnu looked at Dr Sujata with a dry smile. 'I have thought about it, but you are wrong,' he said.

Dr Sujata's brow furrowed and she questioned, 'About what?'

'I will never be absolved of any wrong-doing. Nor me, nor Gopika or Vignesh or probably Mrs. Devi for that matter!' Vishnu's smile gave the statement poignancy.

'What do you mean?' Dr Sujata asked taken aback. 'Don't you want to clear your name?'

'I cannot!' Vishnu said. 'I have to own up to the fact that my inaction led to the death of one young, promising life.'

'What about the others?' Dr Sujata asked.

'Well, I played a part in creating a circumstance that led to Arya's accidental death, but Gopika died of her own doing. Rather she died because of how cleverly Mrs. Devi's played the circumstances presented to her; and probably Vignesh helped her with it. But I have no part in their deaths.' Vishnu's answer was probably not what Dr Sujata had expected, for she seemed a bit agitated. It could even have been that her discomfort stemmed from the aliment she was suffering from, but the true cause wasn't apparent.

Vishnu took a long drink from his glass of water and continued, 'I made a mistake; an inexcusable one by some standards, but I have paid a price. I have lived like a zombie, cut-off from the world for almost a decade. And I will always have Arya's death on my conscience and Gopika's death on my head. I seriously wonder whether two murders and one obliterated life was a proportionate response to one accidental death. But that is for Mrs. Devi to live with. I don't see what good could come off finding her and confronting her if she doesn't want to be found; if she doesn't want to face me.' Every word Vishnu said rang through the room and oozed of confidence and self-realization. It hadn't yet dawned on Vishnu, but he was finally free of all the shackles of his past life. He had come to terms with who had framed him and why; and he also realized that punishment or repentance works only when the offender is willing to face his accuser and accept what comes his way. 'Mrs. Devi has dealt out punishment that she saw appropriate, but she probably doesn't have the guts to face the truth. She probably has no answer to my question – WAS IT WORTH IT? But I accept that she has endured a lot in her life and I would not want to put her in any more pain.'

'So, you don't blame yourself for the deaths of Gopika or Vignesh; or Sita and her father for that matter?' Dr Sujata asked and Vishnu sensed that she was a bit irked.

'If you think of it, all of us could shoulder equal blame for it, but then we all didn't receive equal punishment, did we? I mean I was sent to jail and lost almost a decade of my life, three people died and two were murdered and what did Mrs. Devi get? She didn't get her son back and she didn't get any punishment for her crimes either. Perhaps, she paid her debts through her good deeds,' Vishnu argued.

'Huh?' Dr Sujata grunted.

'I found out that John as well as Shalini were fully funded throughout their education by the trust-fund scholarships facilitated by Mrs. Devi,' Vishnu said and quietly unfolded a piece of paper from his pocket and placed it on the coffee-table in between them. It was the copy of the scholarship letter John had given to Nisha. 'Oh, and there is one other thing you might want to see,' and with that Vishnu placed a small object on the paper as if it was a paperweight. Due to the fold in the paper, the object rolled towards Dr Sujata and came to a stop just at the table's edge.

Dr Sujata's face took on an unhealthy hue and her eyes widened in horror as she seemed to grow smaller in her seat, trying to get away from the thing that was trying to roll up to her. 'W-where did you get that?' she hissed.

'You didn't ask what it is,' Vishnu said with sadness. 'This means, you know where I got it from.'

There was an eerie silence in the room and for a while, no one spoke. Finally, Vishnu got up and said, 'Thank you, Dr Sujata. I don't think we will be meeting again.' With that, he picked up the skeletal finger with the Navaratna Ring still dangling on it and started walking towards the door.

CHAPTER SEVENTEEN

'H-how did you find out?' Dr Sujata asked, and then as understanding dawned on her, she said, 'Of course! You spoke with Dr Prakash.'

Vishnu turned back and nodded, 'He mentioned you were actively involved in charities after your fiancée's death. One of the charities you were very active in is the same one named as the sponsor on John's scholarship letter.' Vishnu looked at Dr Sujata and saw that her face hadn't changed much. 'Everything else fits,' he said.

'HOW DARE YOU THINK YOU KNOW ME?!' she shouted, but her voice was raspy and it was more of a shriek than a shout. It was followed by a violent bout of cough that wracked Dr Sujata's cancer-riddled body. Vishnu ran up to her and settled her down and handed her the cup filled with her golden-yellow drink. She had a couple of careful sips and rested her head back on the chair's headrest.

Vishnu was still standing, looking pitifully at Dr Sujata when he said politely, 'I don't know you and I cannot fathom the pain you have endured throughout your life, but what is done cannot be undone. We can analyze it as many times as we want but in the end, the facts remain unchanged. To avenge an accidental death, Mrs. Devi manipulated circumstances that lead to two murders and my jail term.'

'So that's what you think; one accidental death?' Dr Sujata asked. 'What about the deaths of Sita and Mr. Narayanan?'

'Many people experience grief and yet, they do not die. I didn't when my mother or father passed away.' Vishnu paused and thought if what he was going to say next was worth saying, but then he had nothing to lose, nothing to fear, nothing more to gain. 'Mrs. Devi didn't die when she found out her long-lost son Arya was killed in an accident,' he said pointedly and it had the effect he had hoped for.

'Not killed; MURDERED! He was a victim of your carelessness and Gopika's greed and Mr. Narayanan's mistrust!' Dr Sujata said. 'Devi died with Arya. And Dr Sujata was born.'

All those years of his incarceration spent in agony and all those months of self-doubt he spent after that were all wiped out with that one admission from Dr Sujata. But something else had registered in Vishnu's mind and he said, 'Mr. Narayanan's mistrust? Surely any loving father would want to know about whom his daughter is planning to spend her entire life with.'

Dr Sujata's eyes flared at that statement and she said, 'Nothing wrong in conducting a background search. I would have done the same probably. But to trust a piece of paper without fully getting to the bottom of it and breaking up relationships! That is just not right.'

'Am I right in assuming that you met Sita and Mr. Narayanan?' Vishnu asked.

'Yes, poor child. Sita was utterly broken by Arya's death. And Mr. Narayanan was broken by his daughter's sorrow. That is when he told me what a worthless person Arya was. I too was disappointed at first, but once I found out the truth about that email you stole from his desk, I realized that Mr. Narayanan was wrong.' Tears welled up in Dr Sujata's eyes but her eyes were full of rage. 'I had to go back to Mr. Narayanan and let him know that my Arya was innocent and totally worthy of his daughter. When I told Sita about the truth, she at least had the peace of mind that her Arya, my Arya, was a trustworthy companion to her.' Dr Sujata sipped at her cup again to wet her parched lips.

'So Sita was alive even when you visited them the second time?' Vishnu asked.

'If you call that as living, then yes, she was alive,' Dr Sujata said.

'Mr. Narayanan had tried to fill her heart with poison for my Arya. But when I told them the truth and how mistaken Mr. Narayanan was, she seemed slightly happy again, but only for a moment. She asked her father about when he had called Arya and her father gave no answer, just hung his head in shame. And that's when I left their house, never to see them again.'

'So Sita committed suicide immediately after and Mr. Narayanan died of grief some time later?' Vishnu asked, a complete scenario already forming in his mind.

'Yes, all because of you and Gopika!' Dr Sujata said. 'Will you not share the blame for their deaths?'

'Will you?' Vishnu asked and Dr Sujata looked stunned.

'I am sure you have already figured it out. Deep down, a small voice has already said this to you many times, but you were too self-involved to accept it.' Vishnu's voice had a strength to it that made Dr Sujata uncomfortable. 'If I am to be blamed for playing my part in Arya's death, it seems fair to conclude that you played a part in Sita and Mr. Narayanan's death; in addition to those of Gopika and Vignesh!'

Vishnu saw the conflict of emotions play around Dr Sujata's face. She was clearly struggling with her inner demons. 'Gopika and Vignesh were just poisonous beings. They deserved to die and they got what they deserved. Gopika's greed knew no bounds and neither did Vignesh's. And they both had no qualms about destroying human life in pursuit of wealth.' Dr Sujata's breath came in rapid, shallow gasps. 'I am proud to admit that I rid this world of those two hideous human beings; reptiles really.' The hate she had bottled up for all these years had finally spurted out.

'I wonder how you cannot see that you facilitated Sita's suicide and Mr. Narayanan's death too!' Vishnu's statement had surprisingly little effect on Dr Sujata. 'I mean, Sita hadn't given up the hope to live even after Arya's death. Only when she realized that Arya was innocent and that her father's call to Arya about cancelling their engagement had precipitated Arya's stroke and death, did she commit suicide. And that guilt drove Mr. Narayanan to suffer a fatal heart-attack.'

Dr Sujata bowed her head. Vishnu could see teardrops streaking her cheeks and falling on her lap. It looked as if Vishnu's comment had hit the spot. She realized that she herself was the straw that broke the camel's back. She was the one who made Mr. Narayanan and Sita realize the truth about the scandalous email. Her revelation had pushed Sita to end her life and though Mr. Narayanan had acted hastily, he had definitely done so with the very best for his daughter in mind.

'You are right,' she said in a voice so low, it was almost a whisper. 'I exacted a heavy price for my Arya's death,' she looked up to Vishnu and said, 'Hear me out and you will know why. I doubt if you have ever heard of a more sorrowful tale.'

Vishnu sat back in the chair he had gotten up from and wondered what new information Dr Sujata was about to reveal. He was ready to listen to her every word with rapt attention.

'I was born here in Chennai to a decently wealthy family where my Dad owned a profitable metal forge. My Mom had died when I was young and I cannot really say I ever missed her; in fact, I don't even remember her. I was a talented and pampered child. You know how it is with families with old money; they congregate together. A close family friend of my Dad had a boy about my age. Santosh was his name. We almost grew up together and fast friends. By the time we were finishing our high school our friendship had morphed into a yearning for lifelong companionship. When our parents got to know this, they were overjoyed. Both Santosh and I were interested in serving people and we decided we could best do it by opening a free clinic and hospital for the poor. As our families were rich, money was never a concern, but real social service is what we can do with our own hands. So we both decided to study to be doctors. With our high scores in school and entrance exams, we both were admitted into a reputed Medical college for our MBBS degree. Seeing as both Santosh and I were going to be away from our families but at the same college, my Dad approached Santosh's and asked for our relationship to be official with our engagement. Soon after our engagement, we left for our medical studies.' Dr Sujata stopped for a drink and her eyes fogged up. It seemed life she had been physically transported into that blissfully happy period in her life. Vishnu thought about the similarities his early life and that of Dr Sujata's possessed. Both their families were rich and both their mums had died early but then, their lives had taken completely different turns.

'As we wanted to facilitate free surgeries, both of us came up with a plan. Santosh would pursue a post-graduate specialization in general surgery and I would specialize as an anesthesiologist. We spent the first four years of our MBBS studies quite happily and we were about to begin our year in residency. Obviously, more surgeries take place in the city, so that is where we both aimed to go. Our fathers had enough clout to pull some strings and get us the right allocation. We both got in, but then, I was offered a six-month research assistant's position to study the psychological effects of long-term anesthesia under Dr Prakash. Santosh's family had journeyed to take us both back to Chennai, but with my new assignment, I decided to stay back. On their way back . . .' and Dr Sujata trailed off, unable to recount the first and most horrifying of her life's injustices.

Vishnu looked at her sympathetically and said, 'I know what happened. A real tragedy. How did you come out of that?'

Dr Sujata looked at Vishnu thankfully. Vishnu had ensured that Dr Sujata did not have to explicitly mention the death of the love of her life – Santosh. 'For a long time, I didn't,' she admitted truthfully. 'I quit the position Dr Prakash had offered and just went back home as a recluse. But within a week or so, I realized that I was pregnant. I decided to give birth to our baby; mine and Santosh's. My Dad was quite supportive of me, but he still had an image to maintain in the society and for that matter, so did I. He convinced me that I deliver the baby elsewhere and then come back home and claim that I had adopted the baby as a first gesture towards my social service goals. I was packed and sent away from Chennai, away from prying eyes to give birth. Unfortunately, I was tricked into thinking my child was still-born and . . .,' Dr Sujata began sobbing.

Vishnu realized the dilemma Dr Sujata was facing. She loved her Dad and he had in a sense betrayed her. He had pretended to be happy for her to keep the baby, but all the while he was scheming to get rid of it. And here, he had played a masterstroke! He had told Dr Sujata that the baby was still-born and then had abandoned her very-much alive infant at an orphanage. Vishnu knew that the same baby was adopted and named Arya, who grew up and was in love with Sita. 'How did you find out? I mean, after all those years,' Vishnu asked.

'When I recovered from this second twist of fate, I decided that I will keep Santosh's dream alive – to devote my life to social service. With my life-partner and dedicated surgeon gone, there was no point in me being an anesthesiologist. By then, I had fully realized the havoc grief and bereavement plays on human mind; I had experienced it first-hand. And so, I decided to be a psychiatrist specializing in trauma treatment. But to get to that, I still needed to finish my MBBS. So, I wrote to Dr Prakash if there was any possibility of reinstating me as a house-surgeon student. He was very kind and understanding and luckily by that time, he had been appointed to the position of Dean of the College. He had me reinstated in no time and always looked out for me from then on. He also involved me in a number of his research projects and mentored me throughout my charity work.' Dr Sujata looked at Vishnu and then suddenly remembered that she hadn't yet answered Vishnu's query. 'I had given myself up to charity and other research pursuits and was quite content living like a hermit. My father tried in vain to persuade me to lead a normal life; you know, marriage, kids and so on. But, I guess my zeal to lead a normal life died with Santosh. Now, I was only living to fulfill our dreams, Santosh's and mine.'

Vishnu listened to Dr Sujata's narrative and was really impressed by the strength, resolve and selflessness that she had shown. Yet, she hadn't answered his query and Vishnu thought it would be rude to remind her again of it. So he just waited for her to continue her story.

It seemed like Dr Sujata got the drift, for she gave a start and said, 'Oh right! Well, my father tried everything to get me back to the normal track and that is when he decided to lie to me regarding my baby. Another twist of fate really; though I gave birth to a healthy child but my Dad spirited him away to be abandoned at an orphanage and told me that my baby was still-born. It was more than a quarter of a century later that he told me the whole truth, right on his deathbed. It was again the heart of a loving father that forced him to do that. Once he was dead, he thought I was going to be alone in this whole wide cruel world and so, he wanted to ensure I knew I had someone.'

'Huh,' Vishnu grunted and a very sly smile cracked up on his face.

Dr Sujata was too engrossed in the moment of her story to fully fathom Vishnu's reaction. 'On his deathbed, he disclosed the twisted secret; of my son being alive and abandoned at the orphanage. It took a lot of persuasion, pleading and money exchanging hands, for me to find out where my child had ended up. I was just struggling with the dilemma of whether to disclose the truth to Arya when your cruel misadventure snatched him away from me forever. After his death, his foster parents did not even acknowledge my claim on Arya. They just kicked me out of their house. For them, Arya had just one set of parents and they were it. I had lost the right to be his mother the day I had abandoned him.' With that she looked at Vishnu and was more angered to see a smirk on his face. Vishnu was lost in thought and his brain had not yet corrected his facial expression when Dr Sujata had mentioned about her Dad's seemingly diabolical plan of getting her back to normal by lying about her child. 'You find this funny!' she shrieked.

Vishnu was shaken back to reality and as he realized why Dr Sujata was so upset, he corrected his expression to a more somber one, bowed his head low and said, 'No; not at all, Dr Sujata. What you have been through is the stuff of nightmares!' He took a deep breath, locked eyes with hers and said, 'It does give more weight to a conclusion I am coming to, though.'

'What conclusion?' she asked with anger clearly audible in her voice.

'Never mind that just yet; please continue,' he said.

'Well, once Arya was gone and I had punished all of you who were responsible for his death, I had nothing to live for and I tried to end my life. Unfortunately, the method I chose wasn't very efficient. I ran my car into a tree but instead of killing me, it just left me crippled and disfigured. After almost a year of physiotherapy and two more of facial reconstructive surgeries, I was able to walk up to the mirror. But the person staring back at me wasn't me anymore. My face, my posture everything had changed.' Dr Sujata's eyes were unfocussed as if she was actually looking into her past, trying to recognize the face that was looking back at her from the other side of the mirror. 'I had no one else to go to and so, I went back to Dr Prakash. Imagine my surprise when he just couldn't recognize me! But after a while, he did and he convinced me to continue my social work. I started helping him out with his patients' background-prep when I found that he had been assigned to handle your case. I was furious to see that you hadn't learnt your lesson at all. You were still self-engrossed and when you couldn't bear the punishment, you opted for the easy way out – suicide. That would have deemed my Arya's death pointless. I wanted it to mean something. I wanted something good to come out of all this. I realized that they had framed you using the split-personality argument; something I had experienced first-hand when my physical appearance changed. I wanted to be the same Devi I was earlier, but I just couldn't seem to fit her in my new body and I changed to Dr Sujata. In the past, I was Devi for my family and friends, and Dr Sujata to my colleagues. With Arya's death and my accident, Devi too died, leaving space only for Dr Sujata to live on. I went abroad to gain more insights into your situation, and mine; all the while, I kept in touch with Dr Prakash and unbeknownst to him, kept tabs on your case. My research on the psychological effects brought on by multiple-personality disorder resulted in a doctorate and when I came back to Chennai, Dr Prakash was more than happy to hand over your case to me.' With that, Dr Sujata took a deep breath and picked up her glass. She sipped her medicinal infusion and it seemed to soothe her.

Vishnu looked at her and it seemed as if he wasn't yet satisfied. She looked at him and noticed the slightly confused look on his face. 'Did I miss something?' she asked.

'Yes! You told me your story and it is really a sad one. But you still haven't told me mine!' Vishnu said in an almost exasperated tone. 'How did you frame me? How did Gopika die? And Vignesh?

It was Dr Sujata's turn to smirk and she said, 'Oh right! That was a runaway train and it was bound to wreck!' The excitement and satisfaction in her voice was apparent. 'I didn't have to do much really. I just sowed an idea in your minds and it grew up into a monstrosity that engulfed all your lives. Come to think of it, I didn't even have an idea, you came up with that one!'

'What?' Vishnu exclaimed.

'Yes, don't you remember? I just came to you with a problem; that of two business rivals I needed out of my way. And you were the one who suggested we kill one and frame the other one for that murder.' Dr Sujata was content seeing the look of shock on Vishnu's face. 'I never thought Gopika would go for it. Mind you, I never thought you guys would be such inept detectives as not to realize there was no Sanjana!'

Vishnu's head bogged down. In their zeal, boredom, confidence and oversight, they had totally missed out on checking on the other half of the story. Their search had connected John and Shalini, but they had not bothered to verify John and Sanjana's relationship. Vishnu was just about to ask what Dr Sujata's plan was, had they found out she was lying about having a daughter named Sanjana but then realized it was futile. What had happened had happened and what hadn't, hadn't! There was no point in discussing the hypothetical when the actuality was still unclear.

'When I approached you with the story of John and my non-existent daughter Sanjana, I was worried that my ruse would easily be uncovered and I was scared at first. But when you demonstrated your utter lack of diligence, I just decided to see how far your ineptitude takes you. Obviously, Gopika's greed and your mutual relationship was something I hadn't realized but in the end, was a bonus.' Dr Sujata seemed to be quite enjoying this part of the story. She sounded almost gleeful.

'You know, soon after I left your agency's office that day, Gopika called me and asked for some time. She claimed that she could arrange for my business rivals to be taken care of in the way you suggested, all by her lonesome! I had just wound you guys up and then, all I did was see what you ended up doing. I started following Gopika and that is how I found about her blood-donation and her efforts to rope in Vignesh; if that really was his name. I cared little for what his name was. All I hoped for was that the guy had a price I could buy his loyalty for, and as is often the case with *such* guys, there was; and quite cheap too.' Dr Sujata was in the groove now. It was as if she couldn't believe her luck. That was real-life entertainment for her; like Gopika, Vishnu and Vignesh were mere puppets and she was the puppet-master!

'What do you mean by *such* guys? Do you know where he came from?' Vishnu asked.

'As far as I could find out, he was one of those out-of-city youths who had come in to be a star in the film industry. After a couple of years spent struggling to get a break, he was doing any odd-jobs that came his way. The cut-throat competition, the hardships he had endured and the failure that he had become, had made him quite an unscrupulous character; agreeable to do anything for money. And your dearest girlfriend Gopika . . . well, she had something spectacularly diabolical planned for you!' Dr Sujata looked at Vishnu and saw that he was almost crumbling as it dawned on him that his beloved Gopika had decided to do away with him.

'So, she planned on killing me?' Vishnu asked. 'With the help of Vignesh, was it?'

'What? No!' Dr Sujata pitied the naivety that Vishnu still

demonstrated. 'She didn't want to kill you; she just wanted to destroy you! Even I don't know what her plan exactly was, as she kept things very close to her heart, but she did tell certain things to Vignesh who was all but happy to tell them to me, for a price of course. Gopika didn't want you dead, quite the contrary. She wanted to somehow frame you for her death; or at least her assault and disappearance. And she was going to use Vignesh to accomplish that.'

'And you turned Vignesh against her?' Vishnu asked.

'Well, I didn't have to really. I just told him that if this woman was ok with destroying her partner who was also in love with her, what qualms would she have in getting rid of Vignesh after he was done being useful for her. Mind you, Vignesh wasn't an idiot either. The hard life trying and failing at breaking into the movie scene had sharpened his wits but numbed his morals. Plus, initially, it seemed all innocent. All Vignesh had to do was call you once and keep an eye on you for some time, offer you a glass of cold water from *her* jar once you guys meet up and talk to you for a few minutes. He told me when and I was there, right outside your agency office that night. Gopika had only asked him to talk to you for a minute, give you the glass of cold water and leave. But curiosity and my instruction made him hide and wait. Obviously, Vignesh was shocked to see that you passed out soon after you drank the water and Gopika came in shortly. By the look of things, she had planned to set up an elaborate scene where there was a physical altercation between you and her; and either she had left bleeding or you had murdered her and hidden away her body.' Dr Sujata was now in full flow and the story was so enticing that she couldn't stop narrating it.

'Gopika . . . wanted to frame me for her murder!' Vishnu couldn't believe what he was being told, but deep down, he realized that it was the truth. Gopika was so consumed with greed and the confidence in her own abilities that she thought she needed no one else to succeed.

'The irony of it all! You gave the idea to get rid of my rivals and your partner was using it to get rid of you. Poetic justice, really. And all this to prove to me that she could alone work your plan to solve my problem!' And with that Dr Sujata let out a laugh as twisted as the story had really become. 'Vignesh, in his zeal to understand more of Gopika's plan, was hiding in the shadows when Gopika started creating the scene she had envisioned; the blood and everything. Vignesh, in the heat of the moment, thought she was framing him not you, and he confronted her. In the ensuing argument, he pushed Gopika a bit too hard. She fell and her head cracked open on the table corner. The scene was set! She was dead, there was blood and you were there passed out at your desk. But Vignesh was slyer than I had given him credit for. He ran up to my car and ushered me in. One look and a quick filling up from Vignesh and I understood what had really happened. But as I bent down to check Gopika's pulse for a sign of life, Vignesh snapped a picture of me touching Gopika's neck! I was too frail to take him on and that was not the place to do it either. He gloated about his intelligence and luck and asked me to help get rid of the evidence incriminating him, for if he was incriminated, he had a photograph to prove I too was at the scene. We put Gopika's dead body in the storage freezer along with the phone she had given him and cleaned up the mess. We emptied out the contents of the jar and the glass you drank from and washed them both down thoroughly. I had the presence of mind to take Gopika's purse with me without Vignesh noticing.'

Dr Sujata looked at Vishnu and saw him deep in thought. He was probably appreciating the beauty and precision of how all the events fit perfectly to conspire against him. He suddenly came out of his trance, looked up to Dr Sujata and queried, 'And then?'

'Well, Vignesh wasn't too smart really. As soon as he got into my car, he started with his blackmail pitch. Give me more money or else . . .. Well, I decided to give him *his due* and tranquilized him with the powerful sedative that I had already loaded in a syringe, just in case. I needed time to think. It was clear to me that this low-life had to die, but I needed to make it look good. I realized that making a murder look like an accident wasn't as easy as they say, but making a person disappear was easier. Luck smiled on me when I rummaged through the contents of Gopika's purse and found the deed to an obscure property. Gopika had also given driving instructions there, probably because it was so out of the way. I drove to the property and it was perfect; incompletely developed with lots of loose soil and not a soul in sight. I dragged Vignesh's limp body into Gopika's house and just then, he began to stir. I had no choice but to stand on his throat and suffocate him to death. With great effort, I dug a shallow grave and buried him there, hoping that no one will ever find him, ever again.' Dr Sujata seemed to almost gloat at her efficiency and the stroke of luck she had, but then realized that that wasn't completely true and added, 'But you did find him!' There was awe in that statement.

'It was because of the mentoring you provided, Dr Sujata,' Vishnu said sincerely. 'Of course, I had invaluable help from some really awesome people, but you were the key to getting my brain to function properly after my incarceration.'

'Maybe,' Dr Sujata said. 'Above all, it was your firm belief throughout, that if you somehow found Vignesh, you could in a sense absolve yourself. That was your mental block as well as your support pillar. You couldn't have come out of it had you not found Vignesh; and that led you to focus on, and ultimately succeed in finding him.' Dr Sujata looked down in what seemed to be out of shame and said, 'Once I realized that you were getting close, I even tried to put you off-track by hinting that you really might have split-personality.'

'I remember that conversation,' Vishnu said. 'So, what made you change your mind?'

'Once again, fate forced my hand,' Dr Sujata said ruefully. 'I wanted you to be tormented for life; just like I was. But then, I was diagnosed with final-stage leukemia and that gave me the impetus to think. If you hadn't realized *your* mistake and just lived your life believing that you killed Gopika, not clearly knowing why any of it happened, all those deaths and all the suffering would have been futile. A week ago, I had decided that I will just tell you everything, but then that too would have been pointless. I wanted you to discover the truth for yourself, learn from your mistakes and emerge as a better person than you were.' Dr Sujata was visibly tired now. 'Honestly, I was losing hope. With every passing moment, I feared that I will die and take the secret with me, leaving you to a life of endless and futile torture.'

Vishnu and Dr Sujata both fell silent for what seemed like an eternity. No one moved a muscle as they were both engrossed in assimilating all they had let out in the open. Vishnu looked at Dr Sujata and though she had obliterated his past life and changed him completely, he held no animosity towards her. Dr Sujata looked at the sharp, full-of-promise man sitting in front of her and surprisingly, found that all the hatred she had felt for him was gone.

'You, your father, I, Gopika, Vignesh and Mr. Narayanan – anyone of us could have acted differently and stopped it all from happening,' Vishnu said with emotion. 'I lost many things to this whirlwind, but perhaps, they were all worth losing. In the end, I gained a new zeal, a new perspective for life and along the way; I established some very strong relationships. And for that, I sincerely thank you.'

With that, he stood up, bowed slightly to Dr Sujata and walked to the door. He opened the door and turned ever so slightly to see that Dr Sujata had not moved from her seat and he said, 'But for you; WAS IT WORTH IT?' and walked out, closing the door behind him. Dr Sujata sat there motionless, with a dry smile on her lips.

EPILOGUE

Vishnu was as always, dressed in his expensive linen casuals as he glided down the stairs. He made a beeline to the breakfast table where Aiyya was waiting for him with a small stack of papers to sign. It was Pesarettu and Uppuma for breakfast and Vishnu had his usual heavy fill. Immediately after the breakfast, Vishnu asked for his car to be brought up front, which Aiyya relayed deftly. 'Anything else?' Aiyya asked.

'Yes. With the business safely in your hands and me slowly learning the ropes, I was wondering what I should do?' Vishnu asked.

'You have to make up for lost time, Thambi. What you have to do will soon come looking for you,' Aiyya said with a sly twinkle in his eye. 'The car is ready.'

Vishnu climbed down the porch and got in the front passenger seat of the massive 4x4 Ford F150 pick-up. He had just bought it and decked it out to the specifications he wanted. On the driver's seat, a familiar face greeted him; well not quite greeted him for the face seldom showed any emotion.

'Hi Malai! Doing alright?' Vishnu chirped.

A slow, short nod was all he got back in response. He looked at Malai who seemed thankful for Vishnu's decision of buying the pick-up. But even here, it seemed that there was not an inch of room left for Malai to move about.

'You know where to go,' Vishnu said and was again acknowledged by a nod.

After about an hour of slow but comfortable driving through the hot, humid, bustling Chennai streets, Malai stopped the pick-up close to the pavement. Vishnu looked at his Patek Phillipe.

'We have about forty-five minutes to kill,' he said in Malai's general direction.

Malai fidgeted around at the side of his seat and the backrest tilted far enough to resemble a reclining comfy chair. Malai pulled up a folded newspaper, rest his head on the reclined seat and covered his face with the newspaper, apparently going to sleep.

Vishnu gave a sigh and started browsing vacation spots within India on his new smartphone. It took a while for the forty-five minutes to pass and he said, 'See you back in an hour, Malai.' He got out of the pick-up and the first thing that hit him was the heat and the humidity. A thin line of sweat trickled down his back as he opened the door to the reception. The attractive figure of Nisha was clearly visible, standing behind the counter tidying up her desk. She looked at him and flashed a smile worth a thousand diamonds. Just as Vishnu had covered half the distance from the door to the desk, Nisha picked up her sack-purse and came up to him with a springy step.

'Come on, I am famished! I need to be back in an hour, you know,' she said.

'The usual place then? Idli Wada for you and Parotta with mutton masala for me,' Vishnu said. 'By the way, did you ask?'

'Yes. Shalini madam approved my leave for eleven days, including weekends,' she said.

'Fantastic! How does Arunachal Pradesh sound?' Vishnu asked.

'That would be enchanting! It will be fun to drive around the beautiful countryside,' she said and asked 'We are taking *the Mountain* with us, right?'

Vishnu gave out a throaty laugh and said, 'Of course! Who else is gonna take care of us in that far off place!'

ABOUT THE AUTHORS

Naks is an engineer and a researcher who dabbles in movie making, cooking and traveling. This is his first foray into novel writing!

Cos is an engineer and a researcher who dabbles in wildlife photography, traveling and martial arts. This is his first foray into novel writing as well!

Printed in Great Britain
by Amazon